Intimate Surrender

Also by Laura Landon

Intimate Surrender

LAURA LANDON

Montlake
Romance

The characters and events portrayed in this book are fictitious. Any similarity to real persons, living or dead, is coincidental and not intended by the author.

Published by Montlake Romance
PO Box 400818
Las Vegas, NV 89140

ISBN-13: 9781477805954
ISBN-10: 1477805958
Library of Congress Control Number: 2013931719

There can be no greater honor
than to dedicate this book to my loyal readers.

Prologue

Hannah tried to move, but stabbing shards of burning pain raged from the core of her being. She winced, then pressed her fist low to her belly and sank back into the straw.

For several agonizing moments she did nothing but struggle to take enough air to breathe. This must be what it felt like to die.

She inched her spread legs closer together and cried out when spikes of fiery pain shot through her. She couldn't lie here so…exposed.

Scorching tears streamed from her eyes only to get lost in the straw beneath her. The despicable things the man had done to her and the revolting ugliness of his intrusion clung mercilessly to her.

Humiliation consumed her, and she recoiled from the shame.

Terror paralyzed her when she thought of her father's reaction if he ever discovered how she'd been defiled.

She shifted in the dirty straw. She couldn't let him find out. The beating she'd receive if he did would be worse than any thrashing he'd given her before.

She rolled to her side and clasped her hand over her mouth to keep from casting up the little she'd eaten earlier.

She was desperate to flee from the place where the man had groped and clawed at her, but a rush of burning pain shot through her when she tried to rise.

She hugged her arms around her middle and squeezed her eyes tightly shut. Every inch of her screamed in pain. Over and over she prayed that no one would ever find out what had happened, that she could pretend to the world she was still pure. That when she woke in the morning she'd be safe in her own bed instead of curled up in the corner of a dirty stall in the horse barn. But even if by some miracle that were possible, his atrocious actions would always haunt her. She would never forget what he'd done to her.

She could still feel his hands on her body, touching her in places no one had ever touched her before. She could still smell the sour liquor on his foul breath when he kissed her, when his filthy mouth sucked at her breasts, and she still felt the burning of his whiskers against her tender flesh. Every inch of her throbbed—every muscle screamed in pain. Her flesh was bruised and sore where he'd pawed at her, mauled her, pushed into her.

She wanted to cry to the heavens for the reprehensible acts he'd committed against her, but she was unable to utter more than a raspy moan. Her voice was hoarse from her pleading cries for him to stop. But he had not. He'd touched her in the vilest manner. His large, brutish hands had clutched at her with unrelenting force.

With trembling fingers, she pulled the shredded material of her dress to cover her breasts. She knew what he'd done to her had been a sin. Her father had repeatedly warned her about the sins of the flesh. Over and over her father had demanded her promise not to allow any man to touch her. But she hadn't been able to stop the man tonight. He'd been too strong, too determined. Even her screams hadn't been loud enough to summon anyone to help her.

Hannah recoiled in shame. She was no longer pure and innocent as her father told her she must be. She was no longer a virgin as he'd demanded she remain to be accepted as one of God's children. She could never be one of the select.

She tugged at the hem of her gown wrapped around her waist. With wild fury, he'd pushed it there before he'd...

Hannah cried out in agonizing mortification. A man she didn't know had violated her, had invaded her body, had raped her. The way he'd stroked her and fondled her had been a filthy and disgusting act. Her unyielding flesh had rebelled when he'd entered her as if he'd torn her in two.

Hannah struggled again to move, but another brutal stabbing of pain shot through her.

She lay still a while longer, then attempted to stand. She had to escape before her father discovered her. He'd never believe that what the man had done hadn't been her fault. He'd always warned her of the sins of the flesh. The sins a *woman* caused a man to commit.

Hannah rolled to her side and looked down. Blood—so much blood. *Her* blood.

A pool of crimson still streamed from inside her, turning the straw beneath her an earthen black.

She tried to distance herself from the convicting evidence that proved she'd been violated, but stopped when the door burst open and her father stormed into the barn. There was a crazed look in his eyes, a murderous expression on his face.

"No!" he bellowed.

The roar of his accusation caused the animals still in their stalls to shift uncomfortably. Hannah used the little strength she had to push away from him as he shot toward her.

"I told Brother Jasper he was wrong! That my daughter would *never* behave so wantonly. But he laughed in my face. Laughed!"

"It wasn't my fault, Father!"

"Liar! Brother Jasper told me what you did. How you flaunted yourself, letting him glimpse your breasts."

"No!"

"Don't deny it! I know you! You're the daughter of Satan. I've always known it but prayed I could save your wretched soul if I kept you on your knees in prayer. But I've failed. Even God doesn't want you. He knows what you are. A whore!"

"No!"

"Quiet! You used your beauty to tempt a righteous man. The same as Eve tempted Adam. Brother Jasper told me how you paraded your body like a Jezebel before him. How you tempted him until he could not resist."

"No!"

"You did! Brother Jasper lay prostrate at my feet to ask forgiveness for his weakness. He admitted all to me and the other brethren and begged for us to intercede for him in asking forgiveness."

Hannah shook her head. She knew words were useless, knew her father's rage was so intense he'd never listen to her, never believe her.

"How could you have disgraced me so? You're more wicked and shameless than any of Satan's strumpets!"

Baron Fentington reached for the strap he always carried and pulled it from his belt. "I have begotten a brazen harlot!" He brought the strap down across her tender flesh. "Worse than Delilah!" The strap came down again. "Worse than Eve!" The strap came down yet again.

Hannah curled her body into a tight ball as the sting of the leather flayed her back and her buttocks. Her denials went unheard. Her pleas for her father to stop the beating went unheeded.

With each slash of the strap, she succumbed to the pain. Eventually, the little strength that remained left her, and she prayed that when she lost consciousness she'd never wake again.

A blessed numbness settled over her. And she fell into darkness.

* * *

She wasn't dead. She'd prayed that she wouldn't wake, or that when she did, she would be in heaven. But when she opened her eyes, she was still alive, and condemned to the living hell to which the righteous liar had committed her for the rest of her life.

She was weak from the blood she'd lost, with her body bruised and battered.

In time, she woke enough to take in her surroundings. She was no longer in the barn or anywhere near the house. Someone had carried her down the long lane that led to where her father's land bordered the Earl of Portsmont's estate—where her best friend Grace lived. They'd dumped her body there and left her to die.

Her father's intent was clear—she was no longer welcome in his home. He no longer considered her his daughter. To him, she was already dead.

She slowly rose to her feet and walked to a nearby stream. She stepped into the shallow water and scrubbed away as much of the filth and humiliation as she could from her battered body. But she was unable to scrub away the shame of what the man had done to her—a man of the cloth. A man who claimed to represent God. A man who preached redemption to the lost.

As the sun sank below the horizon, Hannah washed the bloodied gown as clean as she was able—but the body it covered would never be clean again.

She was a wicked, shameless woman. A whore. A woman beyond redemption. That is what a man of the cloth had condemned her to be. But she would not allow him to destroy her.

Somehow she would rise from the hell she faced now. But she'd learned her lesson. She would never trust a man again—especially a man of the cloth.

Chapter 1

Fifteen Years Later

*H*annah nearly skipped as she walked through the flowering meadow. It had been so long since she'd been to the country she could hardly take everything in. The smile on her face refused to dim. She couldn't believe she'd almost turned down an invitation from her friend Caroline, the Marchioness of Wedgewood, to join her family for a two-week summer party at the Wedgewood country estate. And Grace, the Duchess of Raeborn, would also be there. Grace and Caroline were her dearest friends. How could she have refused?

All of Caroline's sisters would also be in attendance, each with her husband and a growing number of children. There were fourteen by latest count, but by year's end Hannah knew there would be at least two more.

Her smile broadened as she remembered seeing Grace when she'd arrived the day before. It was obvious Grace was increasing again. Although Raeborn was probably a nervous disaster, Grace was aglow with happiness.

Hannah savored the warmth that tugged at her heart. She was responsible for Grace and Raeborn discovering one another. Although it had been anything but blissful in the beginning, everything had turned out far better than anyone could have imagined.

She wanted to laugh. Who would have anticipated that a match having its beginnings in Madam Genevieve's famous bordello would ever turn out so perfect? But then, who would have thought Madam Genevieve, one of London's most famous bawds, would be invited to a party hosted by the Marquess and Marchioness of Wedgewood and attended by the Duke of Raeborn, plus a smattering of earls, viscounts, and barons? There were times when friendship far surpassed anything London Society could imagine.

Hannah swung her arms as she continued her walk, then turned to her left when she reached a narrow path at the edge of the meadow. When Lady Caroline heard that Hannah wanted to go for a walk while the rest of her family either napped or took care of the smaller children, she suggested Hannah travel in this direction. According to her instructions, there was a small brook only a little farther, with a perfect little resting place that overlooked a quiet stream.

Hannah was excited for the opportunity to be by herself. She was excited to have the chance to escape London and the worries she'd left behind. Although she knew the city was where she belonged, there were times when she needed to be by herself. When she needed to think. This was one of those times. Things were getting too dangerous for her, as well as for her girls in London, and she feared that when she returned, she'd have to take actions that would cause trouble. But that was in the future. Until then, she intended to enjoy every minute of her time here.

Hannah stopped along the path and listened. Her excitement rose. She was near the brook. She could hear its rushing water. She gathered her skirts and ran toward the sound.

The air left her body when she first glimpsed the sight before her. Huge green trees lined the water's edge. Their arching limbs spread out far toward the middle of the stream. Rocks of all sizes edged the brook, made smooth by the quiet waters. And the grass all along the banks was the deepest green. The sight left her breathless.

She walked to the water's edge and looked down into the depths of the stream, so crystal clear she could see the smooth pebbles at the bottom. Every once in a while, a fish broke through the surface as it swam downstream. It took nearly all her resolve not to remove her clothes and step into the inviting water, though such a thought was out of the question. She couldn't, however, stop herself from removing first her shoes, then her hose, and sitting on the brook's bank. With a cry of delight, she lowered her feet into the stream.

The water was cool and refreshing, and she wiggled her toes beneath the surface like she had as a young girl, when she'd been able to sneak away from her father's watchful eyes. She'd often gone to a stream similar to this one and walked barefoot in the water. That is, until the day her father had discovered her absence and came after her. When he found her, he beat her with the strap he was so fond of using. From then on, she had never returned to the stream if there was a remote chance he might see her.

Hannah shook her head to erase such memories. She refused to think of her father. He'd been dead to her for almost fifteen years—dead to the rest of the world for the past year—and that's where she intended for him to stay.

She swished her feet in the water as if the movement could wash away any thought of him, then leaned back and rested on her elbows. She lifted her gaze to the sun. The warmth of its glow spread throughout her body and let her pretend that the last nearly fifteen years had never happened. She smiled.

"I have no idea who you are," a low, smooth voice said from behind her, "but I'd give everything I possess to capture the vision and never let it go."

"Oh!"

Hannah pulled her feet from the water and turned. Her gaze locked with eyes as deep and rich as the finest Swiss chocolate. Eyes that possessed a warmth unlike any she'd seen before. And a countenance brimming with kindness and gentleness. She started to rise.

"No, don't move. Stay where you are. I didn't mean to frighten you. I mean you no harm."

Hannah lowered her feet back into the water and watched as the man walked toward her.

"Allow me to introduce myself," he said in a voice that wrapped around her like plush velvet. "My name is Rafe Waterford, the Marquess of Wedgewood's brother. I was invited to visit during the summer party. As, I assume, were you?"

Hannah nodded. She tried to speak and couldn't find her voice. She couldn't do anything but stare into the stranger's magnificently handsome face.

He smiled. "Would you mind if I sat?" He motioned to a spot near her on the bank.

"No. Please. Sit."

He lowered his tall, lean body to the ground next to her and pulled his boots from his feet, then his stockings. "I hope you don't mind, but you have the right of it. The water looks entirely too inviting to pass up."

Hannah tried to pull her feet out of view, but there was no place where they could be hidden. Finally, she gave up and relaxed. Lord Rafe was hardly the first man to see her body. Her feet were the most innocent of what men had seen.

"Oh, this is wonderful," he said, lowering his feet into the water.

"Yes, it is, isn't it?" she answered.

His smile, when he turned to face her, stole her breath. There was something about him that drew her to him like metal to a magnet.

"Did you just arrive?" she asked, knowing he must have, or she would have noticed him yesterday when she arrived, or at least last night at dinner.

"Actually, I haven't yet arrived. I'm on my way to the manor house just now. I live a short distance from here in the dowager house. Since it's vacant, Thomas has given me use of the place."

"How fortunate for you. Are you alone?"

"Are you asking if I have a wife?"

Hannah felt her cheeks redden. "Excuse me for being so forward."

"Not at all," he answered. He pressed his hand over his heart and breathed a loud sigh. "Alas, I haven't found my one true love, although not for want of my family's trying. They are forever introducing me to the *perfect* prospect."

Hannah laughed. "I know Caroline and can well imagine her attempts to find you a wife."

"Although Caroline is quite accomplished at playing matchmaker, her efforts pale in comparison to my other sister-in-law, the Lady Prosser, my second brother's wife. She is convinced that matrimony is the ideal life for all men. And now that I've reached the ancient age of thirty, she feels that time has run out for me to find a bride on my own. She considers it her Christian duty to assist me in finding a wife."

Hannah shook her head. "I feel you are doomed then, sir. One woman's efforts to see you married are dangerous enough, but when two females conspire, there is no hope for you."

"I will have to be on guard, then," he said, splashing his feet in the water as if taking a stance.

Hannah could not help but laugh at his antics.

"What about you? Surely you have a husband, although I'm at a loss as to why he would allow you out of his sight."

Hannah felt her cheeks warm. "No. Like you, I have sworn off matrimony."

His expression turned serious. "You have my sympathy, then. Whatever turned you away from marriage must have been very tragic indeed."

Hannah turned her face. She *was* uncomfortable talking about this. Uncomfortable pretending there'd ever been a chance that she would marry.

"Ah, I see I've touched on a painful topic. Please, forgive me." He moved his feet beneath the water for a few moments, then stopped. "I'm afraid you have me at a disadvantage, though."

Hannah turned back to face him. "Excuse me?"

"I don't know whether to call you miss, or my lady, or Your Grace, or Your Royal Highness."

She laughed. "Definitely not Your Royal Highness. You may call me miss. Miss Hannah Bartlett."

"Very well, Miss Hannah Bartlett. Why is it that we've never met before? I assume you are an acquaintance of my sister-in-law."

"Not your brother's?"

"Heavens, no. He doesn't have nearly such good taste when it comes to choosing friends. You are definitely a friend of Caroline's. Her taste is impeccable."

"Actually, I'm friends with all of Caroline's sisters, although I confess to knowing Lady Caroline and the Duchess of Raeborn best. I grew up near them and we were of an age."

"Then you knew my sister-in-law in childhood?"

"Yes. We were friends from little on."

He laughed. "You don't know how happy I am to hear that." He paddled his feet beneath the water. "Perhaps you can be persuaded to enlighten me as to what kind of young lady she was?"

"You want to know about her childhood?"

"Yes."

"Haven't you ever asked *her* about her youth?"

"Yes, but I only hear tales of her best conduct. To hear her talk, she was perfect growing up. As were all her sisters."

"So you want me to reveal the mischief she got into?"

His feet paddled faster. "Yes, exactly."

Hannah shifted on the grass to see him better and saw an impish twinkle in his eyes. "May I ask why you want me to betray one of my best friends with tales of her disobedience?"

"It's very simple. Lady Caroline has contrived to wring from her husband every misstep I made growing up—"

"Of which I assume there were many," Hannah interjected.

"I admit I wasn't a saint as a youth. I didn't acquire that status until later in life."

Hannah shot a look in his direction and saw an expression of innocent sincerity on his face. She couldn't help herself and burst out laughing. "Oh, you are terrible," she said through her laughter.

"My point exactly. That's what my dear, sweet sister-in-law mistakenly thinks. I want to point out that her husband might have given her the wrong impression of me."

Hannah pulled her feet from the water and tucked them under her skirt, then turned to face him. "You want to blackmail her."

Lord Rafe clasped his hand atop his heart and feigned shock. "You wound me, Miss Bartlett. Mortally."

He fell back to the ground and clutched his chest as if reenacting Hamlet's death scene.

She laughed again. It suddenly dawned on her that she'd laughed a great deal today.

She returned her gaze to the man who'd given her such entertainment. "Methinks you will survive, my lord. I'm sure you've had much practice feigning your innocence."

He rolled to his side and rested his cheek in the palm of his hand. His gaze locked with hers.

His movement brought him much closer to her. Hannah fought the rapid pounding of her heart. She didn't want this. She couldn't allow her emotions to sneak up on her as they were doing—as *he* was causing them to do.

"Do you visit Lady Wedgewood often?" he asked, lifting his chin to look her in the eyes. "I would hate to think you were a frequent guest and I'd missed you until now."

Hannah shook her head. "No, this is my first visit."

"Perfect." He sat. "Then you haven't seen the sights."

"The sights?"

"Yes. Wedgewood Estate has many interesting places to see. There's a maze in the south garden. It's quite one of the best I've ever seen. When we were young, my brothers and I repeatedly attempted to lose our younger sisters there."

"You didn't," Hannah said on a laugh.

"Oh, yes. Constantly. Our father finally threatened us with a belt if we ever left the girls behind again."

"I don't blame him," she said. She felt the need to stand up for females being abused by their older brothers. "How old were they?"

"Our sisters?" He thought a moment. "They must have been three and four. Or Estelle may have been five."

"You really were terrible. They were just babes."

"That's what Mother said. She always shielded them from our antics. My brothers and I thought it was just because they were girls and we were boys."

"I'm sure that didn't have anything to do with it," Hannah said.

He looked surprised. "Then what reason do you have for her protectiveness?"

"I think she chose to protect them because they were defenseless and you and your brothers were bullies."

"You wound me again, Miss Bartlett."

Hannah laughed. "Have they forgiven you?"

"Who? My sisters?"

"Yes."

"Of course," he said, focusing on her. "Haven't you realized by now that it's impossible for anyone to stay angry with me for long?"

She couldn't help but smile at him. "That, Lord Rafe, is the first statement you've made with which I can wholeheartedly agree. I don't doubt at all that you have a talent for winning hearts. That you have remained unmarried this long is a miracle."

"Bachelorhood is a state in which I've practiced very hard to remain."

Hannah studied him more closely and wondered how many hearts he'd shattered in his past. She quickly brushed the thought away. She didn't want to consider anything that personal about him. "What other sights would you show me?" she said, needing to stop the direction her thoughts wanted to go. Unfortunately, she was enjoying herself more than she had in a long time. He really was a delightful man.

"Well, next I would show you the brewery."

"A brewery?"

"Yes, have you ever been to one?"

"No."

"Then that is something we must do. I'm sure we won't lack company when the others discover our plans. Bradford Brewery is one of the finest around, and it's not too far away." He stretched out on the grass beside her. "And, of course, we have to have a picnic in the gazebo near Hunter's Lodge."

"Hunter's Lodge?"

"Yes. Every Wedgewood guest votes Hunter's Meadow the most beautiful sight around. I'm sure you will too. Then we will—"

Hannah stopped him with a lift of her eyebrows. "You don't think Lady Wedgewood has events planned for her guests?"

"Oh, I'm sure she does, and I'll look forward to attending those with you too. But it's in my best interest to find opportunities to enjoy your company without my sister-in-law's gigantic family at hand."

Hannah rolled her eyes heavenward in an attempt to ignore his antics. "You really are terrible, my lord."

"Rafe," he said. "Please, call me Rafe."

Hannah considered his request. "I think I should continue to call you 'my lord' for at least a day or two longer. We don't know each other well enough to be on a first-name basis."

"Does that mean I'm to call you Miss Bartlett instead of Hannah?"

She put the sternest expression she could muster on her face. "Yes, Lord Rafe. That's exactly what that means."

"You've dashed my hopes again, sweet lady."

"You'll survive. I have no doubt of it. Now, I've been gone from the house long enough." Hannah reached for her shoes, then sprang to her feet. "It's time I returned, or Caroline will assume I got lost and send someone to search for me."

"It's not that late," he said, getting to his feet. He reached into his pocket to pull out a watch. "Only a little after four o'clock."

Hannah looked at the watch in his hand. "Oh my," she said, lowering her gaze to get a better look at his timepiece. "What an exquisite watch."

"It was my grandfather's. It was his father's before him. He gave it to me on my sixteenth birthday."

He handed it to her so she could get a better look.

She cradled it in her palm and held it with the greatest care. She'd never seen anything so remarkable. Gold filigree etchings covered the lid of the pocket watch creating a tastefully simple design.

"Turn it over," he whispered.

She did. The same gold etching covered the back, except in the center. A saying was inscribed there. She tilted it slightly to read it.

IN ALL THINGS, BE NOBLE.

"That's beautiful," Hannah whispered.

"Press here," he said, pointing to a tiny jeweled knob on the side of the watch.

Hannah pressed the knob and the lid opened. Her breath caught. The face of the watch was inlaid with the most exquisite mother-of-pearl she'd ever seen. Larger rubies marked every quarter hour on the face of the watch, and in the center a gorgeous sapphire held the hands of the watch.

"Oh, my lord, I've never seen anything so remarkable. What delicate workmanship."

"My father was a little upset that Grandfather handed it down to me instead of leaving it to him. But he explained that he wanted me to have it and if he gave it to him, he would hand it down to Thomas, who was next in line for the Wedgewood title."

"He didn't intend for your brother to have it?"

"He told me I was better suited to live up to the saying on the back than Thomas."

Hannah lifted her gaze and looked at him. "That was a very heavy burden to place on a sixteen-year-old's shoulders."

"Perhaps. I've never thought much about it. I treasure the watch because it was my grandfather's and I was extremely fond of him."

A strange emotion washed over her, a warm and comforting sensation that seemed to connect her to him. She wasn't familiar with such a reaction. She'd never experienced bonding with anyone before and it confused her.

"I need to go," she said, feeling a desperation to separate herself from him.

"Allow me to escort you?"

She held out her hand to stop him. "No, thank you. I can find my way alone."

He stepped closer to her. "At least let me help you with your shoes."

Before Hannah could object, he took her shoes from her hands.

"Sit here." He pointed to a large rock nearby.

"I'm capable of putting on my own shoes, my lord."

"Of course you are. I can tell you are a very capable woman. But pray, allow me to exhibit a small bit of chivalry so when my dear sister-in-law expounds on my misbehavior, you can point out that you witnessed a different side of my character."

"Are you always so eloquent with words, my lord?"

He laughed. "Always. Now sit."

He reached for her hand and helped her to sit on the rock. He wasn't wearing gloves, and she tried to pretend that, when his flesh touched hers, a sudden surge of heat didn't travel up her arm and through her chest.

Just as when he knelt at her feet, she tried to pretend that her heart didn't shift in her breast.

And when he put first one shoe on, then the other, she tried to pretend that one molten wave of fiery passion after another didn't rush to her core and set her ablaze.

When he finished, he placed her foot on the ground, then stood and reached for her hand.

She placed her palm in his and rose.

"Are you certain I may not escort you back?"

Hannah concealed the ball of her cast-off stockings as discreetly as possible in the palm of her left hand and tried to speak, but no words would come. No man had ever affected her like this. She hadn't allowed one to. So how had this one broken through the barriers she'd erected to guard and protect her emotions?

She made a second effort to speak, but resorted to shaking her head.

He smiled. "I'll see you later, then. At dinner?"

She nodded, then turned. She needed to escape the net he'd thrown around her. Needed to do everything in her power to avoid being pulled in like a hungry fish snapping at the worm on the end of a hook. But most of all, she needed to avoid giving in to emotions she thought had long been dead and buried.

She had no right to allow them to surface. She was a whore, she reminded herself. A bloody whore!

"I—I have to go," she stammered, then turned and nearly ran in her effort to escape.

"Miss Bartlett?"

She stopped and turned.

"I enjoyed this afternoon."

She took in the warm smile on his face, recognized the sincerity in his voice, and knew she was in more trouble than she'd been in since she'd arrived in London at fifteen—ragged, broken, and abandoned.

Chapter 2

❧

*R*afe arrived for dinner early. He told himself it was because he hadn't seen his brother yet or thanked his sister-in-law for inviting him, but that wasn't the reason. He wanted to arrive early so he would be there when she entered the room, so he could glimpse her before she noticed him.

He couldn't wait to feast his eyes on her again to see if she was as beautiful as he remembered.

He paused in the doorway of the drawing room and found his brother Thomas, Marquess of Wedgewood, deep in conversation with the Duke of Raeborn and Viscount Carmody. He wasn't sure what they were discussing but prayed it wasn't some boring measure that was before the House of Lords. His least-favorite topics were anything being debated on the floor of the House. He didn't have the patience for anything serious tonight. He wanted to focus on only one thing. But she hadn't arrived yet.

"Rafe," Thomas said, motioning for him to join them. "Come help me. I'm outnumbered. Raeborn and Carmody both think Squire Robbins's thoroughbred can run six furlongs in under a minute, and I say it's impossible. He doesn't have the speed. What do you say?"

"I say it would easily take him a minute and a half, if not more. The squire hasn't dedicated half the time he used to spend in training his stable since his wife passed away. All his horses have lost their speed."

"I forgot Robbins lost his wife," Raeborn said. "You seldom saw one without the other."

Carmody nodded. "They were very devoted to each other. I can understand how the man would lose interest in everything."

"Word has it, though, that Robbins's youngest son and his family are returning to the abbey," Rafe added. "They intend to help with the running of the estate."

There was a short silence. Then Carmody said, "I'd hate to think of having to live even one day without Josalyn. When our time comes, I hope I go first."

None of the men said anything for a few moments. Then Rafe waved his hand in front of him. "This conversation has turned much too maudlin. We've come for a party. I refuse to have our two weeks start out on a somber note."

"Good for you," Carmody said.

"Yes, Rafe. I knew I could count on you to bring life to our gathering."

"So what plans has your wife made to keep us entertained?" Rafe asked, then turned his gaze to the doorway so not to miss a certain lady's arrival.

"It's not what Caroline alone planned, but what she and her sisters have concocted. They've been closeted in the Blue Room since everyone arrived, and we've heard nothing but laughter."

"Well, I refuse to play another game of charades," the Duke of Raeborn said with a grimace. "Especially if we have to act out animals like we did at Baldwin's. Deuced frustrating trying to act out a rhinoceros, when none of you have ever seen or heard one."

Wedgewood laughed. "It wasn't that we didn't know what a rhinoceros was. It's just that your imitation of one was so bloody horrible."

"I beg to—"

"Save your breath, Raeborn," Carmody said. "You have to admit that when it comes to parlor games, you come up short on the talent end."

Raeborn laughed. "You have a point. You'll understand, then, when I excuse myself from a game of charades if any of the ladies suggest it."

"I'll support you wholeheartedly."

"Now, what about you, Rafe?" his brother said, slapping him on the back. "Have you come prepared to partner the half dozen single young ladies my wife has invited to draw your attention? She intends to parade a different candidate in front of you nearly every other day for the entire two weeks."

Rafe groaned. "Tell me she hasn't," he said, knowing that Caroline undoubtedly had.

"Oh, I'm afraid tonight will be your only free night. You're on your own for dinner. But I believe Miss Estelle Warden will arrive tomorrow to keep you company for the day. As you remember, her father is a small landowner and well respected in the area."

"I will have to make every effort to enjoy this free evening, then."

Rafe tried to keep his frustration from showing. He didn't need his sister-in-law's help in finding someone to accompany him every day. He'd already met the only person with whom he wanted to spend time. And she wasn't one of the local ladies.

During their conversation, Baron Wexley, Baron Hensley, the Earl of Baldwin, and the Earl of Adledge arrived. Their gathering was complete. They stood in two small groups after they'd helped themselves to the refreshments provided. It wasn't long before the gay laughter of feminine voices filled the air. Their conversations stopped, and the men turned toward the door.

Rafe stepped to the side of the group of men to make sure he could see her when she entered. He experienced a strange sense of excitement that wasn't at all usual.

One by one, Lady Wedgewood and her six sisters entered the room. Their gowns provided a rainbow of colors, and the smiles on their faces seemed to compete with the noonday sun.

"Have you ever seen so many beautiful women gathered in the same room?" the Duke of Raeborn said in a hoarse whisper.

"Never," Wedgewood added. "All seven of them."

"Eight," Rafe commented, unable to look at anyone but Miss Hannah Bartlett.

"There are eight," Wedgewood said, slapping his brother on the back. "Leave it to you to notice that we'd miscounted."

"You didn't miscount," Rafe said, giving his brother a knowing grin. "You're all so smitten with the women you married that you overlooked the most beautiful woman in the room."

The second the words were out of his mouth, the look on his brother's face altered. The change wasn't drastic, and if Rafe hadn't always been able to read his brother's nuances so well, he wouldn't have noticed it. But the slight narrowing of his gaze sent a stab of forewarning he couldn't explain.

"Are you referring to Miss Bartlett?" Wedgewood asked.

"Yes." He returned his gaze to where she stood.

She was even more beautiful than she'd been this afternoon. She wore a gown the most vibrant shade of green. Her neckline wasn't high, yet it wasn't too low. It was just perfectly placed to allow a hint of the creamy skin should one be inclined to look—which, of course, he was. How could he not?

She wore little jewelry, only a single strand of pearls around her neck. Her wheat-colored hair was loosely pulled from her heart-shaped face, and thick ringlets cascaded down her back. A narrow ribbon that matched the green of her gown twined its way through her hair, making every golden glimmer glow with more radiance.

Their gazes met—and held. A smile lifted the corners of her lush lips. His heart shifted in his chest. Such a reaction was very unlike him. That in itself made her effect on him more startling.

Rafe turned a smiling grin on his brother. "Remind me to thank your wife for inviting Miss Bartlett. Her presence promises to make this summer party most enjoyable."

His brother's expression darkened again, but any concern Rafe had concerning his brother's reaction didn't last long. His concentration shifted to the women following Lady Wedgewood into the room.

"Rafe," Caroline said, walking toward him. She wore a smile that reinforced his opinion that his brother was one of the luckiest men on the face of the earth. "I'm so glad you decided to join us tonight. I was afraid you wouldn't arrive until tomorrow."

"Thank you for the invitation," he said, leaning toward her to kiss her cheek. "I was actually excited to have an opportunity to attend."

"Marvelous!" she said. "I've invited several local young ladies to join us for the next two weeks. I hope you're agreeable to that."

He shifted his gaze to where Miss Bartlett stood next to the Duchess of Raeborn. "That wouldn't have been necessary, my lady. I see there's a female guest without a partner here already. It will be my pleasure to fill in where I'm needed."

His sister-in-law's gaze moved to Miss Bartlett's, then darted to her husband's. The arch of Wedgewood's eyebrows reinforced a warning, but Rafe refused to consider it. His meeting with the woman earlier had been far too enjoyable to heed any admonitions.

"If you'll excuse me," he said, raising his sister-in-law's hand to his lips in farewell, "I think I'll make certain Miss Bartlett feels welcome."

"Have you met Miss Bartlett before?" Lady Wedgewood asked with a questioning frown.

"Yes, earlier this afternoon, on my way over. We had a lovely conversation."

He didn't wait to see the reaction to that statement, but nodded his farewell and walked across the room. The smile on Miss Bartlett's face was encouragement enough when he neared her.

"Your Grace," he said, greeting the Duchess of Raeborn. "Miss Bartlett."

"My lord," the duchess said. "It's nice to see you again. It's been far too long since you attended one of our gatherings."

"Yes. I believe the last time was Christmas."

The duchess laughed. "Oh, yes. What a time that was." She turned to Miss Bartlett. "You'll be glad you didn't accompany us then, Hannah. We were all here, like now, and were prepared to leave. We'd been here for two weeks already, and I'm sure Caroline and Thomas were more than eager for us to depart. The night before our scheduled departure, Adledge made some ridiculous wager with Baldwin about…" She looked to him for help in remembering what that wager had been about.

"I believe Lord Adledge wagered that he was a better shot than the Earl of Baldwin," he added.

"Oh, yes. That was it. So, it was decided that we would stay one more day until the wager was settled. But, when we awoke, there was a mountain of snow already on the ground, and the storm that raged outside showed no sign of letting up anytime soon. We ended up imposing on Caroline for another two weeks. And we were housebound for most of the time!"

Miss Bartlett laughed. "Oh, dear. I can't imagine your brothers-in-law being confined for one week let alone two."

"It was difficult indeed. All that saved us was Lord Rafe," the duchess continued. "Every afternoon he occupied the children for an hour or more with stories he would make up."

"Only a few were my own creations. Mostly, I told tales I remembered from my youth."

"Well, your talent was a godsend. The children, down to the babes, were on their best behavior for fear they wouldn't be allowed to take part in the storytelling."

"I think it was more that they didn't want to miss out on the delicious sweets Cook sent up when I finished."

"That may have played a small part in their good behavior, but not the most influential one." The duchess turned to Miss Bartlett. "Once you become acquainted with our storyteller, you'll realize he has a gift."

"Oh, I would never doubt his gift. Lord Rafe impressed me with his ability in telling tales earlier this afternoon."

The duchess's eyebrows lifted.

"Yes," Rafe rushed to explain. "It was my good fortune to meet Miss Bartlett on my way here this afternoon."

"Yes," Miss Bartlett continued. "I'd gone for a walk, and we met by the stream. He regaled me with the most flattering stories. I was quite captivated."

"See, my lord? Even Hannah realizes your talent. It's no wonder that as your life's calling you chose to—"

Rafe was thankful the butler chose that moment to announce that dinner was ready.

There was a time when he'd been more than eager to reveal his life's vocation, but that was no longer the case. He was consumed with doubts that hadn't been there a few years ago and consumed with an emptiness that gnawed at him—that left him hollow on the inside.

"Allow me to escort you in to dinner," he said, offering Miss Bartlett his arm.

He knew when she placed her hand on his arm he'd feel her warmth through the material of his jacket. However, he had no idea the slight pressure of her fingers would leave such a vivid impression. Nor was he prepared for his body's reaction.

A molten heat spiraled throughout his entire being. A weight settled in his chest, then traveled low to his belly. His heart shifted, and he had to take a breath to recover.

He turned his head, and his gaze locked with hers.

The smile on her face captivated him like no woman's smile had ever done before. He felt that, with that slight connection, she'd wrapped her essence around him and possessed a part of him that no woman had claimed before. He read her thoughts as if she'd intentionally opened them up to him. She was attracted to him the same as he was attracted to her. Only, she fought the attraction whereas he welcomed it.

"I'm glad that you have agreed to join us for the next two weeks. Do you join my sister-in-law's family often?" he asked when they were seated at the table.

"Are you?" she answered. "I'm seldom able to come, although not for Lady Wedgewood's or the Duchess of Raeborn's lack of invitations. They are most generous in their offers to include me."

"And the reason you are unable to come is because…?"

"Because…"

There was a hesitation in her eagerness to respond. She paused as the first course was being served, a warm cream soup, and Rafe knew she was using the interruption to decide what to say. From the look on her face, she was debating whether or not what she said would be the truth. Or a lie.

Her hesitation lasted a moment longer. "I have personal responsibilities that keep me in London," she answered finally.

Rafe breathed a sigh of relief. She hadn't lied. She'd avoided disclosing anything revealing about herself, but she hadn't lied to avoid the truth. A ray of sunshine filled his chest. She hadn't been able to lie to him.

He lifted his glass of wine and took a small drink. He felt like celebrating. "Ah, Miss Bartlett. You are indeed one of the most interesting people I have ever met."

His words halted her soupspoon halfway to her mouth. "I assure you, my lord, I am one of the least interesting people you will ever meet."

"Hardly." He placed his wine glass back on the table. "I find I am very intrigued by you. I intend to use the next two weeks to show you how intrigued I am."

Before he could register what happened, she changed. The glint in her eyes turned sharper, the smile that lifted her lips turned less sincere, and the expression on her face lost its pleasant disposition.

"I would like to discourage you from wasting your time and efforts. There is nothing about me that should intrigue you."

She slowly reached for her wine glass and brought it to her lips. Rafe noticed her hand shook ever so slightly. "You are quite wrong about that, Miss Bartlett," he whispered as he took a spoonful of soup. "Quite wrong."

She lowered her glass and, without looking at him, whispered, "For your own good, my lord, don't read more into our meeting than what happened. We will at times during the next two weeks be in each other's company. Then I will go back to my life in London, and you to your life here. I'm sure we will remember our time together with fondness. But nothing more."

Rafe took another spoonful of soup. "Are you certain?"

She looked surprised. Maybe his confidence shocked her. Or, maybe she realized that he was indeed serious.

And that he intended to be a formidable opponent.

Rafe smiled as he finished his soup, then placed his spoon on his plate. He was ready for the next course.

Chapter 3

The following morning the sun rose to herald a perfect day to be in the country. Hannah sat at one of the tables randomly placed on the terrace and watched the various activities enlivening the lawn. Both adults and children were thoroughly enjoying the games Caroline had planned.

The children scampering about ranged in age from seven years to toddlers barely able to walk. Even the nurses had the babes out in their perambulators.

Hannah couldn't help but smile as a gathering of the younger children caught a ball some of the adults rolled toward them, or played with the six puppies that were new to the Wedgewood Estate. A group of older children sat around Lord Rafe as he told them a story.

Grace was right. He had a gift for storytelling. The children were mesmerized with whatever tale he was telling them. And, if she wasn't mistaken, the book he was reading from was a…Bible.

She tried to keep her emotions from rebelling, but doing so was difficult. She'd grown up clutching a Bible in her hands more hours than she wanted to remember. Memorizing chapters from the scriptures was her punishment whenever she did something wrong—and according to her father, she did very little right.

She couldn't imagine what story he'd found that was so captivating, but from the looks on the children's faces, the tale was a fascinating account. Even the female Caroline had invited to accompany Lord Rafe for the day was engrossed in what he was saying. Or perhaps she was only spellbound by the amazingly handsome and unbelievably charming man telling the story. Although, truth be told, he wasn't that young. He'd told her earlier that he was thirty years old—a year older than she was.

Hannah studied him again and wondered how he'd escaped marriage so long. And why. He obviously loved children. He was a perfect candidate for marriage—too perfect not to have every eligible female within traveling distance vying for his attention, and his name.

Which was no doubt why Caroline had invited the lovely Miss Estelle Warden to join them today.

Hannah found herself frowning. She'd only known Lord Rafe for one day, but that was long enough for her to realize that he and Miss Warden were totally unsuited to each other. Where he was vibrant and bursting with life, she was quiet and inexpressive. Hannah couldn't imagine any two people more opposite.

Hannah reached for the lemonade she'd taken from the refreshment table and took a swallow. It tasted good, refreshing—clean. She looked at the glass filled with pale liquid. *Clean* suddenly struck her as an odd choice of word to use, but one she realized fit how she felt since she'd left the city behind her. Clean.

Clean wasn't a word she could use to describe how she felt when she was in London. It wasn't a word she could use to describe how she'd felt even one day since her father had dumped her on the road outside her home and left her to die.

She ran her finger down the sweating glass of cold lemonade and watched the drops of liquid trickle downward toward the table. The drops reminded her of tears… tears that pooled on the table until they'd formed a small puddle…like how her tears had fallen.

She took a linen napkin, sopped up the water, and then placed her glass on the napkin. She didn't want to be reminded of even one day of her past. Nor did she want to be reminded of the life she'd made for herself in London. She'd come here to forget. And for two weeks, that's what she intended to do—pretend that her life might have been different if that one night had never happened.

The excited sound of laughter pulled her away from her musings. She looked up to find the children gathered around Lord Rafe. They were on their feet, and she could tell from their pleading tones that they were begging for another story. But Lady Wedgewood intervened, and the children scampered off to play a game of croquet several of the adults were starting.

Hannah watched them run off, then turned back to where Lord Rafe stood. The lovely Miss Warden was gazing up at him as if he were an immortal being from a heavenly planet. But he wasn't staring at Miss Warden. He was staring at…her.

Hannah's gaze locked with his, and her heart stuttered. The corners of his mouth lifted and he smiled.

A thousand voices shouted their warnings. She'd never met a man with the power to affect her like he did. She'd convinced herself she never would—that there wasn't a man alive who could break down the barrier she'd erected around her emotions. But this man came closer to entering her inner sanctum than any man she'd ever known—and there had been many. *Of course there had been many.*

Hannah smiled politely, then turned her gaze. She wouldn't encourage him. She wouldn't give him the slightest provocation. Forming any sort of close friendship would be dangerous for her and disastrous for him.

He didn't know what she was. He didn't know how critical it was to avoid an association with her. But *she* did. She knew how dangerous even developing a friendship with her would be.

She focused her attention on the group of youngsters sitting in a circle on the lawn. They were engrossed in a game she'd played often when she was fortunate enough to visit Grace and Caroline as children. She couldn't remember the name of the game any longer, but she remembered how anxious she'd been when the person who was *it* would choose someone by tapping her on the head. Then that person would have to jump up and run as fast as she could to be the first one back to the spot that had been vacated.

Remembering those special times brought back one of the few good memories she had from her childhood. For some reason, that thought saddened her. She wished there had been more. She wished her childhood would have been filled with happy times. But it hadn't been, which was probably why she was so determined to rescue as many other young girls as she could and give them a childhood they would remember with fondness.

A shadow passed over her, and she looked up.

"You look entirely too lonely sitting here by yourself," Lord Rafe said.

His voice was deep and rich, and the warmth of his words wrapped around her like a favorite woolen cloak. She tried to shake it off.

"Quite the opposite, my lord. I'm enjoying myself immensely."

"You prefer being alone?"

Hannah smiled. "In London I'm never alone," she said, "which is why I enjoy the solitude of the country so much."

"Is your life in London that full?"

"Yes, quite full. But what about yours? What do you do to occupy your time?"

For the first time, he seemed at a loss, almost embarrassed. But in character, his expression changed, and his charming devil-may-care personality came to the forefront.

Hannah realized that the lackadaisical side of his personality was perhaps an act he put on to hide his true nature. She wondered what deeper traits he felt it was necessary to hide. She was about to delve into his personality to find what he was avoiding having anyone discover, when the danger of being so inquisitive hit her.

It wouldn't be safe to want to know more about him. She couldn't afford to care. She decided changing the subject was her best form of defense.

"Where is Miss Warden? Surely you haven't abandoned her?"

He glanced over his shoulder. "No. The children wanted to play another lawn game, and she decided to join them."

Hannah gave him a censorious look. "Did you frighten the young lady off?"

"Heavens, no. I don't frighten women. They terrify *me*!"

Hannah couldn't help but laugh. "Oh, Lord Rafe. I've never met anyone less terrified of females than you. I'd wager to say that you're accustomed to having every female you meet fall at your feet."

"Every female except you, Miss Bartlett."

Hannah couldn't hold his gaze. She lifted her glass of lemonade and took a drink.

"Why is that?" he asked after sitting in the chair opposite her.

She couldn't avoid his gaze, couldn't help but look at his face.

Hannah hoped she'd see a teasing glint in his eyes, an expression that said his question was a jest. But he was deadly serious. He genuinely expected her to give him an answer. And it would have to be one he would believe.

"I know you have a difficult time believing this," she said, placing her glass back on the table and looking directly at him, "but I have no intention of ever marrying. I therefore think of it as a kindness to both myself and any man who shows me the slightest amount of attention not to offer any encouragement that our acquaintance could possibly develop into anything substantial."

"Have you ever considered what you would do if you met someone you wanted as more than a friend?"

"That will not happen, my lord. I will not allow it."

He arched his eyebrows, then reached for the glass a servant had placed on the table beside him. "How very intriguing," he said, taking a sip of the lemonade.

"My comment was not meant to intrigue you."

"I know, Miss Bartlett. That is what makes your attitude even more interesting."

Hannah knew it was useless to argue with him. She focused instead on Miss Warden, who was entertaining the younger children. "Miss Warden seems like a very pleasant young lady."

"She is," he answered.

"But she doesn't interest you?"

He shook his head, then took another sip from his glass.

"That's all right, my lord. Lady Wedgewood mentioned she'd invited several other local girls during our stay. Six, if I understood correctly. That means there are five more possibilities."

"But the second candidate won't arrive until the day after tomorrow. Which means that tomorrow I will be free. And so will you."

"I'm sure Lady Wedgewood has something planned for tomorrow in which she expects us to participate."

"She did, but she changed her mind when I mentioned that you had never visited a brewery and I'd promised to take you. Of course, the fact that everyone else was eager to go helped sway her. We will leave midmorning, stop for lunch at the Spotted Goose on our way, and then tour Bradford Brewery in the afternoon. If we're fortunate, Lord and Lady Grayson will be there. You'll enjoy meeting them."

Hannah knew she needed to discourage him as much as possible. "Who has Lady Wedgewood invited to partner you the day after?"

Lord Rafe rolled his eyes heavenward. "I'm not certain. I'm not overly interested in my sister-in-law's matchmaking schemes. I'm more concerned with my own efforts."

Hannah wanted to offer a reply that would douse his intentions, but couldn't think of anything that would emphasize her point more than what she'd just said. She was glad when Raeborn, Carmody, and Wedgewood joined them on the terrace.

"You abandoned us," Lord Wedgewood said to his brother.

"Yes, Rafe. We needed you to make the final call," Raeborn said, accepting a glass of lemonade from a nearby servant. "Baldwin and Adledge claimed Wexley's ball tapped Wedgewood's. Anyone could see it didn't come close."

The men would have continued their argument, but Lady Caroline and the Duchess of Raeborn joined them.

"What did I tell you, Linny?" Her Grace said, putting her arm around her husband's waist.

"You were right, Grace," Lady Caroline said, stepping over to her husband's chair.

"Right about what?" Wedgewood asked.

Lady Caroline kissed her husband's cheek. "Grace predicted that there would be a controversy over your game."

"There's no controversy," His Grace said. "Adledge and Baldwin wanted to win so badly they trumped up a foul where there was none."

"Yes, and their influence has corrupted Wexley. He's been in the family for less than two years and already they've turned him into a coconspirator."

"I take exception to that," Lord Baldwin said as he joined them on the terrace. Lord Adledge and Baron Wexley nodded their agreement as they followed him to their table. "We would have trounced you if you hadn't invented a foul."

The six men bantered back and forth for several more minutes, each team insisting that it would have been victorious had it not been for the antics of the other team.

"Well, there is one way to prove which team has the superior talent," the Earl of Baldwin announced.

"Yes," the Marquess of Wedgewood said, rising to his feet. "A rematch! My superior team challenges your inferior team to a rematch."

Baldwin stood. "My team accepts. This time, however, we will appoint a judge for any disputed rulings."

"Who?" Wedgewood asked.

"Your brother, the esteemed Lord Rafe. He will make a fair and honest ruling for every controversy. We'll make him take an oath of fairness. Do you agree?" he said, scanning the men gathered on the terrace.

Both teams agreed with hearty enthusiasm.

Rafe turned toward Hannah. "Would you care to come along?" he asked as the men readied to leave. "You can keep me from making an error."

Hannah shook her head. "I'm sure you'll be fine without me."

"I'll accompany you," Caroline said. "I may be of some use. With the exception of my husband, the others are gentlemanly enough not to argue with me."

"Excellent," Rafe said, extending his arm to Caroline. "We'll return shortly," he said before they left. "Unless the game turns deadly and we're caught in the cross fire."

"I have faith you'll prevent it from going that far," the duchess said with a laugh. "Hannah and I will wait here for the verdict."

Hannah watched as the group left.

When they were far enough from them that they couldn't be overheard, the duchess relaxed back into her chair and breathed a sigh.

Hannah knew Grace was about to say something regarding the attention Lord Rafe was paying her and wanted to be the first to reassure her that she had nothing to worry over. "There's no need to say anything, Grace. I have no intention of causing trouble."

"I know you don't. It's your heart I'm concerned about."

Hannah turned to face her friend. "Then there's nothing to worry about. My heart beats strong and steady enough to keep my body alive and active. To everything else, it is dead. Any capabilities it had to nurture feelings for another human being—especially someone of the opposite sex—died fifteen years ago."

"Don't be so sure, Hannah. It's possible that part of your heart isn't completely dead. I think it has been dormant thus far. Lord Rafe is a remarkable man. If anyone has the power to revive your emotions, it will be him."

"Then I will have to be more determined in my efforts to discourage him."

"Have you considered that his feelings for you could develop into something very genuine?"

Hannah turned to her friend and smiled. "I'm not a novice when it comes to men, Grace. Lord Rafe is intent on pursuing me because I am one of the few females who didn't fall panting at his feet when we first met. I think he is too accustomed to keeping the fairer sex at arm's length. He's attracted to me because I've resisted his charms."

"You may be correct," the duchess said.

"But…" Hannah could tell there was more Grace wanted to say.

"It's just something Caroline said."

Hannah waited.

"She said she'd never seen such an intense look on Lord Rafe's face as when he looks at you."

"Infatuation, Grace. Nothing more."

"Let's hope so. I don't want to see either of you hurt."

"We won't be." Hannah took another sip of her tepid lemonade. "I realize now I've handled this whole situation wrong. I've become a challenge to him." Hannah placed her glass on the table. "I need to change my tactics. I'll begin tonight."

Chapter 4

❋

*I*nstead of joining Grace and her sisters in the music room after dinner, Hannah excused herself and walked onto the terrace. It was a perfect summer evening. The moon was full, and there was a gentle breeze from the east that rustled the leaves on the trees. If ever there'd been an ideal romantic setting, this was it.

She'd plotted her actions all through dinner and knew she wouldn't have long to wait before Lord Rafe joined her. The smiles she'd given him when their gazes met, which had been often during the meal, made her message clear. For the first time since they'd met, she'd encouraged his attention.

A wave of regret washed over her. She felt as if she were deceiving him. But she had no other choice. This afternoon she'd realized that her attempts to discourage him were actually having the opposite effect. He was used to females vying for his attention. When she didn't encourage him at every opportunity, she became a challenge.

Hannah knew what she had to do, but she was loath to follow through with her plan. She was quite fond of Lord Rafe. He was the most unusual man she'd ever met. He was the first man with whom she could be herself. Perhaps the reason was because he didn't know who she was. Perhaps it was because he didn't know *what* she was.

Hannah thought about how easy it was to talk to him, how often she found herself laughing at something he said. She would miss the friendship that was developing between them. But Grace was right in warning her not to let him become attracted to her.

Allowing him to pursue an association with her wasn't wise. It was time to do whatever it took to discourage him. And she realized the answer was to pretend she was as attracted to him as every other woman he'd ever met. Only then would he run from her the same as he ran from any who pursued him.

Hannah prepared herself for the role she had to play, then released a soft sigh when she heard footsteps behind her. She knew it was him.

He stopped when he reached her, but she didn't turn. She wasn't ready yet.

"I thought I'd find you here," he said, stepping to her side. "You've spent a great deal of time out-of-doors since you arrived. My guess would be that you love the fresh air but are trapped indoors much of the time when you are in London."

She turned her head. "Yes, I love it outside. There's a sense of freedom in the country that I don't experience in the city. Do you visit London often?"

"I did when I was younger. I was the second son of a marquess, you know, and expected to make a showing at a certain number of social events each Season."

"When did you stop?"

"Going to London? Or attending the social scene?"

"Either. Would I be incorrect in assuming they both happened at the same time?"

He laughed. "No, you would not."

She kept her gaze focused on his. "When did you stop?" she asked again, keeping her voice soft and low.

He hesitated as if he was thinking. Or as if captivated by the tone of her voice. Which is what she intended.

"When Thomas married Caroline," he finally said. "I felt as if the pressure to find a bride had been lifted. Then, when the two of them provided an heir to ensure the Wedgewood line continued, I knew it was no longer essential that I marry anytime soon."

"And during all that time, you didn't meet one young lady with whom you felt an attachment?"

"No. But I blame that on Thomas."

Hannah felt a giggle bubble to the surface. "Really? How was that your brother's fault?"

"Not only had he already laid claim to the only perfect female in London, but I suddenly realized I couldn't settle for a future that didn't promise to be equally as blissfully happy as theirs was."

"Their marriage does set the standards for happiness quite high."

"Yes, it does. And until recently, I didn't think it was possible for me to find that same happiness."

His admission jolted her insides. She'd have to be dim-witted to miss his implication. And she hadn't survived this long by being naive.

His declaration caused an emotion to consume her that was partly joy, partly elation, and partly terror. Grace had been right. He had become infatuated with her. She should have realized it sooner. And she would have if she hadn't been so infatuated with him, if she hadn't been so reluctant to ignore the emotions she never thought she would experience.

She turned her head as he sat on the balustrade next to her. This brought his face even with hers and allowed him to look her in the eyes.

"Has anyone told you that you are the most beautiful woman in the world?" he asked.

Hannah wanted to laugh, but she couldn't. The look in his eyes was too intense not to take him seriously.

Her beauty had been proclaimed more times than she could count, but never with the intent Rafe meant with his declaration. He was pursuing her on a human level—as a man pursues a woman he wants to get to know better. A woman he wants to court. The men in her past weren't interested in courting her. Nor were they interested in getting to know her on any personal level—except one.

His words confirmed her belief that once she gave in to him, she would no longer be a challenge. Although the thought of severing their budding friendship saddened her, she knew it was necessary—no, *essential.*

Hannah lifted her gaze to meet his. "Not lately. Thank you," she whispered.

He stood, then reached for her hands.

She was surprised to find that her fingers trembled when she placed them in his. She didn't anticipate such a reaction.

With a gentle lift, he brought her to her feet. He was going to kiss her.

Hannah realized his intentions with the same surety that she'd learned to read in every man before they acted.

And this time she would allow him to kiss her—something she never allowed a man to do.

He stepped closer, then wrapped his arm around her waist. The heat that radiated between them was intense enough to ignite a fire; the vibrancy that exuded from each of them was powerful enough to bring a dead man back to life.

With a slow, familiar ease she found endearing—and startling—he cupped his hand to her cheek and rubbed his thumb over her lips. His touch was a gentle caress that brought to life every nerve in her body. With a slight shift of his body, he brought his head closer.

Hannah found herself leaning toward him, reaching to experience the feel of his lips against hers, eager to bring about a completion of what his actions promised.

Then he kissed her.

His touch was soft and gentle, containing a shyness that took her by surprise. And for several long seconds, she reveled in the innocence of their first encounter.

His first kiss lasted but a moment, the briefest of meetings that served as an introduction. Then, with a moan that contained a desire for something more, he pressed his lips to hers and kissed her again.

His arms wrapped more securely around her body and brought her closer to him. Hannah skimmed her palms up the front of his jacket and twined her arms around his neck.

Her movement caused a reaction that intensified the slow-burning fire that smoldered within her.

With a yearning that seemed to border on desperation, he deepened his kiss, drinking from her, demanding from her, giving to her.

Intimate Surrender

The passion she thought their kiss would satisfy was having the opposite effect. She found herself wanting more, desiring something beyond a kiss. And she knew only too well what that something was.

He kissed her with more passion, and the fire inside her burned even hotter. A warmth she'd never experienced before consumed her, and she knew, in only a few more seconds, it would be too late to extinguish it.

She breathed a heavy sigh and attempted to loosen her hold on him. Instead, her hold tightened, as if some unknown force controlled her body and the orders she gave it.

She believed there was nothing of the carnal side of life she hadn't experienced, but never had she faced the upheaval she was experiencing now. Never had she battled an assault so fierce as the war raging inside her because of his kisses. And it was a war she was losing.

He kissed her with more passion, asking more from her, demanding more. And she knew that, whatever he wanted, she would give it to him.

His lips parted atop hers. His tongue skimmed her lips, probing the entrance to her mouth as if requesting admittance.

When it wasn't immediately granted, his finger pressed ever so gently against her chin and she opened to him.

His tongue breached her entrance, dipping, delving, dredging pure emotion from her. He deepened his kiss even more. And all was lost to her.

All reasoning abandoned her. She couldn't think, could only accept what was happening to her and demand more. He left her desperate for something he hadn't given her yet, frantic for more of what he offered, feverish for a place she'd glimpsed he could take her.

Her legs weakened beneath her, and his arms tightened around her when she sagged into him. She was totally dependent on him, needing him to remain upright and requiring his assistance in order to take her next breath. She *wanted* what she knew only he could give her.

This couldn't be happening. Feelings like this were dead to her. She'd killed them long ago, destroyed them when she'd arrived starving on the streets of London fifteen years ago without a farthing to her name. With no one to help her. With little chance to survive. She'd abandoned the last shred of respectability that was left her after she'd been raped, obliterated any sense of decency her father had ingrained in her, and stamped down any integrity that hadn't been beaten out of her. And the man kissing her was resurrecting every emotion she thought she'd buried long ago.

He kissed her again. Even though she thought it was impossible for them to continue further down the path they were traveling, she felt more drawn in by his kisses. And his touch.

His hands caressed her flesh, touched her, and molded her breasts in his palms. Then his arms twined around her. He ran his hands down her spine, traveling lower, and then lower yet.

His all-consuming effect totally controlled her. She knew what step was next. She knew what her body told her she *wanted* to happen. And if she didn't stop their progress, it would be too late. She couldn't allow it. No matter how desperately she wanted it, she...couldn't...allow...it.

She placed her palms against his chest and pushed, gently at first, then with more pressure. Of course he relented. She knew he would. There was never a question that he wouldn't. But a little voice inside her head told her she hadn't stopped him soon enough. That it was already too late.

With an abrupt halt, he lifted his lips from hers.

The separation was painful; the loss unbearable. She regretted her action the minute she no longer felt his flesh against her. She felt the loss as if a part of her had just died, because that was what had happened.

She reminded herself that a future with him was impossible. He was the brother of a marquess, and she was a—

The thought stopped her cold. She could never allow him to do to her again what he'd just done. Stopping him the next time would be harder—perhaps impossible.

She allowed him to wrap his arms around her and pull her close, because it was difficult to stand on her feet without his assistance. She allowed herself a moment to rest her cheek against his chest, because she needed time to slow her breathing. She allowed herself to listen to the racing of his heart in his chest, because it was something she could take away with her—the knowledge that her kisses had the power to cause his heart to thunder as loudly and rapidly as his kisses made her own heart thunder.

When she could no longer battle the resurging desire to kiss him again, she dropped her arms to her sides and stepped away from him.

"Are you all right?" he asked, the tone of his voice husky and filled with an emotion she'd heard often in the voices of men she'd been with, but had never understood its origin.

"No. Are you?"

He shook his head, then took in several deep gasps of air. "I knew it would be like this," he said finally.

She turned away from him and pressed her fist against her stomach. How could he have known? No matter how much experience he'd had with the baser aspects of life, she'd had more. And she had no idea it would be anything like this. *None!*

She walked away from him and took the steps that led to the garden below the terrace. She needed to be alone. She needed to think.

She hoped he wouldn't follow her but knew he would. His concern for others was one of his most endearing strengths. She knew he would have to make sure she was all right; she knew he wouldn't leave her after the earth-shattering kiss they'd just shared.

She walked down one of the paths that led to a small pond in the center of the garden and stopped when she reached the water's edge. The moon was full and bright, and its glow reflected off the water.

"Did what happened when we kissed frighten you?" he asked from close behind her.

She shook her head. "It didn't frighten me. It saddened me."

He turned her to face him. "How could our kiss sadden you?"

"It saddened me because nothing can come of it. What we shared cannot continue. It can never happen again."

"How can you say it will never happen again? I can hardly keep from kissing you again right now."

She shook his hands from her shoulders. "You can't."

"Why?"

"Because I cannot allow it. I can't allow you to continue your infatuation with me."

"Infatuation? You think what I'm feeling is infatuation?"

"It doesn't matter what it is. It can't continue."

He reached for her again and held her at arm's length. When she refused to look at him, he dropped one hand from her upper arm and placed his finger beneath her chin. He lifted until she was forced to look at him.

"I've always believed I would find someone special, just like Thomas found Caroline, and Raeborn found Grace. I knew if I was patient and remained faithful, God would place the woman He'd chosen for me in my path. Well, He did. You're that woman."

Hannah felt her jaw drop and her eyes open wide. "You think *God* placed me in your path? You think *God* intends for us to be together?" She twisted away from him and stepped around him. She needed to put distance between them. She needed to absorb what he'd just said—and remain calm.

"Lord Rafe, God did not play a part in our meeting each other. God does not intend for us to become anything more than acquaintances who happened to meet at a country party hosted by mutual friends. I regret that you felt more from the kiss we shared than what was actually there. I wish you had not, because I cannot allow anything more to develop between us."

"*Can't,* or *won't?*"

"Either," she answered. "Both. Please believe me when I say it is impossible for our friendship to develop further. Because of events beyond my control, or yours, I cannot allow you to think there can be anything between us."

"Why? What events can possibly be tragic enough to prevent us from getting to know each other better?"

"Events that *I* refuse to explain to anyone—especially you. Now, if you will excuse me, I'm quite tired and would like to retire."

His gaze narrowed, and he held back words for several long seconds as if he didn't trust himself to speak. "Of course," he finally answered. "Would you like me to accompany you back to the house?"

"No, Lord Rafe. I can find my way by myself."

Hannah turned and, on shaky legs, walked away from him.

"Miss Bartlett?"

She stopped.

"Sometimes it is impossible to ignore what is meant to be. Or stop it. I believe this is just such an event."

Hannah tried to ignore him, but her feet stumbled as the impossibility of his words struck her.

Chapter 5

❦

*I*t had been three days since he'd kissed her, and Hannah could still feel the warmth of his lips against hers.

As planned, they visited Bradford Brewery the next day. All the adults went—all sixteen of them.

En masse, they exited the house and made their way to the waiting carriages. Rafe hung back, perhaps hoping he'd be able to ride in the same carriage as her, but at the last minute, Hannah asked Caroline to trade places with her. She used the excuse that she needed to discuss something with Grace on the way to the brewery.

If Rafe realized her intent was to avoid him, he didn't comment on it. Hannah hoped her bluntness made her position unquestioningly clear. She also hoped that by keeping his distance, he'd decided to abandon his quest for her attention. And she thought she may have succeeded.

Other than being in the same room with her during their visit with Mr. and Mrs. Grayson Delaney, the owners of Bradford Brewery, he didn't force his attentions on her the entire day. Nor did he find excuses to remain in her company the next day when Caroline had again invited one of the local young ladies to join them.

This second guest was a young widow by the name of Francine Crawley. She seemed close to Rafe's thirty years and had lost her husband almost two years before. This female showed promise of being a much better match than Caroline's first guest. The fact that she had two small children was not a deterrent to Lord Rafe as it would have been to other men. He obviously loved children—another reason why Hannah was not suitable for him.

As she watched the two of them interact during the day, Hannah thought that Caroline's second choice showed promise. The next day, however, she wasn't as convinced.

She'd shared a few words with Rafe over breakfast, and when she'd asked how he'd enjoyed his time with Mrs. Crawley, his response lacked enthusiasm.

Hannah sat back on one of the several blankets scattered on the ground. Today they were enjoying a picnic by the lake. After everyone ate, there were a half dozen boats tied to the dock, waiting for anyone who wanted to paddle downstream.

Hannah watched as four of the boats made their way across the water.

"I swear," Grace said, coming to sit on the same blanket where Hannah sat with Caroline, "our husbands have the ability to turn even the simplest entertainment into a challenge."

"And look," Caroline said, pointing to the boats skimming the water. "Rafe's no better. He was one of the first to choose his partner."

"Yes, Grace," Mary said from a nearby blanket. "You should feel honored. Rafe got to choose first, and he chose your husband."

"That guarantees they will be the winners, then," Josie said from a nearby blanket. "His Grace is in excellent physical condition, and we all know how Lord Rafe spends his free time every winter."

"How?" Hannah asked.

"Making sure everyone in the parish and surrounding area has enough firewood to keep them warm throughout the winter," Caroline answered. "Especially the widows and the elderly. Thomas said Rafe has chopped more kindling than most woodcutters."

Grace and her sisters laughed at that comment, but all Hannah could think of were the hard corded muscles she'd held on to when she'd kissed him.

"What do you think he thought of Mrs. Crawley?" Josie asked. "Did he say anything after she left for home yesterday?"

Caroline shook her head. "All he said was that she was a very nice lady and he sympathized with her over her loss."

"That doesn't sound very promising," Anne said.

"Do you know what Thomas thinks?" Caroline said with a gleam in her eyes. Her question gathered her sisters' complete attention.

"Thomas thinks the reason Rafe has not been receptive to either of the women I've invited is because he is already infatuated with someone."

"Really?" they all chorused. "Who?"

"Thomas doesn't know. He tried to encourage Rafe to divulge a name, or at least tell him whether or not there was anyone in particular to whom he was drawn, but he refused to say anything."

"Oh, isn't that interesting," Francie said. "I wonder who it can be?"

The roaring in Hannah's ears prevented her from hearing anything more. Surely Rafe's thoughts were shifting away from her. She'd given him no cause to think she'd changed her mind as far as he was concerned. She hadn't encouraged him in the least. And he'd avoided her for the last two days. Surely that held some significance.

Shouts of excitement pulled her attention back to her surroundings. Grace and her sisters were on their feet and cheering loudly as two of the boats neared shore.

"Can you see who are in the closest boats?" one of the sisters asked.

"Not yet," another answered. "They are still too far out. But, from the size of the men, my guess would be that Raeborn and Lord Rafe are in the boat that will reach shore first."

"Who's in the second boat?" another sister asked.

"I'm not sure," Caroline answered, "but I think it's Thomas and Carmody."

Hannah rose too. She tried not to appear overly interested, but couldn't help but stare at the two men in the nearest boat. There wasn't a doubt in her mind that the two men were the Duke of Raeborn and Lord Rafe.

"Do you recognize them, Hannah?" Grace asked when she stepped beside her.

"Yes. Your husband and Lord Rafe clearly won the race."

"Oh, dear." Grace sighed. "I'm afraid Raeborn will be ever so difficult to live with for the next few days."

Hannah looked into her friend's face and saw a brilliant smile that reflected her delight. She looped her arm around Grace's arm and gave her a squeeze. "I'm afraid what will be more difficult is the banter and boasting that we will have to endure from our winners for the remainder of our visit. And the excuses by our losers."

Grace laughed. "I'm sure you're right."

"Come along, Hannah. Let's go congratulate the winners so they can begin their crowing."

Hannah wanted to remain behind but couldn't. Her absence would be noticed. She walked at Grace's side as they made their way to the edge of the water.

"Well, Your Grace," the Duke of Raeborn said, pulling his wife into his arms and giving her a quick kiss. "That was quite a race, don't you think?"

"I doubt Baldwin and Hensley think so."

Raeborn turned to watch the last boat come to shore. The smile on his face widened. "Poor Baldwin. Wedgewood hinted last night that he was getting a little thick around the middle. I think he even wagered a side bet that the poor chap wouldn't even be able to finish the race."

When Raeborn's shoulders lifted in what appeared to be smug satisfaction, Grace tapped her finger against her husband's chest. "Need I remind you that humility is a gift to be shared?"

The Duke of Raeborn brought his wife close again and kissed her on the forehead. "Thank you for the reminder, Your Grace. As usual, you are correct to point that out to me."

"You're welcome. I simply want you to realize that had you had Lord Baldwin sharing your oar, you wouldn't be feeling so superior right now. You just had the good fortune to have Lord Rafe at your side."

"Are you insinuating that Lord Rafe is responsible for our win?"

The Duchess of Raeborn tapped her husband's cheek with her finger. "Yes, Your Grace. I believe that's exactly what I'm insinuating."

Rafe was quick to deny Grace's compliment, but Raeborn held up his hand to stop him. "She's right, you know," he said, clapping Rafe on the back. "Just look at him, ladies. He's not even winded. I'll wager he could take another trip around the lake while the rest of us are ready to drop to the ground and catch our breaths."

Hannah made the mistake of focusing her attention on Rafe. Her heart flipped in her chest.

"I believe you have it right, Your Grace. I believe I would enjoy another turn around the lake, but at a much more leisurely pace." He nodded in her direction. "Would you care to join me, Miss Bartlett?"

Hannah tried to think up an excuse to avoid being alone with him, but the words refused to form in her mind. He took her failure to decline as acceptance and held out his hand for her to take. She cast Grace a helpless look, then placed her hand on his arm and let him escort her to the boat.

"I'm glad you didn't refuse," he said when they reached the shore.

"I should have." She said the words more as a reprimand to herself than an answer to his comment.

"But you didn't."

"No, I didn't. But I prefer you don't read anything into my accepting your invitation."

He stopped to help her into the boat, then assisted her as she sat on the wooden bench. When she was settled, he sat, then reached for the oars and shoved the boat away from the dock. He didn't speak again until they were well away from shore. "What I have a difficult time understanding," he said in a relaxed tone, "is why you refuse to accept what is happening between us."

"Nothing is happening between us."

He ignored her and continued. "It's not as if you find my company distasteful, or that you find me personally objectionable. If you did, our experience when we kissed would have been completely different."

"I prefer you didn't mention our kiss."

"I'm sure you do, Hannah. But I can't do that."

"Why not?" Hannah tried as hard as she could to ignore the bulging of his muscles as he pulled back on the oars. Or the way the material of his shirt pressed against his chest when his arms moved. Or the bronzed skin of his exposed forearms because he'd rolled the sleeves of his shirt to his elbows. She realized she'd lost her battle when she was unable to lift her gaze from the V of his open shirt.

"Because the kiss we shared happened to be an important event in our futures."

"We have no future—" She tried to argue, but he didn't give her the opportunity to continue.

"Yes, we have a future. And I venture to say it will be a very interesting one."

"Please take me back." Coming with him had been a mistake. Debating whether or not they had a future together was pointless. Allowing him to think there was a chance she might change her mind was senseless. "I'd like to return."

"We can't," he said, letting their boat drift to shore. "We've reached the other side of the lake, and although I appreciate everyone's opinion of my superior strength and endurance, my energy is nearly used up. I'm afraid you'll have to give me a few minutes to rest before we return."

Hannah looked to the other side of the lake. It *was* a long way, and he had just rowed the distance three times. "I'm sorry. I'm sure you are tired. We can rest here a few minutes. Then we must return."

"Thank you." He jumped to dry ground, then pulled the boat to shore. "Would you like to stretch your legs for a moment?"

Hannah debated, then let him assist her out of the boat.

She stepped onto dry ground and turned. She was desperate to move beyond his reach. Too desperate. She didn't look where she was placing her foot and stepped on a half-buried rock.

Her ankle twisted, and before she could regain her balance, she was falling to the ground.

Suddenly, strong, muscular arms caught her around the waist and lifted her in the air. In one swoop, she was in his arms and being carried up the bank.

"Are you all right?" he asked. He didn't put her down but held her securely against his chest.

"Yes, I'm fine. I just lost my balance."

He smiled at her. "I'm just glad you didn't land in the mud. My reputation for chivalry would have been severely tarnished."

"I'd hate to be the person responsible for the mar against your perfect persona."

He lowered her to the ground and studied her for a few seconds. "Do you think I aim to be perfect?"

Hannah took a few steps away from him. When she turned back, she found him sitting on the ground. Her heart couldn't help but race in her breast. He looked so undeniably handsome in a rugged, masculine way. "I don't think you *aim* to be perfect," she answered. "I think you just naturally *are*."

"Perfect?"

"Yes."

A frown furrowed across his forehead. "Miss Bartlett, please join me." He patted the ground near where he sat, then held up his hand to assist her to the ground. "I'd like to clear up several misconceptions you have about me."

Hannah hesitated, then gave up and took his hand and sat beside him.

"First of all," he said, "I find perfect people boring. And I'd wager you do too. Secondly, all you need to do is ask anyone in my family and they will tell you I am *far* from perfect. And thirdly, I have *never* aspired to perfection. I find people who aspire for perfection to be very frustrated individuals. They also deceive themselves if they think they can ever achieve perfection."

Hannah looked into the serious expression on his face. "I see I touched on a delicate subject. Please forgive me."

He breathed a heavy sigh, then placed his forearm atop his raised knee. He sat that way for several moments looking out onto the water, then turned to face her again. "Please, excuse my bluntness. I am the one who needs to ask your forgiveness. I thought I'd mastered my reaction to everyone's opinion that I am something I'm not. Evidently, I feel comfortable enough with you to let my true feelings show."

She offered no reply to his admission, but not because she didn't have a question or two she wanted to ask. It was merely that being so curious would have exposed more of his true nature than was safe for her to know. Allowing herself to understand him better would have put the wall she'd erected around her emotions at risk. Thankfully, wisdom prevailed and she kept the separation from him intact.

Just then, a strong gust of wind loosened a wisp of her hair and blew it across her face. Before she could pull it back, he reached up and gently pushed it from her forehead. But he did not remove his fingers from her face. He cupped his hand to her cheek and held her.

She knew she shouldn't allow him to touch her so intimately, but when she placed her hand over his to move it away, he turned his palm upward and twined his fingers with hers.

"See how perfectly your hand fits in mine," he said, not as a question, but as if stating a fact.

She wanted to pull her fingers from his grasp, but her muscles refused to obey her orders. She looked to where their hands touched and saw what he meant.

Their hands were not similar—his were much larger, rougher, and calloused. His fingers were thicker, longer, and stronger. Yet together they made a perfect match.

The fit of her hand nestled into his seemed as if two halves had been brought together to form a whole. Where his were large and strong, hers were small but not fragile. Where his were rough and calloused, hers were soft but not weak. Where his were robust and forceful, hers were gentle but not frail.

She suddenly saw how perfect a match he was for her. If only she could erase the last fifteen years.

She felt a gentle tug to her arm and allowed herself to be pulled toward him. She knew what his intentions were and was helpless to refuse him. He wanted to kiss her, and she wanted the same.

He lay back on the grass and pulled her with him. She went willingly.

She leaned over him and pressed her mouth to his. She fed the hunger she felt in his kiss and kissed him with more abandon. She wanted to kiss him because she told herself this was the last time she would allow it.

Tomorrow she would think about leaving. Removing herself from being tempted by him was the only way to ensure she would be safe. She could no longer deny the intense attraction between them. Separating herself from him was the only way she could make certain his fascination for her died.

She deepened her kiss and reminded herself that this was the last time she would kiss him. She offered him as much as she had to give, but only as long as she remained in control. When she felt herself weaken, she lifted her mouth from his.

Her breathing came in rapid and shaky gasps. His breathing matched hers. The fact that their passion could turn to a raging inferno so quickly frightened her to death. It was a warning she could never ignore.

"We should return before Grace sends a search party to find us. We've been gone long enough."

Rafe sat up and pulled his grandfather's watch from his pocket. He flicked the latch, and the lid opened. "You're right. We've been gone more than half an hour. We need to return."

He rose to his feet and reached out his hand to help her stand. "Do you feel it?" he asked when she placed her hand in his.

She thought to pull her hand from his and pretend she didn't understand his meaning, but that would be useless. She felt the same attraction when they touched as he did. "It doesn't matter what I feel. There can never be anything between us. I won't allow there to be."

He didn't argue with her as she thought he would, nor did he reply to her statement. He only looked at her with a knowing smile on his face and walked with her to the boat.

Yes, the sooner she made arrangements to leave, the better.

Chapter 6

*H*annah didn't separate herself from the women for the rest of the day for fear of finding herself alone with Rafe. After dinner, she adjourned to the drawing room where Grace and her sisters had gathered while the men challenged each other to a game of either billiards or cards.

The truth was that she didn't trust herself alone with him. She didn't trust that she would be strong enough to stop him if he tried to kiss her again. And she knew that eventually their actions would go beyond kissing. Passion as intense as what they experienced always did.

She breathed in a shaky gasp and focused her attention back to the various conversations taking place.

"What female have you invited to accompany Rafe tomorrow, Caroline?" Josie asked.

"I've asked Lady Laurin to join us. She's Viscount Canderly's middle daughter. She's a few years Rafe's junior, but she's quite mature for her age."

"I hope Lord Rafe shows more interest in her than he has the other young ladies you've placed in his path."

"I do too. She's just returned from her first Season and was reported to have made quite an impression on the young bucks in search of a wife."

"How did she escape having an offer?" Mary asked.

"If rumors are to be believed," Grace said, "suitors were lined up requesting for her hand."

"She refused them all?" Frances asked.

"Her father did," Caroline added. "Lady Laurin is quite a beauty and supposedly her father's favorite. He is very particular who he considers for his daughter. And none of the men who asked for her hand met his expectations."

"Well, he can't have any objections where Lord Rafe is concerned," Anne said. "I don't know of anyone more perfect."

Sarah laughed. "If Lord Rafe were any more perfect, he'd be a saint."

"Well, what do you expect from a vicar?" Josie replied, and all her sisters laughed.

The sisters continued to recount examples of things Rafe had said or done that qualified him for sainthood. But Hannah didn't hear any of their comments. How could she when the blood rushed with such fury through her head? She could barely breathe. She couldn't think.

Rafe was a *vicar*! A man of the *cloth*!

She wanted to laugh, and would have if the truth weren't so tragic.

The man she'd kissed with such abandon, and allowed such liberties, was a vicar.

A fresh wave of panic rushed through her. She wondered if he knew who she was—*what* she was. She wondered if he realized he'd kissed the famous Madam Genevieve. That he'd declared his interest in a prostitute—a *whore*!

The room swayed beneath her, and she grasped the cushions of the sofa.

"Are you all right, Hannah?"

Hannah turned to find Grace watching her. There was a deep frown on Grace's forehead and a look of concern in her eyes. "No...No, I don't believe I feel well. I think I'll retire early."

She rose, and Grace rose with her. Caroline joined them.

Hannah wished everyone a good night, then walked to the door on legs that threatened to buckle beneath her. Thankfully, Grace reached for her arm when they left the room, and together the three of them walked up the stairs.

Grace and Caroline followed her into her room, and Caroline closed the door behind them. "I have to leave," she blurted out before she could think of how to make her request without such bluntness.

"You want to leave?" Grace asked.

"Yes."

"When?" Caroline asked.

"Tomorrow morning—early."

Caroline rushed to her side. "Why, Hannah? What's wrong?"

Hannah turned on her two friends. "Why didn't you tell me?"

"Tell you what?" they both asked.

"That he was a vicar! A *vicar*, for heaven's sake! And you allowed him to associate with me! You let him talk to me and spend time with me and get to know me, knowing what I am!"

"You're our friend," Grace said. "We've been friends our whole lives."

"I'm a whore!"

"No!" Grace grasped Hannah's upper arms and shook her. "When you're here with us, you're Hannah Bartlett, our childhood friend. Madam Genevieve is who you are in London. Here, you're the Hannah we grew up with."

"Which person do you think Lord Rafe will think I am when he's forced to make a choice?"

Her friends hesitated. Then Caroline answered a little shakily, "I trust that you will be Hannah to him."

"Trust?" Hannah turned her back on them so they couldn't see the hurt in her eyes. "In the life I lead, trusting anyone can get you killed."

"If you give him a chance, maybe you'll see Rafe is different," Caroline said. "You won't know until you see what his reaction is when he finds out."

Hannah couldn't stop the laughter that threatened to escape. "You'll excuse me if I don't want to be around when he finds out." Hannah turned and faced her friends. "I intend to leave first thing in the morning. Unfortunately, I sent my carriage and driver back to London with instructions not to return until the two weeks were over. May I have the use of a carriage and driver to take me home?"

"Are you sure you can't stay?" Caroline asked.

"I'm sure," Hannah answered. "I should never have come."

"Yes, you should have." Grace rushed to her side and gave her a warm hug. "You are always welcome in any of our homes. Don't ever forget that."

"I know I'm always welcome," Hannah said when both Grace and Caroline released her. "But that doesn't change how things are now. I need to leave. I'm not brave enough to see the disgust and revulsion on Lord Rafe's face when he discovers my identity."

"He won't—"

Hannah held up her hand to stop Grace's and Caroline's denials. "It doesn't matter. I don't wish to be around when he finds out."

"Very well," Caroline said. "I'll have a carriage ready for you whenever you want to leave."

"At dawn," Hannah said. "I'll be ready to leave by dawn."

"You're certain?" Caroline asked again.

Hannah nodded. "I'm certain."

Caroline and Grace gave her a final hug, then left.

When she was alone, she collapsed on her bed and curled in a tight ball. She wanted to laugh at the cruel joke God had played on her by placing Rafe in her life. But no matter how hard she tried, she couldn't find any humor in the feelings his kisses had awakened.

Chapter 7

Rafe glanced at the group of women approaching and smiled, although the last thing he felt like doing was being cheerful. The disappointment he experienced was overwhelming. She hadn't come down from her room yet. Perhaps she was more ill than Caroline's sister Mary thought. All he knew was that she'd retired early last night, complaining that she didn't feel well and wanted to rest. No one had seen her since she'd gone to her room.

"So what opinion have you drawn of her?" Thomas asked from behind him.

"Who?"

"Lady Laurin. The young woman your sister-in-law has invited to tempt you into joining the ranks of the married instead of enjoying your freedom as a single person."

Rafe looked at the charming young lady walking between Caroline and the Duchess of Raeborn and smiled. "She's very pretty."

"That's all? Just pretty?"

"No, she's very pretty—and very young."

Thomas laughed. "That's what I told Caroline when she informed me she was going to invite Lady Laurin. But she's convinced Lady Laurin's other attributes will outweigh your age difference."

"What attributes would those be?" Rafe asked.

"The fact that my wife, as well as Lady Laurin's mother, considers the two of you perfect for each other."

"I'm always amazed at how expertly everyone seems to know which two people are perfect for each other. Do they ever consider that the people involved are the only ones who are privy to such information?"

Thomas shook his head. "I don't think it enters their minds. They are too intent on forcing the bonds of matrimony on every acquaintance they know."

"Perhaps, when you have a chance to speak privately with your wife, you can inform her that she may cease her matchmaking schemes. They are no longer needed."

Thomas clasped his hand on Rafe's shoulder and turned him toward him. "Are you hinting that there's already someone you're interested in?"

"It's possible."

"Do I know her?"

"Is there anyone you *don't* know?"

Thomas laughed. "I grant you that my circle of acquaintances is rather extensive, but there are undoubtedly a few people with whom I'm not familiar. Is the lady who has captured your interest someone I know?"

Rafe smiled. "Perhaps."

"This is indeed cause for celebration," Thomas said. "Wait until Caroline hears that you have found someone on your own. When will we get to meet this amazing woman?"

"Soon, Thomas. Very soon."

Rafe turned away from his brother to watch the females come near them. "I noticed that Miss Bartlett is still absent. Has anyone gone to check on her?"

"Check on her?" Thomas repeated, as if Rafe had spoken a riddle.

"Yes, Lady Adledge mentioned that she'd retired early last night. She indicated Miss Bartlett wasn't feeling well. Is she still ill?"

A frown deepened across his brother's forehead, and Rafe watched the look in his eyes darken. "You seem to be quite interested in Miss Bartlett," Thomas said.

"How can one *not* be interested in her? She's a very unique person."

Rafe felt as if Thomas intended to say something more, but Caroline approached them with Lady Laurin at her side.

"Here you are, Rafe. I told Lord Canderly it wouldn't be too late before we returned his daughter. Would you be so kind as to see her home?"

Rafe smiled. Her matchmaking scheme was so obvious even the most naive person on earth couldn't miss it. "Of course. I'd be delighted. Lady Laurin." Rafe extended his arm for her to take.

The young lady looked up at him with stars in her eyes—the same starry gaze he was used to seeing in every female who was searching for a husband. Only Hannah didn't look at him like that. And she was the one female he wanted to have that look in her eyes.

"The carriage is ready," Caroline said, "and Lady Laurin's maid is waiting."

"Perfect," he said with a smile on his face. "Shall we?"

Lady Laurin gave him a demure smile, then walked at his side.

Rafe kept up a pleasant conversation as they made their way to Viscount Canderly's estate, then spent the appropriate amount of time visiting with Lord and Lady Canderly before he said his good-byes. But his thoughts dwelt elsewhere—on Hannah and returning to make certain she had recovered and would join them for dinner.

As he counted the miles, he could think only that it had been almost a full day since he'd seen her. That it had been more than a day since he'd been alone with her. Since he'd kissed her.

He slapped the ribbons against the horses' rumps and urged them to return to Wedgewood Estate faster. When he arrived, he handed the reins to a waiting stable hand, then raced up the steps and through the door the Wedgewood butler held open for him.

"Good day, Lord Rafe," Carver said in greeting as he took Rafe's hat and gloves. "Lord Wedgewood is in the library. He asked that you join him."

Rafe breathed a sigh of impatience. He was more interested in finding Caroline and making sure Hannah was improved. "Can it wait, Carver?"

"No, my lord. Lord Wedgewood expressed that you should join him as soon as you returned."

"Very well," he said, then turned toward the library. As soon as he found out what Thomas wanted, he was going to find Caroline and…

A footman knocked twice on the library door, then opened it for him.

Rafe stepped into the room and stopped short. Thomas wasn't alone.

Seated on the floral settee in the center of the room were Caroline and her sister, the Duchess of Raeborn. In the two matching wing chairs facing them were Thomas and the Duke of Raeborn. A third chair flanked where his brother sat. It was empty. After the footman closed the door, Thomas pointed to it.

"Come in, Rafe. Join us."

Rafe walked across the room and sat in the empty chair. "This looks like a pleasant, although ominous, gathering," he said, taking the glass of brandy his brother handed him. "From the expressions on your faces," he said, scanning the four people who made up the circle, "the topic of conversation isn't all that pleasant."

"It's not as bad as all that—" Thomas started to say before Caroline interrupted him.

"Not *bad*," Caroline said, "but *serious*."

"Has something happened to Miss Bartlett?"

His question seemed to take everyone by surprise. The frowns on their faces deepened.

"Not really," Caroline continued, "but what we need to discuss concerns Hannah."

"What? Is she seriously ill?" Waves of concern rushed through him. "Have you sent for Doctor Blains?"

Thomas held up his hand. "Miss Bartlett doesn't need a doctor."

"Then what?"

"Hannah has gone," Caroline said. "She left. She returned to London."

Rafe didn't move. He felt as if someone had knocked the air from his body.

"Why?" he asked, but he already knew. She'd gone back to London because their attraction for each other frightened her, because he'd gone too fast. Because he'd taken liberties he never should have taken. Liberties a lady like

Hannah wasn't used to a man taking. "This is my fault. I have to go after her."

He rose to his feet, but his brother's stern voice stopped him. "You can't."

Rafe studied the dark expressions on the four people gathered with him and fought the dread that washed over him. He sat back down and waited.

The Duchess of Raeborn took a deep breath and reached for Caroline's hand before she spoke. "The attraction between Hannah and yourself has been obvious to both Caroline and me since the two of you arrived. I mentioned it to Hannah, but she assured me that although she realized that you felt a certain…fascination for her, I didn't need to worry. She would do everything in her power to discourage you. Instead, it was obvious that every day that attraction only seemed to grow stronger."

"And you object?"

The two sisters looked at each other.

"To me?" Rafe asked. "You object to me? You don't think I'm good enough to pursue Miss Bartlett?"

"No." Caroline answered. "It has nothing to do with you."

"Surely you can't object to Hannah. She's your friend. You invited her because you said that you consider her as close as one of your sisters."

"We do," both the Duchess of Raeborn and Rafe's sister-in-law said at the same time. "Each one of us considers Hannah a part of our family."

"Then what? What is it you object to?"

"There are things about Hannah you don't know," the Duchess of Raeborn said. "Things no one knows."

"What things?"

"First of all," she continued, "what I am about to share with you I am saying in the strictest of confidence. Hannah would not approve of me telling you—of telling *anyone*. She does not want anyone's pity."

"Pity? Why would anyone pity her?" Rafe took a swallow of the brandy Thomas had given him. From the looks on everyone's faces, he thought he might need it.

"Hannah's father is the late Baron Fentington. Perhaps you've heard of him?"

Rafe thought. "I vaguely remember hearing the name. If it is the same man, he was known as a religious fanatic who wore only white and focused his efforts on condemning all women for Eve's sin."

"That's him," Caroline said. "Baron Fentington's estate neighbored ours, and Hannah was of an age with Grace and me. The baron was beyond strict when it came to raising his daughter. He forced Hannah to her knees in prayer for hours a day and severely punished her at the slightest provocation. It was nothing for her to sneak out of the house and come to us for comfort when her father went on one of his tirades. And she most often came with huge welts from the beatings he'd given her."

Rafe found it hard to breathe. What kind of father would do that to his child?

"Unfortunately for Hannah," Caroline continued, "she grew into a beautiful young lady. Her father became more irrational where she was concerned. He was harsh and inflexible, and made her suffer for being beautiful."

Caroline's voice thickened with emotion, and the duchess continued for her. "Hannah tried to make herself as unbecoming as she could, but her beauty came through no matter what she did. Instead of being proud of the woman she was growing into, her attractiveness enraged her father. He forced her to spend more hours in prayer, asking God to take away her sinful pride and vanity."

The duchess stopped for a few moments, as if she needed to control her emotions. Then she continued. "When Hannah was fifteen, Baron Fentington hosted a gathering of fellow clergymen. Of course, none of these men were leaders of their own congregation. They were what Hannah referred to as renegades and sanctimonious zealots. Because of their radical beliefs, no organized religion would have anything to do with them. Therefore, they roamed the area and held meetings in the homes of other extremist leaders."

The duchess paused, and Caroline reached for her hand and held it. "During one of their religious celebrations," she finally continued, "one of the pious members of Baron Fentington's gathering found Hannah alone in the barn. He raped her."

"No!"

Rafe knew the voice belonged to him, but he was so livid he couldn't control his anger.

"When her father discovered what happened," Caroline continued, "he, of course, blamed Hannah. He accused her of enticing a man of the cloth and charged her with tempting him the same as all wicked women tempt righteous and blameless men. He beat her within an inch of her life, then dumped her on the road with only the shredded dress she was wearing."

Rafe couldn't stand to hear any more. He bolted to his feet and stormed to the window, then turned back. "Is her father dead?"

"Yes," the duchess answered.

"Good," he ground through clenched teeth.

"Hannah crawled to our home and asked for refuge," Her Grace continued. "Of course, our father refused because he was as unforgiving and judgmental as the baron. So…" Her Grace paused as if unable to tell the rest of Hannah's story.

Caroline patted her hand and took up the tale where Her Grace left off. "Grace and I carried Hannah to an elderly woman who was known as a local midwife and reputed to have the gift to heal. She took Hannah in, but after she looked at her, she told us she probably would not survive. And she nearly didn't."

Rafe walked back from the window to his chair. "Is that why she left? Was she afraid I would find out about her past and think what happened was her fault?"

Caroline and her sister shared a look of embarrassment.

"No, Rafe," Thomas continued for them. "Hannah didn't leave because she thought you wouldn't understand. There's more."

Rafe sat in his chair. "Go on."

"Hannah recovered from what happened, but when she did, she was left with no place to go, with no one to take her in. She had no choice but to go where she could earn a living. And she thought London would provide the best opportunities for survival."

"You said she was only fifteen. She was merely a child. What work did she hope to get with no references or experience?"

"She found that out after she arrived in London," Thomas added. "To avoid starving, she turned to an occupation many young women turn to—especially women with the looks to attract men. She became a…a woman of ill repute."

Rafe felt as if he'd been punched in the gut. As if someone had belted him in the gut with both fists. "What?" He turned his gaze to his sister-in-law and the Duchess of Raeborn. Their downcast gazes told him he'd heard his brother correctly. "Hannah was a prostitute?"

"Not *was*. *Is*. I doubt that you are familiar with the name," Thomas continued, "but have you heard of Madam Genevieve?"

"Of course," he said, his tone more hostile than he wanted. "There's hardly a man who's spent any amount of time in London who hasn't heard of the famous Madam Genevieve. But what does that have to do with—"

He sank onto his chair as if he'd been struck dumb. He opened his mouth to speak, but no words would come.

The room spun around him in dizzying circles, and he couldn't breathe. He wanted to call his brother a liar—but he couldn't. He wouldn't dare defame Hannah's character with Caroline and the Duke and Duchess of Raeborn sitting there. The words had to be true, but he didn't want to believe them.

He rose on legs that trembled and staggered to the other side of the room. He had no purpose for going there except the need to escape the pitying looks on everyone's faces. It was as if they realized that she was the first woman with whom he'd ever fallen in love and knew they'd just destroyed his future.

"Why didn't you tell me before now?" he said in a voice that sounded raspy to his own ears.

"We didn't imagine that you and Hannah would be attracted to each other," his sister-in-law said.

"When we saw what was happening," the duchess said, "I talked to Hannah, but she assured me she could handle it. She was certain she could discourage you."

"She tried," he whispered.

He turned to face his family. "What happened to make her leave now? She intended to stay until the two weeks were over. Why did she leave so suddenly?"

Caroline and the Duchess of Raeborn looked at each other, then focused their gaze to where he stood.

"Why?"

"She discovered you are a vicar," Caroline answered.

For one second, Rafe's heart stopped and he reached out to keep from sinking to the floor.

"It's not your fault, Rafe," Caroline said in a voice that sounded very far away. "The two of you would never…"

Rafe didn't hear the rest of what Caroline said. Without a look back, he grabbed a full bottle of whiskey and went where he could be alone—and get drunk.

Very drunk.

Chapter 8

Hannah made her way to her private suite of rooms on the third floor of Madam Genevieve's and turned the key. She stepped into the room, then pressed her back against the closed door and looked around. This was her *home*. This was where she felt the most comfortable. Not the floor below, where she'd learned to be another person.

Here there were no lavish bouquets of flowers from ardent admirers. There were no gifts from men seeking her favors. No perfume-scented letters overflowing with undying devotion. Here she was alone with her thoughts and the comforts of her humble upbringing.

She walked to the table where Dalia, her friend and silent business partner, had a pot of piping-hot tea waiting for her, and poured the steaming liquid into a cup. With the cup in her hand, she walked to her burgundy brocade wing chair and sat.

The colors of the fabric weren't as rich as they'd been years ago when the chair was new, and the upholstery was worn in spots, but she didn't mind. It would be several years before she'd have to think of replacing it. And perhaps she never would. Perhaps she would keep it as a reminder. The chair had been the first purchase she'd made with money she'd earned giving her body to men who wanted her favors. Money she'd earned by sacrificing her self-respect. Money she'd earned because she'd given up the life she'd always dreamed of having.

She took a sip of her tea before it cooled, then leaned her head back. She closed her eyes, even though she knew the minute she did her thoughts would shift to him. They always did. He'd taken possession of such a huge part of her heart that it was impossible not to acknowledge him.

She wondered what he was doing now.

It had been nearly a month since she'd left. The house party would have ended weeks ago, and he'd no doubt gone back to the dowager house where he lived. Or perhaps returned to the parish he'd left. Or gone to a new one. He'd undoubtedly gone back to the life he'd lived before they met in an effort to wash the filth he thought clung to him through his association with a prostitute.

She wondered if any of the females Caroline invited during the remainder of the party had piqued his interest. She hoped one of the females he met while he was there captivated him. He deserved to be married. He deserved a house filled with children. He would be too perfect a father not to have a family of his own. His capacity to love was too great not to have a wife and children on whom to shower his affection.

She took another sip of her tea and chastised herself for letting her thoughts return to him so often. She wondered if he'd given her a thought since she'd left, and hoped that if he had, his opinion of her wasn't too unforgiving.

She smiled. She knew he hadn't thought of her as often as she'd thought of him because that would have been impossible. She'd thought of him constantly—at least once an hour every hour of every day.

She wondered if he relived the kisses they'd shared as often as she did. Or if he recalled the conversations they'd had and the details they'd learned about each other as often as she did.

She breathed a sigh. Probably not. He undoubtedly forgot about her as soon as he realized her identity— her profession. His display of passion was something he undoubtedly wanted to erase from his memory. She was, after all, used goods.

She tightened her fingers around the arm of the brocade chair and called herself every kind of fool imaginable. She'd never allowed any man to lay claim to as much of her heart as he managed to possess. And he was the last man she wanted anything to do with. He was a vicar. A man of the cloth. The last man on the face of the earth with whom she would ordinarily associate.

She wanted to hate him as she did every other pompous, overly righteous man spouting scripture and condemning her for the life she led. But she couldn't. She'd come to care for him too much.

It was the others she despised. The ones who thought she should have chosen death rather than turning to the only occupation left to her in order to survive.

They didn't know what it had been like to be so hungry you lost consciousness. They couldn't imagine what it was like to stare death in the face and have to make a choice between dying or using your body to buy a loaf of bread. They didn't know how helpless and terrifying it was for a young girl alone on the streets of London. Nor did they care. They saw only the choice she'd made, and judged her guilty for eternity.

Except she couldn't put Rafe in the same category as the rest of the *men of God* who stood outside the doors of Madam Genevieve's on a regular basis, calling down fire and brimstone on anyone entering or leaving her establishment. She could never hate him. She could hate only that he consumed her thoughts and her dreams like he did, and prayed he wouldn't intrude much longer.

She didn't want to relive every moment they were together. But the memories he'd given her were the best remembrances she'd had in her life. Her heart would be left with an empty chamber if she let them go.

A knock on the door pulled her thoughts away from the sparkle in Rafe's eyes and the broad smile on his handsome face. With a sigh, she pushed thoughts of him to the special place in her heart where she kept him.

"Come in," she said, setting down her tepid cup of tea.

The door opened, and Dalia entered.

"I thought I'd find you here," her friend said, closing the door behind her. "You've spent a lot of time here since you returned from the country."

"Have I?"

Dalia sat in a chair facing Hannah. "Anything you want to share?"

Hannah smiled, then shook her head. "Someday, maybe. Not yet."

"Very well. But you know I'm here when you want to talk."

"Yes, I know. You always have been. I don't know what I would have done without you over the years."

Dalia laughed. "You'd have managed. You're a survivor. You would have found someone else who thought the same as you and had the same goals."

Hannah looked into Dalia's dark eyes and smiled. Dalia returned her smile. The two of them were friends, as close as Hannah was to Grace and Caroline. Although Dalia was a few years Hannah's senior, the prostitute still possessed her striking beauty. Hannah often told her she didn't appear any older than the day she'd rescued Hannah from the street and brought her to Madam Genevieve's.

Dalia claimed the reason she didn't age was because she was part French, part Italian, part Greek, and part Gypsy. She believed the Gypsy in her refused to age, and none of the other parts were strong enough to fight the Gypsy.

Even though she was well past thirty, she had the figure of a woman ten years younger. Which was why Dalia was still one of the most asked-for courtesans at Madam Genevieve's. A request she often agreed to. Something Hannah hadn't done since she'd saved enough money to buy Madam Genevieve's.

She set down her cup and saucer. "What have you discovered?"

"It's not good, Hannah. Skinner, Flanks, and Crusher have joined forces."

"Well," Hannah said, leaning back into her chair. "That's an unlikely partnership. They must consider me an exceptionally dangerous adversary."

"Rumor has it they intend to destroy you. They're tired of losing their girls to you. Alone, they haven't been able to defeat you."

Laura Landon

"But they stand a chance if they unite," Hannah finished for her.

"That's the word on the street."

Hannah rose to her feet. She was too angry to remain sitting. "Don't they know if they'd recruit their women from the prostitutes already in the business, I wouldn't be a threat to them? I'm only after the innocent girls they press into service. We both know once a girl enters into the business of her own free will, it's almost impossible to get her out. I only want to save the innocent ones who turn to prostitution rather than starve to death on the streets. Or are forced into it by men like Skinner and the others and can't escape."

"They know it, but we both know there's more money in selling virgins."

Hannah turned to look out the window. Below were the streets of London. This area wasn't near Saint Giles or close to the slum area on the East End, but neither was it in the middle of Bond Street. She didn't know why Skinner and the others took such an interest in her when she was so far from them. "We must have affected their profits lately more than I realized. How many girls have we rescued from their clutches?"

"Six in the last two weeks," Dalia answered.

Hannah turned to look over her shoulder. "That many?"

"Yes. And Delores is out right now because she heard rumors that there's another girl on the streets who needs our help."

"She didn't go alone, did she?"

"No. Humphrey went with her."

Hannah breathed a sigh of relief. "Bring them up when they return."

"I think we need to warn the other girls to be careful until this blows over," Dalia said. "Flanks and Crusher aren't brave enough to do anything that might draw attention to them, but Skinner's another story. He's a mean one."

"Talk to everyone, Dalia. Tell them never to go out alone—always in pairs or even three. And to take one of the men with them."

Dalia stood, but paused when there was a knock on the door. "I'll get it," she said and opened the door. "Hello, Martha," she greeted one of the girls.

"Hello, Miss Dalia. I came to tell Miss Genevieve that Mr. Skinner is below. He's demanding to see her."

"He is, is he?" Dalia said.

The tone of Dalia's voice indicated she intended to tell Martha to send him packing, but Hannah knew it was better to find out what he wanted—although she already knew what that probably was. "Show Mr. Skinner to the Lilac Room, Martha," Hannah said. "Tell him I'll be down momentarily."

"Are you sure, Miss Genevieve?" Martha said with a worried frown on her face.

"Yes. I think it will be best to let Skinner have his say. Maybe I can prevent some of the trouble he intends to cause."

"If you say so," Martha said, then turned and left.

Dalia faced her. "Do you want me to come with you? I'm not sure it's wise to meet with him alone."

"No, I think he'll reveal more if I'm alone. I don't want him to think we're ganging up on him."

Dalia smiled. "But we are. We have been ever since we started rescuing girls from his grasp." An admiring look filled Dalia's eyes. "Can you believe that was almost twelve years ago? How many girls do you think we've saved from the life of hell he'd forced them to live?"

Hannah shook her head. "Hundreds, Dalia. And nearly that many babes."

"Yes," Dalia said on a sigh. "The babes." Her eyes grew damp. "That's what I'm happiest about, Hannah. The babes we've saved. They'd have died if we would not have rescued them and found homes for them."

"Yes. Now it's time for me to meet our enemy and see what threats he intends to make."

"Just be careful," Dalia said before she left the room.

"I will," Hannah answered, but this was one meeting she wasn't looking forward to. She followed Dalia down the hall, but took another set of stairs that led to the main part of the bordello. The part where Skinner was waiting for her.

She didn't knock when she reached the door but opened it and stepped inside the room. The man standing on the opposite side turned to face her.

If Hannah hadn't seen Skinner before, the long scar that ran down the side of his face would have frightened her. As it was, the evil glare in his eyes alarmed her. He was a man to be reckoned with—to be feared.

"What an unexpected pleasure, Mr. Skinner," she said, entering the room. "Shall I ring for tea?"

"I doubt my presence is a pleasure, Madam Genevieve, and tea isn't necessary. I won't be staying that long."

"As you wish." She sat on the lilac settee and pointed to the chair opposite her. "Won't you have a seat?"

He hesitated, then walked to the chair she'd indicated and sat.

"Now, what can I do for you, Mr. Skinner?"

"It's not what you can do for me, but what I can do for you."

"And what would that be?"

"If you stay out of my business, I might allow you to live a little longer."

"My goodness," she said, putting up a front of bravado, "you are very blunt."

"I've found that's the best way to be. It gets everything out in the open where there aren't any misunderstandings."

"And what exactly do you mean by 'staying out of your business'?"

"You know what I mean. I'm talking about all the young fillies you and your girls are stealing from me."

"Stealing? I can hardly steal something from you that you don't own. And unless I'm mistaken, it's illegal to *own* another human being in England."

"You know what I mean, Madam—"

"Unfortunately, I do, Skinner. You want me to stop rescuing innocent young girls who fall into your clutches. You want me to allow you to continue to abuse and misuse children for your low-class clientele's perverted pleasures. You want me to look the other way when young girls die because of the atrocious acts that are committed against them. And that," she said, rising to her feet, "I refuse to do."

The glare in his eyes turned deadly. "You'll regret this."

"No, Mr. Skinner. What I regret are the scores of innocent young girls I was unable to reach before you got them."

He slowly rose to his feet but didn't turn to leave. Instead, he stared at her for several long, chilling moments. "I'm going to enjoy making you regret your words. Enjoy it immensely."

Hannah stormed past him and opened the door.

With a smile on his face, Skinner walked past her, but stopped before he reached the outside door. "You have a real fancy place here," he said, letting his gaze lift to the ornate ceiling. "I'm going to enjoy taking it away from you."

On trembling legs, Hannah walked past him and threw open the front door. "Get out."

The sneering darkness in his eyes sent a wave of terror through her. She wanted to shift her gaze away from him but knew that would be a show of weakness.

Hannah hardened her glare. She tried to stand up to him with a sense of bravery far beyond what she felt. She knew she'd failed when the corners of Skinner's mouth lifted as if he intended to laugh at her. But his murderous glee didn't last long.

The malicious smirk on his face died when a low, angry voice spoke from behind them.

"I believe the lady asked you to leave."

Hannah didn't turn to the far corner behind her where the voice came from. She knew whose voice it was. She'd imagined hearing it every night since she'd left Caroline's.

She gripped the doorknob to keep from sinking to the floor and held on tightly.

"It seems you always have a knight in shining armor nearby to come to your rescue, don't you?" Skinner said as he walked past her and out the door. "But the day will come," he said before he took the steps down, "when it will be just you and me, Genevieve. Just you and me."

Hannah stared at Skinner as he mounted his carriage and sped away. But she didn't feel safe even after he was out of sight. A larger danger waited for her inside her home. She turned and came face-to-face with the man who'd haunted her dreams every night for more than a month.

"Hello, Rafe."

Chapter 9

❧

Hannah stared at him from across the room. She was unable to move, barely able to breathe. He was every bit as handsome as he'd been the last time she'd seen him, every bit as stunning to look at. And yet…

There was something different about him. Something she couldn't put her finger on. He somehow seemed harder. Darker. A distant figure that was almost unapproachable. It was as if he had aged several years in the month they'd been separated.

"May we talk?" he said, his tone more a demand than a request.

"Of course. Come with me."

Hannah heard his footsteps behind her as she moved toward the Daffodil Room. When she arrived, she reached out her hand to open the door, but his arm reached around her and turned the knob first. With a push, he opened the door and she entered.

He followed.

"Please, be seated. I'll ring for tea."

He didn't ask her not to, which meant he intended to drag this meeting out long enough to make it uncomfortable for her, long enough to give her the dressing-down he thought she deserved.

Perhaps she owed him a bit of retribution. But not too much. He wasn't the only one who'd been deceived. She had too.

She rang for tea, then sat in a chair near him. From the hardness of his features, she could tell he did not intend to make this easy on her. Well, she told herself, she'd handled difficult men before. Although it had been a while and she was a bit out of practice, she could do it again.

"How have you been?" she asked when she was settled.

"Fine. And you?"

"Very good. Did you have business in London?"

"No. I came to see you."

"Oh."

"You left without saying good-bye."

"I thought that was best—considering…"

"It wasn't. I expected more from—"

He was interrupted by a soft knock. The door opened, and a maid brought in a tea tray and set it on the small table in front of Hannah. "Thank you, Livy."

"You're welcome, miss."

Livy gave Rafe an appreciative glance, then bobbed a polite curtsy and left the room. They were alone again.

"Does she think I'm a…customer?"

Hannah wanted to smile, but the anger she heard in Rafe's voice stopped her. "No. We're not open for business yet."

Hannah ignored the tightening in Rafe's jaw and poured him a cup of tea, then handed it to him. He took it, but didn't take a sip before he set it back on the table with a decided clash that caused the tea to slosh in the cup.

"Why didn't you tell me?" he demanded. His voice was harsh. His tone strained with anger. The look in his eyes was as cold as steel.

She tried to hold her irritation to a minimum but failed. His question enraged her. "Tell you what, my lord? That I was leaving? That I was not Miss Hannah Bartlett, an innocent country miss who had grown up near Grace and Caroline, but was instead the infamous Madam Genevieve, a prostitute? That my father was the ill-reputed Baron Fentington? That the business I had to return to was a bordello? Or that in my other life I was a whore? Which ones of those questions are you angry that I didn't answer? And I have a question of my own, Lord Rafe. Why didn't you tell me you were a *vicar*?"

Hannah took advantage of Rafe's stunned silence to continue. "A *vicar*, my lord. If it weren't so unbelievably tragic, it would be funny. Let us hope your saintly parishioners never find out that you spent a week of your summer holiday with a whore."

"Stop it! You're not a whore!"

"But I am. That is what a man like you forced me to be. That is the only life a man of the cloth left me to live after he raped me."

Hannah couldn't stay seated. She couldn't bear to stay where she was forced to look him in the eyes. She rose and walked to the other side of the room. "Why did you come here?"

For several long moments, she didn't think he would answer. Then she heard the heavy sigh he breathed. "I couldn't stay away. I tried. I thought if I drank enough, I'd forget the first time we met and the first time I kissed you."

"Don't," Hannah ordered, but he either didn't hear her or he chose not to.

"When that failed, I tried to work myself until I was so exhausted I didn't even have the energy to think. But no matter how exhausted I was when I fell into bed, you wouldn't let me sleep. I relived every conversation we had, remembered the way my flesh tingled every time I touched you, remembered how hard you tried not to laugh at some of the things I said, and the excitement I felt when you failed."

"Don't," she said again.

"Did you think of me even once after you left? Were your dreams as consumed with me as mine were with you? Were you as afraid that you'd never see me again as I was that I'd never see you?"

Hannah turned to find him standing close behind her. She hadn't heard him walk toward her, but how could she when the blood rushed inside her head so ferociously that the room could have exploded and she wouldn't have heard it? "It doesn't matter what I remember or miss or try to recall, Vicar. The truth is that you are a man of the cloth and I am a prostitute."

"But you don't have to continue what you're doing. You can give it up. We could go away someplace where no one knows you and start a new life."

She stared at him, unable to believe he'd just said what she'd heard. "I'm not a seamstress, who can pack up her bolts of materials and open a shop in another village. I'm a prostitute. My reputation will follow me wherever I go."

"Then we'll move. If you are discovered, we'll go to another town where no one has ever heard of you and—"

"And what, my lord? How long will you be able to stand up in front of your congregation of saints and preach your sermons on righteousness and morality with a prostitute sitting in the front pew? How long before you realize you're not only living a lie, but preaching one too?"

He didn't move but lowered his gaze as if she'd opened his eyes and now he saw the ugly truth. "Go home, Vicar Waterford. Go back to your parishioners and forget you ever soiled yourself by associating with me."

"I'm not sure I can, Hannah. I tried when you left, and failed. I can't give you up."

"You don't have me, Rafe. You never did. I told you that from the start."

Something akin to a smile lifted the corners of his mouth, but the sadness on his face told her the gesture wasn't a smile. "You did, didn't you?"

"Yes. We don't have a future. And nothing we say or do will change that."

Hannah watched him as he struggled to make a decision. Finally, he took a step away from her as if he needed to separate himself from her.

Hannah bit her bottom lip to keep her eyes from filling with tears and hoped he would leave before she embarrassed herself.

"Maybe we could—"

Hannah lifted her hand to stop his words. She heard the pain in his voice and recognized the hurt he felt. She felt the same pain. "You cannot afford to have anything to do with me," she countered. "I'll destroy you, and in the end, you will hate me."

"No, I—"

"You will," she interrupted with more force than she thought she was capable of.

He stared at her for several long, torturous seconds, then walked across the room and opened the door. "Why was that man threatening you?" he asked before he left.

"That man?" Hannah had to think a moment before she realized what he meant.

"The man you asked to leave."

"Oh, him. It was nothing. Just a misunderstanding."

"It sounded like more than a misunderstanding. Are you in trouble?"

Hannah shook her head. "Nothing I can't handle."

"Are you sure?"

She wanted him gone before she couldn't hold back the tears any longer. "Yes. Good-bye, Lord Rafe. Have a good life."

He gave her a curt nod, then softly closed the door. And was gone.

Hannah sat on the nearest chair and let the tears fall. Because she couldn't have stopped them if she'd tried. Her heart hurt too much.

* * *

Rafe forced the fresh air to fill his lungs as he stood outside Madam Genevieve's bordello. He tried to order his feet to carry him away from her, but they wouldn't obey. He felt as if an empty pit had opened up in his chest and swallowed the heart he needed to exist.

He'd lost her again. Even though he'd known there would be numerous barriers they'd have to face, he had prayed that when she saw him, she'd be willing to undertake the challenges. Instead, she'd shown him how impossible a life with her would be.

For years he'd searched for just the right woman, a woman who'd match him as perfectly as Caroline matched Thomas. A woman who'd make his blood turn hot and his heart race.

When he'd met Hannah that first day by the stream, she'd caused all those things to happen—and more. There was something unique about her, something he'd searched for but hadn't found in any of the women he'd met. Yet the more he pursued her, the harder she fought to separate herself from him. But once he kissed her, he knew it didn't matter how hard she fought the feelings blossoming between them. He had no intention of ever letting her go.

Thomas once told him that he knew for sure after he'd kissed her that Caroline was the one woman in all the world he couldn't live without. At the time, Rafe didn't believe him. After all, he'd kissed scores of women, and although kissing a woman was a pleasant experience, there was nothing *that* mind-shattering in the experience. Now he knew how wrong he'd been.

The second he lifted his lips from Hannah's, he knew what Thomas meant. He knew that this was the woman with whom he wanted to spend the rest of his life. The minute he ended their first kiss, he wanted to kiss her again—and again. Until he'd found out the truth about Hannah's past—her *present*.

The fact that she'd lived her life as a prostitute destroyed any hopes for a future with her. She was right. How could he preach morality and righteousness to a congregation of saints when the woman he brought into their midst was the blackest of all sinners? How could he look his parishioners in their eyes and tell them their shepherd was living with a woman who'd made her living lying with men to whom she wasn't married? And yet…

How could he survive the rest of his life without her?

He stared at the entrance to the famous Madam Genevieve's one last time, then turned to walk away from her. Perhaps in time he'd be able to convince himself that he was lucky to have escaped the embarrassment and humiliation of a relationship with her. Perhaps in time he'd realize that her past was too great a barrier for him to breach. And most of all, perhaps in time he wouldn't be so desperate to discover a way for them to be together.

And yet he knew that would never happen. He'd never be content to live his life without her. He'd always be desperate to find a way for them to be together. And a part of him would die if he couldn't find it.

The street that took him from Hannah loomed before him with devastating emptiness, but he had no choice but to force his feet to carry him away from her. Their lives were too divergent to find a middle ground. How did he think he could ever expect a congregation to accept her once they found out who she was? And they would. He had no doubt of that. The bad always came before the good.

And what would he do if he were no longer a vicar? It's what he'd been called to do. What he wanted for his life's vocation.

He supposed he could always go back to Thomas and live in the dowager house. He could help Thomas run the estates. But he would never be happy doing that. He needed to do something whereby he could help someone. He needed there to be some kind of purpose in his life. He needed…

He paused. He needed Hannah. But that would never be.

He forced his feet to take the first step that would carry him away from her.

If he hadn't been so lost in thought, he might have seen the woman racing down the walk, towing a young girl behind her. At the last second, he stepped to the side, but the woman was focused on the path behind her and they collided. The woman fell to the ground.

"Oh, excuse me, ma'am," he said, rushing to help her to her feet.

The woman scrambled to rise, but she stumbled back to the ground when she tried to put weight on her ankle. "Run, Betty!" she ordered the young girl.

"He's coming," the young girl called Betty cried as tears streamed down her face. "I'm scared!"

"Go, girl. It's that big house right there," the woman said, pointing to Madam Genevieve's bordello. "I'll stop him until you get inside."

"But—"

"Go!"

"Run, Betty," Rafe encouraged. "I'll help your mother."

The girl looked toward the man racing toward them, then back to the woman on the ground, then turned toward Madam Genevieve's and ran.

Rafe watched to make sure she was safe, then waited for the man as he raced toward them. It was the same man

Hannah had ordered to leave when Rafe arrived. "Stay down," he told the woman. "I'll deal with this."

Rafe stepped onto the middle of the walk and raised himself to his full height. He knew he presented a forceful figure and thanked the hours of wood chopping for the assistance. He braced his feet wide and glared at the approaching man. "That's far enough," he said when the man was near enough to hear him.

The man Hannah called Skinner stopped.

"It's you again," Skinner said, glaring at him with fury in his eyes. "This is the second time you've come to Madam Genevieve's assistance. I find that very irritating."

"This is the second time you've bothered Madam Genevieve and her friends in the short time I've been here. I find that very disturbing."

"What you'll find even more disturbing is what I do to make you pay for sticking your nose into things that don't concern you."

"Anything that concerns Madam Genevieve concerns me."

Rafe hadn't had the opportunity to study Skinner earlier, but he did so now. The man was truly ugly. The long, jagged scar that ran down his cheek gave his face a permanent sneer. One could become accustomed to that, just as one grew accustomed to a person with a mole or a mark from birth. But the malicious glare in his deep-set, beady eyes was something Rafe doubted anyone could become accustomed to. The man exuded meanness. Cruelty emanated from every pore of his body. Rafe didn't know how Hannah could call anything associated with him a *misunderstanding.* Or how she could believe she could handle whatever was between them.

"Then you are a fool," Skinner said, his mouth curling into a snarl.

The smirk on his face fell when the door to Madam Genevieve's opened and three burly men walked toward them.

"Ah, I see help has arrived," Skinner said, taking a step back. "But be warned. This is not over. You can tell Genevieve she has stolen one too many girls from me. Her victory will be short-lived."

With that, Skinner turned and walked away from them.

Rafe watched until the man turned the corner, then looked over his shoulder to make sure the young girl had made it to safety. Hannah stood in the open doorway.

The three men raced to assist the woman who'd fallen, and Rafe slowly made his way back to Madam Genevieve's. His gaze didn't leave Hannah.

As he'd done so often when talking to his parishioners, he studied the expression on her face. The look in her eyes. What he saw revealed volumes—including several details he was sure she didn't want exposed.

Some of what he saw in Hannah's eyes didn't surprise him. *Fear*—she had good reason to fear Skinner. *Independence* and *self-reliance*—she'd taken care of herself her whole life and thought she was strong enough to take care of Skinner by herself. *Regret*—she was disturbed to know he'd been involved in the confrontation with Skinner and upset that he'd discovered that she was in danger. But he was past caring. She needed help but thought he was too weak to help her. She intended to protect him. To shield him as if he were some weakling.

The closer Rafe got to her, the angrier he became. She was in danger, and she would have allowed him to leave her. Her stubborn independence told her she had to face Skinner on her own. Didn't she realize she wasn't a match for him? Didn't she realize the man was capable of anything—even murder?

By the time he reached her, he was livid. What was wrong with her? Did she think that because he was a vicar he was incapable of handling confrontation? Did she consider him a milksop?

He stormed past her and headed toward the room where they'd spoken earlier. "We need to talk," he said without looking at her.

"I need to make sure Delores is all—"

"Now!"

He threw open the door to the Daffodil Room and waited for her to enter. When she walked past him, he followed her into the room and closed the door. She turned at the decided *thud* when the door slammed shut.

Her gaze narrowed, and he recognized her preparation to form an attack. He couldn't let her begin first. He couldn't allow her to take charge of this conversation. He couldn't permit her to have the upper hand—not when she refused to admit how much trouble she was in.

"You can start by explaining what's going on," he said without any pleasantries.

"Noth—"

"That's not the correct answer. Let's begin again. Who is Skinner? And why he is threatening you?"

She stared at him for several long moments, then the air rushed from her body and her shoulders dropped. "Please leave, Rafe. Please go home before you get hurt."

The pleading tone in her voice caused a powerful pull on his heart. "What about you, Hannah? Where can you go so you won't get hurt?"

"I can go nowhere. I'm where I belong. I'm doing what I need to do."

"And what is that? What are you doing that has Skinner so irate that he's resorted to threatening you? Stealing innocent young girls from him to use in your own bordello?"

She stared at him in stunned astonishment. Then the look in her eyes turned hostile. She took one step toward him and stopped. "What kind of person do you take me for?"

"I don't know, Hannah. You tell me. What kind of person are you to take girls away from Skinner?"

Anger flashed in her gaze. "Why don't you tell me what kind of person you think I am that I would take innocent young girls away from Skinner and bring them here?"

Hannah's reply forced him to consider what answer to give her. When he did speak, the tone of his voice was more controlled. "I know you, Hannah. I know you would never deal in children."

"Do you? How many times did you kiss me without realizing you were kissing a prostitute?"

He couldn't answer her.

"Go home, Rafe. Go back to your congregation of saints and stop bothering me."

Rafe knew she intended to say more, but a knock on the door stopped her. The door opened, and an attractive woman a few years older than Hannah entered.

"Everything's taken care of," the woman said. "Delores just twisted her ankle when she fell. But she'll be fine."

"And the girl?" Hannah asked.

"She's frightened, but she's safe."

"Good. Lord Rafe was just leaving, Dalia."

Then she turned her back on him.

Chapter 10

✤

Hannah listened to the door softly close behind Rafe before she let herself breathe. She needed him gone. Needed him to leave before something happened to him. Skinner was dangerous, and associating with her put Rafe in harm's way.

Oh, how tempted she'd been to ask for his help. How desperate she'd been to lean on his strength and rely on him to help her. But that wasn't a possibility. She'd never forgive herself if something happened to him. And something would if he remained close enough that Skinner could get to him.

"I'm not leaving you, Hannah."

She spun around and faced him. "Go. Please."

He shook his head. "Not until I know what you're involved in."

"This is no place for you. You're not capable of fighting Skinner. You can't even imagine how his mind works. He's evil through and through."

"But you can understand how he thinks? You believe that you're a match for him?"

"More than you! You belong in a church preaching to *good* people who are eager to listen to you. Not here, where men like Skinner don't think twice about sticking a knife in someone's back, or cutting a stranger's throat because they don't like the way he looks."

"What did you do to make him your enemy?"

Hannah paused a moment before she allowed herself to smile. "Let's just say he disagrees with what I'm doing."

"What would that be?"

"What it is can't concern you."

"Everything about you concerns me."

"No! Forget me. You don't belong here."

He shook his head as if he wouldn't consider what she'd said. As if he was blind to who and what she was because he wanted her to be something she wasn't. His next question confirmed it.

"What does that young girl have to do with this? Why does Skinner want her? Why do you?"

"Rafe, stop. Go back to Thomas and Caroline. Go someplace far away from me."

"I don't want to be any place where you're not."

"You have to! You can't stay here. You're not safe."

"Neither are you. Let me help you."

"No! Go back to your congregation of saints. Shepherd *them*!"

He paused. "I can't. I don't have a congregation to shepherd."

His revelation stunned her. "Why don't you have a congregation?"

He hesitated for several long seconds. "The reason isn't important. We're not talking about me. We're talking about you. And I'm not going until you tell me what this is about."

Hannah studied the determined look on his face and realized how serious he was. "I can have you thrown out."

"Then you'll force me to stay outside and pray Skinner doesn't see me and decide to repay me for helping you take that girl away from him."

A wave of fear raced down her spine. He would do it. He was naive enough to stand in front of Madam Genevieve's until she let him in. Or Skinner saw him and killed him. "You're a fool," she whispered.

"Thomas used to tell me that quite often when we were younger."

Hannah squeezed her eyes shut and took a deep breath. She had no choice but to tell him what she was doing—what she'd been doing for several years already.

A part of her was eager to tell him. A part of her wanted to have someone who could shoulder some of the burden. Not that he could do anything to help her. But at least someone would know about Coventry Cottage in case something happened to her. And who better than Rafe?

She breathed a deep sigh, then nodded.

He walked into the room and sat in the chair she indicated. Before she joined him, she walked to the table where she kept several decanters of liquor and poured a glass of brandy for Rafe and a glass of wine for herself. A knock on the door interrupted them.

"Are you all right?" Dalia asked, stepping into the room.

She nodded. "I'm fine, Dalia. Come in. I'd like you to meet someone."

Dalia closed the door and walked toward them.

"Dalia, this is Rafe Waterford—Vicar Waterford. He's a…friend. Rafe, Miss Dalia Cavendau. Dalia's both a friend and a business partner. She helps me run Madam Genevieve's."

"Vicar?" Dalia asked. Her questioning gaze locked with Hannah's. "Vicar Waterford?"

"Yes, Dalia. Vicar."

"Miss Cavendau," Rafe greeted.

Dalia cast Rafe an evaluative glance. Her hesitation was obvious. She finally spoke. "I'd like to thank you for helping Delores like you did. And the young lass. She wouldn't have made it without your help."

Rafe's gaze shifted from Dalia to Hannah. "I'll accept your thanks once I make sure the girl didn't exchange one owner for another. Not before."

A frown covered Dalia's brow.

Hannah pointed to a third chair. "You might as well join us, Dalia. I was about to explain about the young girl Vicar Waterford rescued."

The frown on Dalia's forehead deepened. "Do you think that's wise?"

"I don't think either of you have a choice," Rafe said. "I'm not leaving until I know what you intend to do with that young girl."

Dalia's eyebrows shot upward. "*Do?*"

"Yes, *do.*"

Dalia cast Hannah a look of concern, then slowly sat.

Hannah walked to the chair opposite Rafe and sat. "Unlike Skinner and his associates," she said once she had his attention, "we are not in the habit of selling children. The ladies who work at Madam Genevieve's are here because they *choose* to be here. Their reasons vary. As hard as this may be for you to understand, some are here because they enjoy the work."

Hannah enjoyed the color that flooded Rafe's face.

"Some are here because society turned their back on them, and this was the only occupation open to them. They are all, however, free to leave Madam Genevieve's anytime they choose."

"But they don't," Dalia added. "Madam Genevieve's reputation is known far and wide. Ladies come here to work because our clientele is of a superior quality. We don't allow mistreatment of any kind, and that's very important to our girls."

Hannah looked at Rafe. "How did you find me?"

"Caroline told me where you were."

"If they told you that much, I assume they told you how I came to be here and why I've stayed."

The nod of Rafe's head was slight but told her he knew most of her story.

"When I reached London, I arrived with nothing more than the clothes on my back. I hadn't eaten for several days and was near starvation. I tried to find respectable work, but no one would hire me. None of the *good* people of London wanted anything to do with me. There was only one occupation left me."

"There were churches here," Rafe said. "Why didn't you go to one of them for help?"

The tone of his voice contained a hint of censure, and Hannah's temper rose. "Excellent suggestion, Vicar Waterford. I knew the good Christians in London would surely rescue me from near death, even if my attacker had been a member of that elect group. I was certain I could rely on them to help me."

Hannah rose to her feet and paced the space between them. "Do you think I didn't go from one church to the next to beg for help? For at least a scrap of bread? And from one or two, that's what I received. A scrap of bread! Yes, Vicar Waterford. From a few of the Good Samaritans of this world, I received a scrap of bread—before they slammed their door in my face."

Hannah stopped. "Do you know who saved me?" She didn't wait for his answer. "One of Madam Genevieve's ladies. Yes, Vicar Waterford. A whore. Not a man of the cloth, or any of the good Christians in the church. But a whore. Her name was Claudette, and she half-carried me to Madam Genevieve's because when she found me, I wasn't strong enough to walk on my own."

Hannah took a deep breath, then sat again. "Claudette and several of the other girls here nursed me back to health. When I was strong enough, they gave me the choice of staying or leaving." Hannah paused. "I had no place to go. So I stayed.

"I worked hard and saved as much money as I could from my nightly take. When the previous Madam Genevieve decided she wanted to retire, I offered to buy her business. I wanted the security owning my own business would give me. I never wanted to be as helpless as I was when I arrived in London as a fifteen-year-old. I paid her what she asked and became the new Madam Genevieve."

Hannah fixed an unwavering gaze in Rafe's direction. It was important that he understood her goal. "I made a promise the day I took possession of Madam Genevieve's. I vowed that I would never miss an opportunity to rescue as many young girls as I could from living on the street."

A lump formed in her throat when she thought of all the girls she'd saved. That lump threatened to choke her when she thought of all the girls she hadn't reached in time.

As if Dalia realized how close to tears Hannah was, she continued the story for her.

"At first Genny went out every day by herself," she said. "When the rest of us discovered what she was doing, we took turns going out too."

"Is that what happened today?" Rafe asked. His voice was softer and filled with less censure than before.

"Yes," Dalia answered. "Skinner and his cohorts cater to the more depraved of your species. Of high demand are children and virgins. He either lures them into service, or he steals them."

Rafe's gaze lowered to the floor.

"Yes, my lord," Hannah said. "They steal them. That's why it's so important that we keep a close watch and move as fast as we can."

"Surely you realize you're not safe?" Rafe asked.

Concern filled his eyes, and Hannah felt a tug at her heart. He cared about her. No one had ever cared about her. She swallowed hard. "Neither are the children. They need me. They need all of us to save them."

Hannah looked at the man who'd caused such turmoil in her life and reminded herself that they didn't have a future together. They were worlds apart, and no amount of wishing or dreaming or praying could bring their worlds closer.

A knock on the door kept her from saying more to him.

"I just left the girl," one of the prostitutes known as Ruthie said from the open doorway. "She lives with her granny and ran away 'cause she said it was boring there." Ruthie smiled. "She doesn't like the excitement here and has decided to go home."

"I'm glad," Hannah answered. She was thankful she didn't have to make room for the girl at Coventry Cottage. It was overcrowded as it was. "Has Humphrey returned? Was he hurt?"

"He has a cut on his arm, but other than that, he escaped his tussle with Skinner's men unharmed."

"Good. As soon as he's able, have him take the girl to her grandmother. And send Clemmons with him. Everyone needs to take special care from now on."

"Yes, ma'am."

Dalia stood. "I'll make sure the girl gets on her way," she said.

"Thank you," Hannah answered, then watched as her friend left the room. She and Rafe were alone.

He stood and stepped closer to her. "You can't stay here, Hannah. It's not safe. Come away with me."

His entreaty was serious. He really wanted to have a life with her. Except, in time he'd regret his rash decision. How could it be any different?

Her past would be a constant hurdle. It didn't matter where they went; eventually someone would recognize her. In time he wouldn't be able to endure the comments and accusations. She wouldn't be worth the humiliation he suffered—a man of the cloth married to a prostitute. When that happened, he'd hate himself because he'd been infatuated by someone so flawed. And he'd hate her because of who and what she was.

She shook her head. "No, Rafe."

"You have feelings for me. I know you do. You may not be brave enough to face them yet, but you care for me. I know you do. I knew it the second we kissed."

"It doesn't matter what I feel for you, or what you feel for me. All that matters is that you are a vicar searching for a parish where you can do what you've been called to do. And I am a prostitute. A whore."

"You're not a whore! Madam Genevieve is a *role* you've played but not who you really are. Beneath your fancy clothes and beautifully styled hair, you're a good, pious woman. Madam Genevieve is someone you were forced to become because of what happened to you when you were young."

Hannah stared at him in disbelief. "Listen to yourself, Rafe. Listen to the lies you're telling yourself about me." She slashed her hand between them. "You're trying to *pretend* I'm the same as the other females who sit in the pews every Sunday morning. But I'm not!"

"Don't say that. You can't help what that man did to you when you were young."

"No, I couldn't help what he did. But that doesn't change *what* he did. Or what I became because of what he did. You are the one who can't face it. You want to pretend my past never existed."

"Then you'll change. You can become respectable. We'll go away and start over. No one will ever know who you were."

You can become respectable.

Hannah slowly turned and walked to the other side of the room. With her back to him, she pressed her fists against her stomach. The ache there nearly doubled her over.

"A person doesn't *become* respectable. Respect is something that's earned. And being a prostitute doesn't earn a person respect."

"I didn't mean that, Hannah. You know I didn't."

"Leave, Rafe. Go home. Find a parish where you can devote your time to being a shepherd to the saints of this world. Leave me and the sinners of this world alone. We don't need you. *I* don't need you."

"Hannah—"

"Leave!"

A long, agonizing silence stretched before the door opened then closed. The room echoed with a hollow emptiness, and this time she knew he was gone. Her heart ached with a devastating void that only came from knowing that all was lost.

And in that moment, Hannah knew she'd lost the only person who would ever mean anything to her.

She'd lost the only man she would ever love.

Chapter 11

❀

Hannah entered Madam Genevieve's through her private entrance and handed her cloak to the waiting butler. She headed toward the stairs that would take her to her suite of rooms on the third floor. She was tired. She wanted nothing more than to sit down with a chilled glass of wine and hope it would help her forget.

"Did you find who you were looking for?"

Hannah looked to the top of the stairs and saw Dalia. She stood as if she were Hannah's mother and had postponed going to bed so she could reprimand her daughter for coming home late.

Hannah shook her head, then began her climb up the steps. "I wasn't looking for anyone in particular. I just thought there might be a young girl out there who needed our help."

"How much longer are you going to torture yourself like this?"

"Like what?" Hannah said when she reached the top of the stairs. She walked past her friend and went to her rooms. "I'm not torturing myself."

"You are and have been since your vicar left."

"I don't know what you're talking about." Hannah opened the door to her sitting room and entered. Dalia followed her. "And he's not my vicar."

"Taking chances like you are isn't going to help. It's only going to get you into trouble."

"I don't take chances. I don't go out alone. Humphrey is always with me."

"Except when you go off by yourself and tell him to stay with the carriage."

"Who told you—" Hannah stopped. She should have known Dalia would demand Humphrey report any risks she took. Dalia was worried about her. They all were. She could tell from the way they watched over her.

It had been two weeks since Rafe left, and everyone treated her as if she were something fragile and about to break.

"I've never seen you like this, Genny. I know you're keeping yourself busy to forget him, but it's not good for you."

"Don't be ridiculous. I'm not trying to forget anyone. I just remember the promise I made myself years ago. I'd forgotten it for a while."

"You didn't forget. None of us forgot. But we knew to be careful. We didn't underestimate the danger like you're doing now. It's as if you *want* a confrontation with Skinner."

"Don't be ridiculous," Hannah repeated, although that was *exactly* what she wanted. This war wouldn't be over until one of them came out on top. Skinner wouldn't be stopped until he was eliminated.

"When I think of the girls Skinner's already got his hands on, I get sick. It's never been more important to save as many girls as we can."

"That's what we've always done," Dalia said, "but we've never searched for them night and day."

"Well, maybe we should have. Maybe we could have saved more girls. Even one more would have been a blessing."

Dalia walked to the table where several crystal decanters sat and poured two large glasses of chilled wine. When she returned, she handed one to Hannah, then sat in a chair facing her.

"Why don't you tell me what's really behind this," she said after she'd taken a sip of her wine. "And spare me the denials. We know each other too well to test our friendship with lies."

Hannah lifted her glass to her mouth and drank a swallow of the wine. She and Dalia often sat in these same chairs and shared parts of their pasts that no one else knew. That's what best friends did; they listened to each other without judging.

"It's Rafe. I've tried, Dalia, honest I have, but I can't forget him."

"Your vicar?"

"Yes," she whispered. "My vicar. I'll be thirty next month, and I've been a prostitute nearly half my life. I've slept with scores of men and have never given any of them a second thought. Why now? Why him?"

"Because he's special. Because he's opened some of the doors you'd slammed shut years ago by telling yourself that you didn't deserve to be loved the same as other women are. Unfortunately, even though we lock the doors to all the chambers of our heart, when you least expect it, someone comes along with a key to unlock those doors."

"But why *him*? Why a *vicar*?"

Dalia smiled. "Because God has a unique sense of humor, and He often plays tricks on His creations." Dalia laughed. "I have to admit, He played a real good one on you."

Hannah looked at her friend. "That's the first time I've heard you talk about God. I didn't know you were a religious person."

Dalia laughed. "I doubt your vicar or any of the good people who attend church on a Sunday morning would call me a religious person, but I was raised in a good home. My granny was a churchgoer, and she read my sister and me a story from the Bible each night before we went to bed. Those were my favorite times."

Hannah took another sip of her wine. "Do you ever wonder what your life would be like if your granny and sister hadn't died of a fever?"

"I used to a lot, but not so much anymore." Dalia sat back in her chair. "How about you? Do you ever wonder what your life would have been like if you'd had a different father?"

Hannah shook her head. "It doesn't do any good to want to change your life. I learned early on to accept the life you were given and make the best of it."

"But you're not ready to accept your vicar? Or the fact that he might truly care for you?"

At first, Hannah thought to answer Dalia's questions with a flippant reply, but something stopped her. She needed to face the feelings she had for Rafe, no matter how much they hurt.

"When we first met, I knew he was attracted to me. I'd seen that look in men's eyes plenty of times when they first saw me. I know I'm passably attractive—"

"You're more than passably attractive. You're beautiful and you know it," Dalia interjected.

Hannah smiled. "I'm pretty—nothing more. And I know how to please a man. Over the years I've met several men with whom I could have easily fallen in love. But didn't. Love wasn't something I thought I'd ever experience. Then, when I least expected it, there he was. A man who was everything I wanted a man to be—mild yet possessing an inner strength that made me feel safe and secure. Kind and gentle and honest and giving. He's the first man I thought could accept who and what I am."

"If you're sure he can accept you, what's stopping you?"

Hannah rose from her chair and walked to the window on the other side of the room. "He's a vicar, Dalia. He stands up in front of a congregation each and every Sunday and preaches about godliness and virtues. A connection to me would make every word he utters a lie."

Dalia didn't speak for several long seconds. Her silence told Hannah she agreed. A future with Rafe was impossible.

"Have you considered turning your back on your life here and going away with him?"

Hannah turned with a smile on her face. "You sound as naive as Rafe." She took a comforting sip of her wine. "How long do you think it would be before someone recognized me? How long before Rafe is driven out of one church, then another, because of me? How long before he comes to hate me because I've ruined his life?"

Dalia's silence indicated she knew Hannah was right. Her question confirmed it.

"What are you going to do?"

Hannah walked back to her chair and sat. "What I've always done. Run Madam Genevieve's. We need to turn a profit to keep Coventry Cottage open. And I'll try as diligently as I can to save as many girls as possible from Skinner's clutches."

"What about your vicar? It's obvious he means a lot to you. He's not going to be easy to forget."

Hannah breathed a heavy sigh. "For now, I'll keep myself as busy as possible. Maybe in time I won't think of him as often as I do now."

"Which is?"

Hannah tried to hide the tears that filled her eyes. "All the time, Dalia. All the time."

A sharp knock saved Hannah from embarrassing herself with the tears that threatened to fall. The door opened, and one of the girls stood in the entryway with a paper in her hand.

"Miss Genevieve, this just came for you. It came from that whore who works for Skinner who's been telling us when the blackguard leaves to get a new girl."

Hannah reached for the note. "Thank you, Molly."

The girl smiled, then left.

Hannah opened the note and read it. She rose from her chair. "Dalia, tell Humphrey to ready the carriage. Skinner left to pick up another girl."

"I don't like it, Genny. That's the second girl today. Something's not right. Send Converse with Humphrey and you stay here."

Hannah laughed as she headed for the door. "The poor girl would probably run to Skinner for help if she saw both Converse and Humphrey come after her. They're big as barns."

"Then take Converse with you too."

"Who will stay here in case one of the girls needs him?"

"When's the last time one of the girls needed either Humphrey or Converse? They're only needed when one of us goes out to rescue another girl."

"I'll be fine, Dalia. You're fretting like a mother hen."

"Take Converse too. Please."

Hannah gave up her arguments. "Very well. I'll take Converse too. Now go. Have Humphrey bring my carriage to the back door and tell Converse he'd better be there or I'm leaving without him."

Dalia breathed a sigh Hannah heard across the room, then did as she asked.

Hannah followed Dalia to the door, but stopped before she left her room. Even though she didn't think she had anything to worry about, it didn't hurt to be extra cautious.

She walked back into the room and opened the drawer at the back of the small table that sat beside her chair. She reached inside and wrapped her fingers around the small pistol there, then tucked it into a pocket in her skirt.

She wouldn't need it, she was sure. But it didn't hurt to be prepared.

Chapter 12

A light mist fell as Hannah made her way to London's seedier side. The first time she came here in search of a young girl to rescue, she'd hated it. Everything about this part of London reminded her of what it had been like when she'd first arrived nearly fifteen years ago. And even though she'd been here scores of times since, she still didn't like it. She wasn't as frightened now as she'd been then, but she still didn't like the memories that surfaced when she came here.

The carriage turned a corner, then slowed.

"Are you sure this is where the note said, ma'am?"

"Yes, Humphrey. Let Converse out here, then drive ahead, but stay in the shadows."

Hannah sat back against the squabs. There was no use peering out the window. Humphrey would keep watch like he always did. When Skinner or one of his associates showed up, he'd let her know. Then they'd wait until the girl arrived.

If Skinner followed his regular routine, someone would bring her—either one of Skinner's henchmen or the woman called Maude, who ran the holding house where he kept the girls after he pretended to rescue them from the streets. When Maude came, she usually had a guard with her. Hannah always thought she'd rather deal with the guard than with Maude. She was one of the few women who frightened Hannah, and Hannah would hate to have to defend herself against her.

Hannah leaned her head back against the cushion and closed her eyes. Her thoughts drifted where they always did when she had a quiet moment—to Rafe. She wondered what he was doing. Wondered if he'd started his life again. If he was having as hard a time forgetting her as she was him.

She pressed her fingers to her lips and remembered the last time he'd kissed her. There were moments when she swore she could still feel his lips against hers. She prayed she'd never forget what that had been like.

She heard a noise outside and came alert.

"There's a wagon coming, Miss Genevieve. It's that Maude woman and that rotter they call Fish. They have the young'un with 'em."

"Can you see Skinner?" she asked through the open carriage window.

"No. The driver seems to be alone, as always."

"We won't do anything until—"

"Wait," Humphrey interrupted. "Here comes someone."

"Is he alone?"

"Yah, he's alone."

"Good. We'll wait until they exchange the girl, then we'll follow him. Stop the carriage before he reaches the next street if you can."

"That shouldn't be a problem. I'll—*Oomph!*" Before Humphrey finished what he was saying, the carriage lurched, and then the door burst open. Strong, brutal fingers clamped around her arms and pulled her from the carriage.

Hannah struggled, but her efforts only caused the two men to tighten their unyielding grasps. She looked around and spotted two more men standing over Humphrey's limp body.

Her heart pounded frantically. This was Skinner's doing. He'd set a trap, and she'd walked into it. She knew whatever he had planned, it wouldn't be pleasant. "Let go of me," she ordered.

"We ain't lettin' go, missy. Skinner said he got you first, then we could all take turns. I'll be the one after Skinner, just so you know. You won't be sorry."

They all laughed, and Hannah's heart thundered so hard inside her that she thought she would be ill. She tried to twist away from them, but their painful grasps only tightened.

She looked down at Humphrey. Blood seeped from a gash in his head, but his chest rose and fell with each breath. He was hurt, but still alive.

She needed to go to him, needed to stanch the bleeding, but she couldn't free herself. She lifted her gaze to find Skinner before her.

"Well, well, well, Genevieve. What have we here?"

"How dare you, Skinner," she hissed, trying to sound confident. Trying to hide how frightened she was.

"I dare because you have come to my part of town, and everyone knows how dangerous that is."

"I demand you—"

"Demand all you want, Genevieve. It won't do you any good." He laughed. "Look around you. There ain't nobody who will help you. Nobody cares down here."

Hannah didn't need to look. She knew no one would be there who could help her. Or would risk helping her.

Skinner took one menacing step toward her, then another. She was glad it was dark and she couldn't see the arrogant gleam in his eyes. She knew how menacing and terrifying he would look. A cold shiver raced down her spine.

"I'm glad I finally have you to myself," he said, clasping her chin between his thumb and forefinger. "I've wanted to teach you a lesson for a long time. It's time I repaid you for stealing those young girls that belonged to me."

His hand cupped her cheek. Then his fingers traveled down her neck toward her breasts. She struggled harder, but all she earned from her efforts were bawdy guffaws and crude comments from the men holding her.

"Touch me and you'll be sorry, Skinner." She tried to free at least one of her hands. If she could reach the pistol in her pocket she might have a chance to—

Skinner's hand closed around her breast, and she couldn't think. He was going to rape her. He was going to use her like she'd been used the first time. And this time she wasn't sure she could survive it.

"See what happens when you interfere in my business?" Skinner reached up to the neckline of her gown and clamped his fingers around the material. He was going to rip it from her body. He was going to expose her to—

"Get your hands off her. Now!"

Skinner's grip on the material at her neck loosened.

Hannah knew it wasn't possible, but in her mind the voice belonged to Rafe. But it couldn't be. He'd left weeks ago. She only thought it was because she'd always considered him her safe harbor. She thought of him as the anchoring rock to which she could cling in times of trouble. But she knew it was only her mind playing tricks on her—she *prayed* it was her mind playing tricks on her.

She slowly turned toward the voice, and her heart fell to her stomach. Rafe stood in the shadows and faced Skinner with more courage than she'd ever seen from anyone in her life.

He looked anything *but* a vicar.

She didn't know whether to feel relief or collapse from fear. Rafe wasn't a match for Skinner and his men.

"You heard me," Rafe repeated.

There was a threatening tone to the voice, and Skinner turned to face the stranger who'd issued the warning. "If it isn't Genevieve's knight in shining armor."

Skinner dropped his hand from her bodice and took a step away from her. "Have you come to save your lady again?"

"Tell your men to let her go."

"And if I don't?"

Rafe lifted his hand and pointed a pistol at Skinner. "You'll probably regret it."

Hannah took a moment's pleasure in seeing Skinner's eyes widen. Her pleasure didn't last long.

"This is the third time you've crossed me," Skinner said. "Most men don't live long after they cross me the first time. I think you're long overdue for a lesson."

"Let her go," Rafe repeated.

"Or you'll—?"

Rafe fired his pistol, and his bullet struck the cobble-stones at Skinner's feet. Skinner jumped back.

"You'll pay for this," Skinner growled, "and I'll enjoy seeing you suffer." He slowly signaled his men to release her.

Hannah felt the confining grasp loosen around her arms and experienced an immense sense of relief. The moment she was free, she rushed to Rafe's side.

"Go to your carriage," he ordered.

She didn't want to leave him. She didn't want him to face Skinner and his men alone.

She looked down at Humphrey, still lying on the cobblestones, and considered her options. She didn't have a choice. She couldn't leave him. He'd never escape alive.

She shook her head and waited to see what he intended to do next. She knew she'd receive the full extent of his fury as soon as they were alone, and she'd already decided she'd let him get his anger out of his system. Besides, she deserved it. Coming here had been a mistake. Dalia had warned her that this might be a trap, but she was too stubborn to listen.

"Then go check on Humphrey," he said when he realized she wouldn't leave him.

That she would do. She nodded and stepped to where Humphrey lay.

"Take your men and get out of here, Skinner," Rafe ordered.

Hannah knelt beside Humphrey and breathed her first sigh of relief. It was almost over. As soon as Skinner and his men were gone, they could take Humphrey home and this would be over.

She lifted her gaze, expecting to see Skinner and his men slink away. But that wasn't what was happening. Instead of leaving, Skinner stood where he was. The malicious grin on his face broadened, and his arrogant demeanor became more apparent.

A wave of fear washed over her. Something was wrong.

"Stand up, Genevieve," Skinner said. "I don't want you to miss this."

Confusion seeped into every pore. She glanced at Rafe. A frown covered his face as if he realized something was terribly wrong. His gaze darted from Skinner to each of the men with him, then back to Skinner.

"Stand up," Skinner repeated.

She slowly rose to her feet.

Suddenly, as if giving a silent order, Skinner shifted his gaze to a figure in the shadows behind them and gave a curt nod.

Hannah turned to where he indicated and saw the woman Maude raise her arm. She pointed a pistol at the center of Rafe's back and fired.

Before Hannah could shout a warning, Rafe jerked forward. His expression was one of pained surprise. The gun in his hand clattered to the ground, and the men with Skinner charged toward him.

"No!"

Hannah tried to reach Rafe first, but Skinner grabbed her by the arm and pulled her back.

"Now you'll see what happens when you interfere in my business."

Two of the men held Rafe while a third man stepped in front of him. With a leering grin on his face, the man pulled back his arm and slammed his doubled fist into Rafe's gut.

Rafe groaned in pain.

"No! He's not the one you want, Skinner. I am. Do what you want with me, but leave him alone!"

Rafe struggled as much as his wound would allow him to, but the man in front of Rafe pulled his arm back again and pummeled his fist into Rafe's jaw. With a loud groan, Rafe's head snapped to the side and blood poured from his nose and mouth.

Hannah attempted to free herself, but Skinner's grasp was too firm. "Stop! He's had enough!"

Skinner laughed. "You should have thought of that before you interfered again. I told you you'd regret sticking your nose where it doesn't belong." He nodded and the man in front of Rafe hit him again. Then again.

"Enough!" Tears streamed down her face as she pleaded for Skinner to tell his man to stop. But her entreaties were met with Skinner's ribald laughter.

With each blow, more color faded from Rafe's face. Blood streamed from his mouth and nose and the cuts on his face. His legs were limp beneath him. All that kept him from falling to the ground were the two men holding him. And still the beating continued.

"Stop!" Hannah pleaded, begging Skinner to call off his man. But he didn't. The beating continued until Hannah thought she would become ill.

"You want him dead?" the man beating Rafe asked after several minutes. "He's close to it."

"You decide, Genevieve," Skinner said. "He probably won't live anyway. You want George here to put him out of his misery?"

"No! Stop!"

"George will when you promise we'll never see you or your girls down here again."

"I'll stop!" Hannah cried out through the tears that streamed down her face. "I'll stop!"

"Are you sure?"

"Yes!"

A commotion caused Skinner to pause. One of his men rushed toward him.

"There's a group of men coming. One of them looks like Frisk."

"What the hell," Skinner said. He turned back to where Rafe hung limp between the two men still holding him. "Let him go," Skinner ordered.

The two men holding Rafe released him, and he crumpled to the ground. Only then did Hannah see the large bloodstain that darkened his jacket.

She twisted out of Skinner's arms, and this time he released her.

Hannah rushed to Rafe's side and sank to her knees beside him. Bruises were already darkening on his face, and some of the blood was already dry. He was hurt badly—*very* badly.

"If I ever see you down here again," Skinner barked, "I'll go after your girls next. It won't be safe for them to leave the house. You understand?"

Hannah nodded, but only a small part of her mind heard what Skinner said. How could she care about anything except getting Rafe home—if he survived that long.

* * *

Hannah heard the pounding of footsteps behind her but didn't look to see who was coming. All that concerned her was Rafe and how badly he was hurt.

"Miss Genevieve?" a voice said from over her. "Miss Genevieve?" it repeated when she didn't answer.

Hannah slowly lifted her gaze to where Converse stood beside her.

"We have to leave here," he said when he hunkered down near her.

"I don't think we should move him," she said, wiping some of the blood from Rafe's face. "He's—He's been shot. And they beat him."

"That's why we need to get him to a doctor, Miss Genevieve. He needs to be looked after."

Hannah looked at Rafe's battered face resting in her lap. She cupped her hand to his cheek and let the tears fall.

This was her fault. She should have realized this was a trap. She should have brought more men with her. She should have known that Rafe wouldn't leave her. She should have known that he would stay close to protect her.

She thought of the inscription on the watch he carried. IN ALL THINGS, BE *NOBLE*.

It was suddenly important that she make sure his watch was still in his pocket. That he hadn't lost it while Skinner's men were beating him.

She searched the pocket in his jacket until she felt the lump that was his watch. With trembling fingers she reached inside and lifted it out. It was safe. It hadn't been harmed in the scuffle.

"There's a wagon waiting, Miss Genevieve."

Hannah nodded. She knew Rafe needed to be moved. She knew he needed to get to a doctor fast. But he was alive now, and she was terrified that he wouldn't survive the trip to Madam Genevieve's.

"Is Humphrey all right?" she asked.

"I'm right here, Miss Genevieve. Let me help you."

Hannah carefully lifted Rafe's head from her lap and gently placed it on the cold, hard street. When she looked up, Humphrey stood with his arm outstretched. She grasped his fingers and rose to her feet.

"Be careful with him," she said when a group of men picked Rafe up and placed him on a long board.

"We will, miss," one of the men said as they rushed Rafe to the wagon.

Humphrey helped her into the back of the wagon, then sat down beside her. When they slid Rafe into the wagon bed, she nestled his head on her lap again and held him tightly.

"How did these men get here?" she asked after the horses moved forward.

"Your friend sent Converse for help when he saw what was happening. Converse went to Frisk, and he came with his men."

Hannah touched Rafe's swollen face, then placed her hand atop his chest. She needed to make sure he was still breathing. She needed to know that he was still alive.

How had her life gotten to this point? What was she going to do with Rafe when he healed?

How was she going to survive if he didn't?

She couldn't allow herself to think about that now. She didn't want to imagine a world that didn't have Rafe in it. She didn't want to imagine her life without Rafe in it.

Someone had placed a blanket over Rafe, and Hannah tucked it around him as the wagon rumbled through the streets.

"We're almost home, Miss Genevieve," Humphrey said when the wagon turned a familiar corner.

"Send someone for a doctor right away, Humphrey."

"I will. Your friend will get the help he needs in no time."

Hannah felt her hand lift slightly with Rafe's shallow breathing and felt a sense of relief that weakened her entire body.

The wagon stopped at the back entrance to Madam Genevieve's, and several of the girls, along with Dalia, rushed out to meet them.

"Are you all right?" Dalia said, taking Hannah in her arms the minute her feet hit the ground.

"I'm fine. But Rafe's not."

Hannah watched the men take him from the back of the wagon and carry him into the bordello.

Dalia wrapped her arm around Hannah's waist, and they followed the men carrying Rafe. "The doctor's on his way," Dalia said.

Hannah nodded, then slowly climbed the stairs as they carried Rafe up to a room. They were met by all the girls who worked at Madam Genevieve's.

"What can we do?" Delores asked.

"Water. We'll need water and blankets and lots of cloths. And someone wait for the doctor. Bring him right up when he comes."

Without a word, the girls rushed to get the items Hannah had asked for.

Hannah hurried into the room. Rafe was on the bed, and Humphrey and Converse were removing his clothes. To move him as little as possible, they were cutting the material from his body. When they finished, they pulled a cover up over him.

Hannah rinsed a cloth in some water and dabbed at his bruised and swollen face. He'd been hurt because of her. He'd risked his life to save her.

How could she ever repay him?

She reached for his hand and nestled it in her own. And she did something she hadn't done in half a lifetime.

She prayed.

Chapter 13

The door to Rafe's room opened, and Dalia stepped inside. "How is he today?" she whispered.

Hannah looked at the bed and blinked to keep the tears at bay. She'd shed more tears in the last three days than in her entire lifetime. "He's still unconscious."

Dalia walked to Hannah's side and placed a hand on her shoulder. "I think that's a blessing," she said. "The longer he sleeps, the less pain he'll remember and the more he'll have healed by the time he wakes."

"That's what I keep telling myself. But…what if he never wakes? I've heard of that happening. There was a man who made his living in the ring. He was hit so hard he—"

"Don't borrow trouble, Genny. Your vicar is strong. He'll pull through this."

Hannah reached out to hold Rafe's hand. She gently squeezed his fingers but, as usual, he didn't respond. "I promised God that if He let him live, I'd make sure he returned to the profession God called him to do."

"You tried that once and he didn't leave."

"This time I'll make sure he does."

"What about you? How will you survive if he does?"

Hannah didn't have an answer for Dalia. She wasn't sure she could.

Dalia pulled up a chair and sat beside her. "The girls had a meeting this morning."

Hannah looked at the serious expression on Dalia's face and suddenly knew what Dalia was going to say next. She decided to spare her the embarrassment. "Tell them I don't blame them. After what happened, I wouldn't want to live and work where it wasn't safe either. Have they decided where they want to go?"

Dalia smiled. "Leaving wasn't even mentioned, Genny. They met to decide how they're going to get past Skinner's threats."

"No!" The fear in Hannah's voice was harsh even to her own ears. "It's too dangerous. Just look what Skinner's capable of." Hannah lowered her gaze to the bed where Rafe lay, and the tears welled again and spilled down her cheeks. "I couldn't live with myself if this happened to one of them. I couldn't, Dalia."

"You won't have to." Dalia placed a comforting hand on Hannah's arm. "You're not the only one fighting Skinner anymore. He's lowered his heavy hand against nearly everyone on the East End. All the independent dealers below the Strand or Haymarket, even the ones who only have one or two girls working for them, are afraid of him. He's threatened them all."

"How do you know this?"

"About a dozen of them came this morning to sit in on the meeting."

Hannah's jaw lowered, and Dalia laughed as she placed her finger beneath Hannah's chin and lifted. "Unbelievable, isn't it?"

Hannah was too dumbfounded to speak. She could only nod her head.

"They know Skinner has to be stopped or none of their girls will be safe. And, as unlikely as it sounds, a lot of them object to Skinner's dealing in children."

"What did they decide?"

"Well, as you know, all the bosses use at least two or three men to protect their women. Starting tomorrow, at least four of them will show up to guard our girls when they go out."

So many thoughts raced through Hannah's mind that she was incapable of speech.

"I know you're worried, but don't be. This wasn't your idea, so you're not responsible for anything that happens. Skinner's been asking for this for a long time. He wants to own every prostitute on the East End, and everyone knows if they don't stop him now, he'll eat them up one by one."

"It's dangerous, Dalia. You didn't see the satisfaction he took from nearly killing Rafe."

"Saving innocent girls has always been dangerous. Skinner's made it worse. That's why he has to be stopped."

Hannah looked from Dalia to the bed where Rafe lay. Yes, Skinner had to be stopped. No one was safe until he was.

Dalia stood. "I've got to get ready for tonight. It's been unusually busy lately. And the Earl of Parnes will be here tonight. Clorise and Fanny always argue over which one gets to entertain him, so I'd better separate the two before they have words."

"I'm sorry I'm not helping you—"

"I'm fine. You stay here. Your vicar needs you more than I do."

Dalia gave her shoulder a reassuring squeeze, then left the room. When Hannah was alone again, she turned her concentration back to Rafe.

A sheet covered his body. Except for the bandage around his back from the gunshot wound, he was naked beneath it. Bruises covered every part of his body that she could see, as well as areas beneath the sheet she couldn't. Not that she hadn't looked. She had. He was as beautifully formed as any man she'd ever seen—and she'd seen more than her share. But never any who were as bruised and battered as he was.

Hannah walked to the table beside the bed and rinsed a cloth in a basin of fresh water. Several of the cuts still bled, and she placed the damp cloth over a particularly ugly cut on his forehead. When she cleaned it as the doctor ordered her to do several times a day, she dried it, then applied the salve the physician had left. She did the same to several other cuts, both on his face and on his chest. When she finished, she lifted the bowl of warm broth Cook had sent up. The doctor had left orders to get as much liquid down him as she could, but this was the most difficult part. How did you get an unconscious man to eat?

She dipped a piece of twisted cloth into the bowl and let the cloth soak the broth. Then she slipped the cloth into Rafe's mouth and prayed he would suck on it. Thankfully, his throat moved and he swallowed at least a little. She repeated the process again and again.

Eventually, he refused to open his mouth for her, and she set the bowl of broth back on the table and gently washed his face. When she finished, she placed the damp cloth back in the basin and sat in her chair to watch him sleep.

The doctor who'd come to tend Rafe had warned her that he might not recover, but Hannah refused to accept that. He *would* live, and he would recover. She couldn't live with herself if he didn't. It was her fault he'd been shot and beaten, her fault he'd placed himself in danger. And she asked herself for the thousandth time why he hadn't gone home when she'd told him to.

Rafe moved, and she leaned over to hold his hand in hers. He was more restless than he'd been earlier, but the doctor said that was to be expected. Even though he wasn't conscious, deep in the back recesses of his mind he still remembered what had happened to him. His mind realized he was in pain.

Before she could protect herself, Rafe pulled his hand from her grasp and swung his arm in the air. His fist hit her hard. She grabbed on to the corner of the bed to keep from toppling to the floor.

As if he were trying to escape Skinner's men, as he had when they held him and beat him, Rafe thrashed from side to side.

"Rafe, lie still. You're going to hurt yourself." Hannah was afraid he'd undo all the good the doctor had done to the open wounds that covered his body.

She tried to calm him and hold him steady, but he was too strong. He pushed her off him with such force she landed on the floor.

Hannah pushed herself to her feet and ran to the door. She needed help. She needed someone who was strong enough to hold Rafe down.

"Humphrey!" she yelled, hoping someone would hear her and get Humphrey for her.

Thankfully, someone heard her, because in a short time, Humphrey ran into the room.

"Help me, Humphrey," she pleaded, and was relieved when Humphrey's strong arms pinned Rafe to the bed.

For several long minutes, Humphrey struggled to keep Rafe calm. "Those bastards hurt him bad," he said. "If you get a chance to take Skinner down, you make sure I'm there."

The indomitable expression on his face was filled with such bitterness it took Hannah's breath. She swallowed past the lump in her throat and knelt at the side of the bed so she was closer to Rafe. She needed him to know how anxious she was for him to heal, how desperately she needed to know he wouldn't die. She wouldn't feel better until he had healed and she knew he was living a productive life someplace—even if that someplace wasn't anywhere near her.

She leaned toward him to whisper in his ear. "Did you hear that, Rafe? Humphrey is concerned about you." She lightly brushed her fingers across his forehead. "All the girls are worried about you too. They ask about you every day."

She continued talking to him, soothing him with her voice and her touch. Eventually, he calmed.

Humphrey slowly eased his grip and stood. "You want me to stay, Miss Genevieve?"

Hannah shook her head. "No, Humphrey. We're fine now."

"I know you won't want to hear this, but the vicar's hurt real bad. You should prepare yourself in case he doesn't make it."

Humphrey's words were like a blow to her heart. She knew Rafe was badly hurt. When Dalia had first seen him, she didn't recognize him.

"Sometimes there's damage done on the inside of a person's body you can't see from the outside."

Hannah tried to block out Humphrey's warning, but she couldn't. She knew what he said was true. The doctor had cautioned her with the same advice.

She tried to tell Humphrey she was prepared for the worst, if it happened, but she couldn't speak the words. She would never be prepared.

As if he realized there was nothing more he could say or do to help her, he said, "Well, I'll be going, then, if you'll be all right here by yourself."

"I'll be fine, Humphrey. Thank you for your help."

"Call if you need me again," he said, then walked away from her.

Hannah held back her tears until she heard the door close behind Humphrey, then the river of pent-up emotions rushed to the surface. Tears welled in her eyes, then streamed down her face. Uncontrollable sobs racked her body.

She didn't know how she'd manage if he didn't survive. She wasn't sure she could. How would she ever be able to live with herself, knowing a kind, generous man was dead because of her ignorance?

She thought of all the girls she'd rescued from a horrible existence and would never regret what she'd done to save them. She remembered how she'd struggled to make Madam Genevieve's a success—*not* because she took any enjoyment in running it or felt any pride in what she was doing, but because Madam Genevieve's provided her with the income she needed to support Coventry Cottage.

But none of that would mean anything if it cost Rafe his life.

She remained on the floor at his bedside for hours and held his hand. With trembling fingers, she gently brushed back the hair that fell to his forehead. She'd give anything to be able to relive the night she'd walked into Skinner's trap, and change her decision to go. Then Rafe wouldn't be lying here near death.

She brought his hand to her mouth and pressed her lips to his flesh. His hands were the only part of his upper body not bloody and bruised. That's because Skinner's men hadn't given him the chance to use his hands to defend himself. She could still see two of Skinner's men restraining him. Every time she closed her eyes, she relived the beating he'd received.

Rafe moaned, and Hannah rose to dampen a clean cloth and press it to his lips. Then she dampened another cloth in cool water and dabbed his face. When she finished, she felt his forehead for any sign of a fever. The doctor had warned her to watch for a fever. He'd said the wounds weren't nearly as dangerous as a fever.

She was relieved that he wasn't hot to the touch. Maybe he'd be spared the worst and would heal more quickly. With a sigh, she sat on the chair beside the bed and waited.

Tonight would be another long night. Just as the last three had been.

Chapter 14

Hannah sat at Rafe's bedside and continued to do something she hadn't done in fifteen years—she prayed. Over the last five days, she'd prayed more fervently than she'd ever prayed. She'd even considered making promises she knew she wouldn't keep—such as stop searching for the innocent children Skinner wanted, or close Madam Genevieve's—but had stopped short of making a promise God knew she couldn't keep.

God knew what was in her heart, and He knew she had no intention of doing either of those things. Allowing so many innocent children to fall into Skinner's hands was unthinkable. And the income from Madam Genevieve's supported Coventry Cottage. Without the revenue Madam Genevieve's took in, she couldn't feed or clothe her children.

No, God already knew what she would do, so she simply prayed that He would spare Rafe's life. She closed her eyes and began her request again. A soft moan stopped her short.

She focused on Rafe's injured body just as he slowly opened his eyes.

He tried to move his head and stopped on a moan. "Bloody hell," he hissed, then lay quiet again.

"Don't move," she whispered. She placed a hand on his shoulder to hold him steady.

"Hannah?"

"Yes." She reached out and took his hand. "I'm glad you decided to finally wake up."

"I'm not sure I am."

"No, I don't suppose you are." She moved so she was close enough that he could lift his gaze and see her without moving.

"You look tired," he whispered.

She smiled. "I look better than you." She reached for a decanter on the bedside table and poured some water into a glass. "Would you like something to drink?"

"Yes."

She held the glass to his lips, and he took a few sips.

"Where am I?"

"We brought you here—to Madam Genevieve's."

"I'd laugh if it didn't hurt so badly. I'd lay odds that I'm one of the few men of the cloth who's ever spent a night in a bordello."

"That would be something your parishioners might not find amusing."

"No, I don't suppose many of them would."

Hannah placed the glass back on the table and sat in her chair. "Do you remember what happened?"

"Not everything. But Skinner was there."

"Yes, Skinner and several of his men."

The frown on his forehead deepened, and she knew he remembered at least some of what happened that night.

"How long have I been here?"

"Five days."

"No wonder you look tired. You haven't gotten any rest since then, have you?"

Hannah rose from her chair and walked away from him. "Why were you still here? I thought you'd returned to Wedgewood Manor. Why didn't you?"

"I couldn't."

She turned. "Why?"

"You know the answer to that."

"I know that because you stayed, you almost got your-self killed."

"You were in danger. I wouldn't have been able to live with myself if I'd have left you and something happened to you."

"You're a vicar, Rafe. A *vicar*! Not an officer in Her Majesty's army who's been trained to kill."

"I could have been."

"Could have been what?"

"An officer. In Her Majesty's army."

Rafe's words confused her. She stopped to focus on his face. His eyes were closed, but there was a lift to his swollen lips. He was teasing her. He'd nearly gotten himself killed and he was *teasing* her! "You're impossible, do you know that?"

"I try my hardest."

For the hundredth time since he'd been hurt, she real-ized how much she loved him and how desperately she'd miss him if he died. A knot formed in her throat and tears filled her eyes. She walked to the chair where she'd spent endless terrifying hours over the last five days and sat. "Go back to sleep now."

"I've slept long enough. I want to stay awake."

He was tiring. She knew she should let him sleep, but she couldn't deny his need to stay awake for just a little while. She reached for his hand and held it. "Why did you become a vicar? Why not an officer?"

He breathed a shaky sigh. "The uniforms."

A laugh she couldn't stop escaped. "The uniforms?" she said when she stopped laughing.

"Yes, have you ever seen them?"

"Yes. Often, as a matter of fact. I find them very attractive—as well as the men wearing them."

"Women always do."

Hannah thought. "I suppose we do. But you don't?"

"Have you ever asked a soldier how he likes wearing a uniform?"

"No."

"If you had, they'd tell you they hated them. They're hot in the summer. Scratchy year-round. And very uncomfortable. They're…"

He stopped to take a breath. A sheen of perspiration covered his forehead. "They're only appealing to the people looking at them. Not the ones wearing them."

Hannah stopped to rinse a cloth in some cool water and dabbed his face. "I hadn't thought of that. No wonder you chose to be a vicar."

His answer was a moan.

He was in pain. The doctor had warned her he would be when he woke.

"You've talked enough. It's time to sleep." Hannah reached for the dark bottle on the bedside table and poured a small amount of the liquid into a glass of wine.

After she stirred it, she lifted his head and held it to his lips. "Here, drink this."

"What is it?"

"Laudanum. The doctor said to give you some when you woke. It will ease the pain."

Rafe drank from the glass, then sank back into the mattress. "Get some rest, Hannah. You need it."

"I'm fine."

"No, you're not. You're exhausted, and you can't afford to let down your guard. You're in trouble." He breathed a heavy sigh. "You won't be able to protect yourself from Skinner if you can't even stay awake."

She straightened the covers around him and made sure he was comfortable, then sat back in her chair. "I'll stay here until you're asleep, then I'll go to my room. I'll get someone to stay here with you. If you need anything, tell them. They'll come for me."

She sank back into her chair and closed her eyes. He was already asleep when she checked on him a minute later.

Hannah looked at his battered and beaten body and knew what happened to him was her fault. Her goal was now to protect him—and the only way she could accomplish that was to make sure he left London.

A knot formed in her stomach. Forcing him to leave was the only way she could keep him alive.

And it would kill the part of her heart she needed to live.

* * *

Rafe opened his eyes and shifted his gaze to the chair where she always sat. It was empty.

He looked around the room and found her looking out the window.

She wore peach today, the deepest, richest shade of peach he'd ever seen. Her hair was loosely pulled back from her face, and a fistful of golden ringlets was allowed to cascade down her back, fastened at the crown of her head by an intertwining comb made from pearls. The only term that described her was *gorgeous*. He stared at her for a while longer before he spoke. "What kind of a day is it?" he finally asked.

She turned and smiled. "It's a picture-perfect spring day."

"I'm sure it can't equal the picture-perfect woman I'm looking at right now."

She smiled and favored him with a graceful curtsy.

"Perhaps I can escort you outside, then?" he said.

She pursed her lips and gave him a strict glare. "Perhaps you'll stay in bed as the doctor ordered you to do."

"That was a week ago. He didn't realize how quickly I was capable of healing when he issued that ridiculous order."

"He knew exactly how much time it would take you to recover from the beating you took. As well as the bullet wound."

"Has anyone told you how impossible you are?"

She shook her head. "No. I've never had anyone try to go against my orders."

"Are you serious?"

She gifted him with a look of superiority. "Of course I am. Everyone at Madam Genevieve's understands the wisdom in my directives."

Rafe opened his mouth to refute her boastfulness, then stopped. She was serious. He laughed, but not too hard because of the pain he'd suffer if he did. "You are the most remarkable woman I've ever met."

"I'm glad you realize that fact."

"You're also exceedingly stubborn and unwavering."

Her delicate eyebrows arched. "Thank you, my lord. I appreciate your candid opinion."

"And you are tenacious to a fault."

Several furrows deepened across her brow. "Take care," she warned. "Your compliments are taking on a more negative tone."

"I assure you that is not my intent."

"What is your intent, then?"

"I was hoping that you would question your determination, Hannah. I admit I am not well enough to do much, but I am well enough to do more than lie in this bed and be waited on."

She pursed her lips as if considering his argument, then walked to his bedside.

"Going out-of-doors is out of the question." She paused. "But perhaps you could sit on the edge of the bed for a while."

"And stand?"

She laughed. "Let's see how you manage sitting first. Then we'll see about standing."

She pulled back his covers and held out her arm for him to take. He slowly sat, then gingerly swung his legs over the side of the bed.

A pain shot through his back, and he stiffened.

"Not too fast," she warned.

He shifted his body so he was steady, then stretched to test the limits of his endurance. "See, Hannah. I can manage sitting quite well."

"I have to admit, I'm impressed. It's to your advantage that you were in excellent physical condition before Skinner got hold of you."

The mention of Skinner's name shifted the mood of their conversation. "You didn't have to bring up such an unpleasant reminder."

"Yes, I did. I don't ever want you to forget his name, or what he is capable of doing. I want you to remember what a danger he is to you. And how the next time you meet, he will not hesitate to kill you."

"Why do I have the feeling you're trying to scare me away?"

"Because I am."

Rafe patted the bed beside him. "Here. Sit."

Hannah hesitated, then sat.

When she was settled, he reached for her hand and held it. The feel of her flesh against his caused the same reaction as always—a growing warmth that rushed from where their hands touched to every part of his body. "I don't claim to understand everything Madam Genevieve's is involved in, and I can't condone what goes on here, but I admire how you're trying to help the children." He paused. "That's what this is all about, isn't it? The children."

She didn't answer, and he took her silence as a yes.

"I know you are concerned for me. Just as I'm concerned for you. But please save your breath if you think that I will consider leaving you to face Skinner by yourself. I won't do that."

She sighed, and her shoulders lowered in defeat. "Why, Rafe? Why, even after you know how dangerous it is for you?"

"Don't you know?" He took her by the shoulders and turned her toward him. When she faced him, he lowered his head and pressed his lips to hers.

Her kiss was just as he remembered. Heat soared and raced to soothe every aching tendon. His heart tumbled in his chest, and a euphoric energy swelled inside of him.

He loved her. He'd known it for quite some time—suspected it at first, then knew it beyond a shadow of a doubt the minute he saw her walk into Skinner's trap and feared he might lose her. At that moment, he knew he'd never survive if he lost her.

He deepened his kiss, skimming her lips with his tongue, then delving inside her honeyed cavern when she allowed him entrance. He could never have enough of her. Could never love her completely enough. And he would never allow her to push him out of her life.

Rafe held her closer and kissed her again and again. No matter how hard she insisted he leave her, he never would.

He never could.

Chapter 15

❦

Hannah told herself over and over that she'd never allow Rafe to kiss her again. Each kiss was like the pounding of a chisel that chipped away at the barricade she'd erected around her heart to protect it. Every time he kissed her, he exposed more of her heart and her emotions. Every time he kissed her, he possessed more of her soul.

His arms wrapped around her to pull her closer, and she went willingly. All her resolution and determination evaporated the moment she went into his arms. She'd never experienced an overpowering weakness where any man was concerned. Never felt as if she wasn't a whole person unless she was at his side.

She met his deepening kiss and pressed harder against him. She wanted to crawl inside his body and be a part of him—if that were possible. He possessed so much of her heart, she already felt as if he were a part of her. Now she wanted to be a part of him—and she knew it would be easy. He'd already told her that he loved her. He'd already proved that he loved her. Loved her enough to give up his life to save hers.

That was the indicator she needed to halt this kiss and not let it go any further. That was the cautionary warning she required to pull her back from the emotional depths of his kisses…to remind herself what would happen if she fooled herself into believing it was possible to have a life with him.

She permitted herself one final kiss, then lifted her mouth from his.

She lowered her head to his chest and listened to the rapid thundering of his heart. It echoed the pounding in her own breast. It made the two of them seem as if they were one. And in several ways, she knew that they were. He was the other half of her heart—the other half of her soul. And she possessed his heart and soul as well.

She pulled away from him and shifted on the bed to put some distance between them.

"Don't be afraid, Hannah."

She wanted to laugh. "Of course I'm afraid. Skinner's—"

"I wasn't talking about Skinner. I was talking about you and me."

Hannah turned toward him and focused on the gentle features of his face and the tenderness in his eyes. He embodied all that was kindness and peacefulness. He was the antithesis of her life up until the day she met him. He erased the days in her father's house, the hours she'd spent on her knees asking God to forgive her for being such a wretched sinner. He removed the horridness of what the rapist had done to her and made her feel as if she were someone capable of being loved. And he wiped away the ugliness of selling her body to men because she hadn't been strong enough to starve on the streets. He wiped away the foulness of the unthinkable acts she'd committed in order to stay alive.

He was the first man who'd understood the choices she'd been forced to make and didn't judge her for the life she'd chosen.

"I'm not afraid, Rafe."

"Yes, you are. But I'm telling you that you don't have to be afraid of what's happening between us. The love we feel for each other is a gift. I've lived thirty years thinking I'd never find that kind of love—and then I met you. Don't ask me to give you up, Hannah. I won't."

Hannah stood, then walked across the room. The window looked out on the street where fancy carriages drove by. Some of them stopped to drop off a passenger. "You said once that you didn't have a parish to return to. What did you mean by that?"

"Exactly that."

Hannah looked over her shoulder. The expression on his face told her he was serious.

"I preached at a parish in Hertfordshire for a couple of years. Essex a couple of years before that."

"Why did you leave? Didn't you like it there?"

"I was very happy there. Both parishes had wonderful people—good people. They did everything possible to make me feel welcome and appreciated."

Hannah was confused. "Why did you leave?"

The corners of Rafe's swollen lips lifted. "You'll think I'm crazy. Thomas did when I told him, but…"

Hannah walked to the chair near his bed that she'd spent so many hours in, and sat. "Why did you leave a parish where everyone loved you?"

"I left because I wasn't needed. I always felt as though God had something *more* He wanted me to do. I was simply biding time until He showed me what that *something* was."

"You were bored."

"Yes. I was preaching to a congregation of saints." He looked at her and smiled. "Oh, there were the occasional funerals to conduct and grieving families to comfort. There were weddings and baptisms, and the old and infirm to visit. But other than that, I spent most of my time fighting off mothers and fathers with eligible daughters to marry. Every Sunday I was invited to someone's home for dinner. When we finished eating, everyone at the table conveniently had something to do—except the daughter with whom I was invited to spend time."

Hannah covered her mouth to stifle the giggle that wanted to sneak out. "No wonder you took exception to the girls Caroline invited to partner you."

He lifted his gaze and looked deep into her eyes. "You were there. I would have been perfectly content being your partner every day of the two weeks."

"Except everyone knew how impossible that was. They all knew who and *what* I was."

"Why can't you believe that none of that matters? If we love each other enough, we'll find a way to be together."

"And what will we do, Rafe? Look down the road five— even two years. What will we do? I don't fit in your world, and you don't fit in mine."

"Then we'll make another world. A world in which we do fit."

"What world would that be? You have a gift. I've seen you. You open your mouth and people are drawn to what you say. Children sit at your feet in awe. Adults listen to your every word." Hannah paused. "You have a calling, and it would be a sin to turn your back on what you've been called to do." She sighed. "I don't belong in that world."

She lifted her hand to stop him from rebutting what she'd said. "Because of my past, I don't belong in the same circles as you. We would both live in terror every day for fear that someone would discover who I am—what I'd been. Being the well-known Madam Genevieve is impossible to hide."

Rafe opened his mouth to speak, then closed it.

"You know I'm right, Rafe," she whispered. "You've always known it, just as I have. We were both given a magical week this summer in which to experience a love we've never known before. I will never forget you, or the emotions you allowed me to feel. But here is where it must end. You must heal and get well enough to search for the perfect place in which to use your gift. And I must stay here, where I belong, and where I can use the gifts I have been given."

Hannah knew Rafe intended to argue, but a knock on the door stopped him from saying anything more.

"Yes," she said, and the door opened. Dalia stood in the entryway.

"You need to come upstairs, Genny. Delores found one of Skinner's girls. She needs our help."

"I'll be right there."

Dalia nodded, then left.

Hannah stood, but Rafe's voice stopped her from leaving.

"What did Dalia mean 'one of Skinner's girls'? Surely you're not risking your life by going out after more girls?"

"It's not like you think."

"Are your girls still going out to rescue girls or not?"

"Yes, but—"

"Bloody hell, Hannah! Wasn't what happened to me enough? Do you want there to be more?"

Hannah felt her temper soar. He didn't understand. No one understood except someone who'd gone through the same thing. "I have to go. We can talk about this later."

"You're bloody right we will."

She walked across the room, then closed the door firmly behind her.

She needed to leave the room before either of them said words they'd regret later.

* * *

On her way up the stairs, Hannah said a quick prayer that when she reached the girl Delores had rescued, she wouldn't be injured as badly as the last girl they'd found.

She rushed into the room without knocking. A bed was in the corner on the opposite side of the room, and the girl was huddled in a tight ball as far away from where anyone could reach her as she could get. Delores sat on the edge of the bed and talked to the girl. Her voice was soft and sweet, exactly how they'd all learned to speak to the girls they'd found.

So far Hannah hadn't glimpsed the girl's face to see how badly she'd been beaten, or checked the other parts of her body to evaluate how badly she'd been abused. But if her torn clothes and how she was protecting herself was any indication, she'd been raped—and probably more than once.

Hannah looked at Delores, who shook her head in answer to Hannah's unspoken question.

"Look, Lilly," Delores said in a happy tone. "Here's the lady I told you would come. Now everything will be all right. She'll take care of you. She won't let anyone hurt you ever again."

Hannah walked to the bed. "Hello, Lilly. My name is Genny." Hannah sat on the edge of the bed where Delores had been. "Delores, why don't you go down and have someone bring up some warm water. I'm sure Lilly would like to bathe. Wouldn't you, Lilly?"

The girl nodded.

She was glad the girl reacted to what she said. That was a positive sign. But then, Hannah remembered how desperate she'd been to bathe. How frantic she'd been to remove the feel of the man who'd raped her. How eager she'd been to feel clean again.

"I'll send water right up," Delores said, then walked to the door. "And something warm to eat and drink. Who knows the last time the poor thing ate anything."

When Delores left the room, Hannah slid close enough so she could touch the girl. She knew she wouldn't want to be touched at first, but eventually she'd want some soft arms to hold her. Hannah brushed her hand down the girl's tangled hair. "Where are you from, Lilly?"

The girl didn't respond to her question, but Hannah didn't expect an answer. She hadn't asked a question that warranted a strong reaction.

"Are you from London?"

No response.

Hannah smoothed her hand down the girl's long wheat-colored hair. "Would you like me to send for your family? I'll find them and you can go back to them."

"No!"

The girl turned with a jerk, and Hannah got her first glimpse of what had been done to her. Her face was bruised in several spots, and there were at least three cuts across her cheek and jaw where a heavy fist must have hit her. Hannah guessed her eyes were a pretty blue, but they were so swollen it was hard to tell. The only thing she couldn't miss was the terror in Lilly's eyes. She was obviously as terrified of returning home as she was of what had happened to her tonight.

"That's all right, Lilly. You don't have to go home." Hannah opened her arms in hopes that the girl would take refuge in her embrace. She did.

With a bound, the girl fell against Hannah. She was small and fragile, and if Hannah were to guess, she'd estimate Lilly wasn't more than thirteen or fourteen years old.

Hannah held her tightly and rocked back and forth with her in her arms.

"I don't want to go home," the girl cried as she held on to Hannah. "Please don't make me go back there."

"I won't. You can stay right here. I'll take care of you."

Hannah continued to rock her and, finally, the tears came. Step one of the healing process. She feared most for the poor girls who didn't cry but held their hurt and pain inside. They were the ones who healed most slowly.

"It's all right, Lilly," Hannah said, noticing for the first time her ripped clothing and the blood on her skirt. "It's all right. No one will ever hurt you again."

Hannah held the young girl until the last of her tears dried. When the bath water arrived, she helped Lilly bathe, letting the girl stay in the water even after it had grown cold. She would always remember how long she'd stayed in the stream, how hard she tried to scrub away the vile things the man had done to her. Lilly was the same—all the girls they found were. They scrubbed their bodies until they were raw, then scrubbed them some more.

Hannah didn't have a chance to evaluate how badly the girl had been hurt until she finally crawled out of the water. Hannah put salve on the scratches that were raw and bleeding, and ointment on the bruises, but those were the easiest wounds to care for. The wounds that would take the longest to heal were those on the inside. Those wounds would take years, perhaps a lifetime to heal—if even then.

When the worst of the bruises and claw marks were taken care of, she gave the young girl a cup of hot tea, then put her to bed. She'd sit there until Lilly fell asleep, in case she had nightmares. Then, in a week or two, when the bruises had time to fade, she'd take her to Coventry Cottage. Lilly would be fine there. She would be with others who had gone through the same horrors.

Hannah sat on the bed with Lilly's head in her lap. The girl had fallen asleep more than an hour ago, but her grip around Hannah's body hadn't loosened. It would in time. Hannah would sit there until it did.

For some it took longer. The stronger ones didn't take as long. The more fragile ones...well, they would need more care and comforting.

Hannah leaned back against the bed's headboard. The first few hours with a girl they'd just rescued were the hardest for her. Especially the hours after the girl fell asleep and Hannah sat in the quiet with her. Times like this forced Hannah to relive the night everything had been stolen from her. When her dreams had been destroyed.

She thought of Rafe and pushed aside the thought of what a future with him would be like. That dream had been taken from her when a man raped her, the same as with the man who had raped Lilly tonight. That man took everything from her and left her with…

One tear after another streamed down her face, and Hannah let them fall. Very seldom did she allow herself to wallow in self-pity. Seldom did she allow herself to think about what had been taken from her, of what she couldn't give a man.

The most important were children. That ability was taken from her when she lost her innocence and her reputation.

She thought of Rafe and the children he would someday have—children she could never give him. And fresh tears spilled from her eyes.

Hannah breathed a deep sigh and swiped at her wet cheeks. She'd wallowed in self-pity long enough. It was time to forget what she would never have and concentrate on the blessings she'd been given.

She shifted Lilly's head from her lap to the pillow and quietly stood. She needed to wash her face to get rid of the tearstains on her cheeks before anyone saw her. It wouldn't do her reputation any good if they discovered she wasn't as strong as she let everyone believe she was.

Hannah slowly inched backward toward the door, making sure not to awaken Lilly. When she reached the other side of the room, she turned and came face-to-face with the last person she wanted to see her so vulnerable—Rafe.

Chapter 16

Rafe stepped aside to let Hannah walk through the door, then softly closed it behind her. His mind tried to sort through everything he'd just witnessed because he knew it was significant. He knew he'd just beheld a very private part of Hannah's life.

"What are you doing out of bed?" she demanded when they were far enough away from Lilly's room that their voices wouldn't wake her. "Who allowed you to get up?"

Rafe couldn't help but smile, although he was sure his swollen features didn't make his smile too obvious. "No one *allowed* me to get up. Besides, I didn't realize I had to ask permission."

"Where was Humphrey?"

"Dalia sent one of the girls for him. Lord Marlin arrived in a state of inebriation, and in his present condition, Dalia wouldn't allow him the…pleasure of any of your girls. When he was asked to leave, he wasn't agreeable to the idea."

"Damn Marlin. He knows we won't allow him to stay when he arrives drunk."

"Is that a house policy for all your customers?"

"Only the customers who tend to get rough when they've had too much to drink."

Rafe stopped, then reached his arm out to the wall to steady himself. He'd been on his feet longer than he probably should have been.

"You're going to pay for getting up," she warned as she stepped close to him. "Put your arm around my shoulder before you fall and injure yourself more."

Rafe placed his arm around her shoulder and let her help him back to his room.

He was exhausted when he reached his bed, and sank onto the mattress with a sigh of relief. She pulled back the covers and helped him back to bed, then turned to go.

"Don't leave yet, Hannah."

She stopped. "I don't want to talk about what you saw," she said without looking at him.

"Then we won't."

She hesitated, as if deciding whether or not to believe him. She turned. Her eyes were still red from the tears he'd seen her shed, but she held her head high as she made her way to the chair beside his bed, then sat.

"How is she?" he asked.

"She'll survive. At least on the outside. The inside will take longer to heal."

"When she's up to it, do you care if I speak with her?"

She hesitated. "You can try. I don't know how she'll take talking to a man. Not after what happened to her."

Rafe tried to smile. "I can be pretty easy to talk to when I try."

Hannah smiled. "Yes, I know you can."

"What's her name?"

"Lilly."

"She didn't look very old. Do you know how Skinner got her?"

"He took her off the street. She'd run away from home. I don't know why, but she's terribly afraid of whoever is there and doesn't want to go back."

"How does Skinner find them?"

Hannah's laugh surprised him. "Young girls from the country aren't hard to spot. They stand out from city girls like they're wearing signs around their necks to announce their arrival. Skinner has men searching the streets for them all the time."

Rafe leaned back against his pillow and sighed. The clock on the mantel chimed the half hour past ten o'clock.

He reached into his pants pocket but remembered he hadn't seen his watch since the night he'd been attacked. He tried not to panic and told himself that as soon as he was well enough to leave the bordello, he'd start a search of the local pawn shops. If someone from that area had found his watch, they would no doubt sell it.

Rafe looked back to where Hannah stood and saw her outstretched arm. His grandfather's watch lay in her palm.

He slowly took it in his fingers and reverently held it. "Thank you."

"You're welcome. I know how special this is to you and didn't want anything to happen to it."

Rafe rubbed his fingers over the stones on the top and the inscription on the inside. He knew every raised bump and notched indentation by heart. The relief he felt knowing that he hadn't lost his grandfather's watch was indescribable.

The muffled sounds of laughter and voices sifted up from one floor to the next. According to what he'd been told, in the evenings the bordello was always overflowing with customers. Madam Genevieve's was busy on the two floors below—on the ground floor in the receiving rooms where some of the patrons simply wanted to spend time with a beautiful young female, and on the floor above, where Madam Genevieve's girls would take their clients for a few hours of enjoyment.

Tonight was very typical. This was no place for a young girl.

"What will you do with the girl? She can't stay here."

"No, she can't."

"Where will she go?"

Hannah locked her gaze with his. "I'll take her home."

* * *

Hannah gently closed the door to Lilly's room and quietly walked down the hall. The young girl had woken up screaming, and by the time Hannah reached her she was nearly frantic. Hannah remembered the nightmares she'd had after she'd been raped and the terror that engulfed her with each one.

She walked back to Rafe's room and slowly opened the door. The room was dimly lit. The only light came from the smoldering embers in the grate. She stepped inside and looked to the bed. It was empty.

She scanned the room.

"I'm here," he said from a chair in the corner near a window.

"You're out of bed again."

"Yes. I needed to stretch my legs."

Hannah pulled a chair close to him and sat. "Are you in pain? Can I get you anything?"

"I'm fine. How is Lilly?"

"She's sleeping—for now."

"Earlier you said you were going to take her home. What did you mean by that?"

"Just that. I have a home in the country. It's called Coventry Cottage. I intend to take her there as soon as she's up to it."

"How soon will that be?"

Hannah shook her head. "A week. Perhaps two."

"May I come along? I'd like to see your country home."

Hannah thought of all the reasons she should refuse to let him accompany them, all the reasons she should keep Coventry a secret from him—from everyone. And yet she was anxious to show him her home. Anxious to show him that she was so much more than a prostitute.

She stood, then walked to the small cupboard against the wall and opened the door. She removed a crystal decanter and two glasses. She poured a little wine into each glass, then handed him one. For several relaxing moments, they sat in peaceful stillness and sipped their wine. Finally, Hannah broke the silence. "What are your plans when you are well enough to leave here?"

"Are you telling me I *have* to leave?"

"I think you know the answer to that. You know you can't stay."

"Are you trying to protect me again, Hannah? Do you expect me to run back to the country and hide?"

"No, I'm telling you something you already know—that you don't belong here."

He slowly sipped his wine. "Do you want me to go, Hannah?"

"You have to. You don't have a choice."

"Would you want me to go if you weren't Madam Genevieve and I wouldn't be in danger if I stayed?"

Hannah hesitated. Of course she wouldn't want him to go. She'd want nothing more than for their lives to be different and for them to be able to have a future together. But that would never be. "What I want is for you to leave here before Skinner kills you and I will have to live with the guilt of knowing your death is my fault."

"What if I told you it's impossible for me to be happy without you?"

"You can't let that happen, Rafe."

"Can you be happy without me?"

How could she answer such a question? She didn't know what happiness was until she met him. Now that she knew, there was no way she could be happy without him.

"Can you?" he asked again.

"I'll have to be. I can't let you stay. I can't risk Skinner killing you and forcing me to live the rest of my life knowing that you aren't somewhere near here doing what you were meant to do."

Rafe leaned his head back against the chair. For several minutes they sat in silence and stared into the dying embers in the fireplace.

Finally, Rafe placed his glass on a nearby table and turned to her. "Let me go with you when you take Lilly to the country. Let me see where you live. Then I'll be ready to do what I have to do."

"Will you be up to the journey?"

He laughed. "Of course, Hannah. You're the only one who doubts my strength."

Hannah was shocked. "I don't doubt your strength. I know very well how strong you are on the inside as well as the outside. I simply understand better than you how ill equipped you are to handle the life I live. Your goodness doesn't allow you to fathom how evil men like Skinner can be."

"Perhaps you're right. But I'm learning."

"But that's a lesson I don't want to see repeated."

"Neither do I," Rafe said with a heavy breath.

Hannah heard the exhaustion in his sigh. "You need to get back to bed. Would you like me to help you?"

"If you'd like."

Hannah helped Rafe to his feet, then placed his arm around her shoulders to steady him as they walked to the bed. She stepped in front of him to ease him down onto the mattress, but he placed his hands on her shoulders and held her. With a gentle caress, he placed his palm to her cheek. His fingers slowly moved downward to her jaw, then he tipped her chin upward.

For several intense moments, they stared into each other's eyes. Hannah knew if there would be a light bright enough to see him clearly, she'd detect the depth of emotion they each harbored for the other. In the darkness, she could only sense it.

He slowly lowered his head.

He intended to kiss her. She knew it deep down in her body, just as she knew she should step out of his arms. Just as she knew she should stop him with a word, or the pressure of her hand against his chest. He'd stop, she knew he would—but she couldn't do it.

She wanted him to kiss her. She wanted more than his kisses and his caresses. She wanted every part of him. She wanted him to love her the way a man loves a woman, with the physical contact that joins them as one. But that could never happen.

So, when his lips touched hers, she eagerly accepted what he offered. She met his contact with an urgency that defied her order not to kiss him. His kisses were like food to someone starving, and she welcomed him as if he possessed manna from above.

His tongue skimmed her lips as if searching for an unknown quarry, and she opened to him. She surrendered without hesitation. The initial touch caused fireworks to erupt inside her body, shooting lovely, spiraling tendrils of heat permeating every part of her. No one's kisses had ever affected her like his did. No one's kisses had the power his had.

Hannah wrapped her arms around his neck and met his demands with an eagerness that defied all reason. She returned his kisses with a desperation that challenged her resolve. She craved his touch with an ache that felt no relief. And she deepened her kisses to match the intensity of Rafe's.

She didn't realize how tired he was getting until she felt his body lean heavier against her. With a gentle pressure, she grasped him around his upper arms and lifted her mouth from his. "You've been up long enough," she whispered.

He smiled and leaned over to kiss her on the forehead. "I hate to put a halt to what we were doing, but perhaps I'll agree with you this once."

Hannah helped him into bed, then pulled the covers over him. When she was sure Rafe was settled for the night, she turned toward the door. His voice stopped her.

"I'll be well enough to go with you when you take Lilly to the country," he said from the other side of the room.

Hannah turned, nodded, then left the room. Every day that she was with him made it harder and harder to convince herself that she could live without him. Some days she knew for sure she couldn't survive.

Today was one of those days.

Chapter 17

❦

Hannah kept a close eye on both Lilly and Rafe as they traveled through the English countryside. Lilly had improved over the last week, but without warning, bouts of terror would consume her. More and more she looked to Rafe for comfort. Thankfully, she felt comfortable with him.

He'd spent time with Lilly each day, just a few minutes at first, then longer as time went by. Hannah had no idea what they talked about, but the fact that Lilly was talking was a wonderful thing. That was something Hannah discovered working with the girls who'd been raped. They needed to talk. It made their adjustment much faster and easier.

Lilly was asleep now. At first she huddled in the corner, but when the carriage hit a bump that jarred them all, Rafe pulled her against him and held her close. Lilly didn't fight him or move away from him.

That should have surprised Hannah, but it didn't. Rafe had a gift. He had a way with people, especially those who were hurting. He could comfort them like no one she'd ever seen.

Rafe, however, was a concern to her. He'd improved since he'd been attacked, but he wasn't completely recovered. Some of the cuts where he'd been beaten hadn't fully healed and needed care, and the bullet wound on his back still pained him, although he tried to hide the pain from everyone—especially Hannah. But she knew he suffered from a great deal of discomfort. She'd be glad when they reached Coventry Cottage and he could rest.

Hannah looked out the carriage window and recognized the familiar countryside. "We're almost there," she said. "Just a few more minutes."

Rafe gave her a blinding smile. "I can't say I'll be sorry." He rolled his shoulders and moved as much as he could, then looked down at a sleeping Lilly. "What will happen to her now?"

"We'll take care of her and train her to survive on her own."

The frown on Rafe's face said he didn't understand. Thankfully, they'd turned down the long drive that took them to Coventry Cottage.

"We're here," she said as they drove down the long rows of beautiful linden trees that lined the drive on both sides. She loved coming here, loved the peaceful feeling that consumed her each time she passed beneath the spreading boughs. She felt sheltered here, protected. Safe.

Humphrey stopped the carriage in front of Coventry Cottage, and Rafe was able to look at it for the first time.

Hannah took great pleasure in watching his reaction. The drop of his jaw and the lift of his brows evidenced his shock. But his amazement soon turned to admiration. This reaction was the same for everyone when they saw Coventry Cottage for the first time.

"I don't believe this," he whispered in awed incredulity. "I expected a—"

"I know," Hannah finished for him. "A *cottage*. And it is. It's just a very *grand* cottage."

Rafe laughed. His eyes sparkled with enthusiasm and appreciation. "Coventry Cottage is a mansion. A magnificent and beautiful mansion."

Hannah sighed in approval of his assessment. "Yes, it is, isn't it? A magnificent and beautiful mansion."

Rafe looked back out the window. "How did you ever find it?"

Hannah laughed. "I didn't. It found me."

Rafe frowned.

Hannah moved to the door. "Let's go inside. We'll get where it's comfortable, and I'll tell you how my owning it came about."

A footman opened the carriage door, and the disturbance woke Lilly. She opened her eyes with a start, then buried herself deeper into Rafe's side.

"It's all right, Lilly," he said. "We've arrived. Come, look at your new home."

Lilly's initial reaction was the same as Rafe's had been—awestruck admiration. Her gaze constantly shifted back to the Cottage as if she needed to check to make sure it hadn't disappeared.

A footman held the carriage door, and the Cottage's longtime butler, Danvers, assisted them from the carriage.

"Is Mrs. Grange ready for our guests, Danvers?" Hannah asked when she stepped onto the shelled drive.

"Yes, Miss Genevieve. She's been ready since she heard you was coming. And Mrs. Rosebury is anxious to meet her new charge."

Hannah looked up as Rosie—as Francine Rosebury was called by the girls—rushed toward them.

"Mrs. Rosebury, I'd like you to meet our newest guest." Hannah reached for Lilly's hand. "Lilly, this is Mrs. Rosebury. You may call her Rosie when you feel more comfortable here. All the girls do. Mrs. Rosebury, this is Lilly. And this," Hannah said, turning to Rafe, "is Lord Rafe."

"My lord," Rosie greeted, then turned back to Lilly.

"Oh, gracious be," Rosie said, clasping her hands over her ample bosom, "aren't you a pretty one. We're so glad to have you with us, Lilly. The other girls can't wait to meet you."

The uncertainty on Lilly's face eased a little. Rosie had a way of making that happen.

"You'll be sharing a room with Mary for at first," Rosie explained.

"Very good," Hannah said. Mary was the perfect choice for Lilly.

"Are you ready to see your room, Lilly?"

Lilly nodded, and Rosie wrapped her arm around the girl's shoulders and led her into the house.

Hannah watched Lilly go with a sense of relief and satisfaction. Lilly may have had it rough for a while, but her time at Coventry Cottage would help her heal. The days she spent here would be good for her.

Hannah turned to Rafe. His gaze was focused on her. She tried to read the expression on his face but couldn't. "Are you all right?" she said, thinking maybe he wasn't well.

"I'm fine. Actually, I'm more than fine."

"I don't understand."

"I'm sure you don't. I'll explain it to you sometime, but not right now. Right now I'd like to find a soft place to lay my aching body. Do you suppose this magnificent mansion might have such a place?"

Hannah laughed. "I'm sure it does. Let's go inside. I promise you the softest bed in all of England."

Rafe held out his arm for her to take. "That sounds wonderful," he said as they walked into the house.

Hannah suddenly felt as if she owned the world. As if nothing was beyond her grasp. As if she'd been given the greatest gift anyone could receive.

She continued to rest her hand on Rafe's arm, knowing the man she was holding on to had the power to make all her dreams come true.

* * *

Hannah woke the next morning more rested than she'd felt in months. She'd shown Rafe to the room Mrs. Grange had readied for him, then went to her own room. As usual when she came to Coventry Cottage, she was asleep as soon as her head touched the pillow. She hoped that Rafe had slept well too. She also hoped he'd stayed awake long enough to eat the food she'd had sent to his room, but she doubted it. As long as he got a good night's rest, though, that was all that mattered.

Hannah walked into the breakfast room and stopped short. Rafe sat at the table with a plate in front of him piled high with food. When he saw her, he placed his fork beside his plate and rose.

She hesitated to call any man beautiful, but she couldn't think of another word that described him as accurately. Especially when he looked at her. Especially when he smiled. Especially when the expression in his eyes changed from blatant admiration to something so obvious that it could only be called what it clearly was—love.

"Good morning, Hannah. You look radiant this morning."

"You look like you had a good night's rest," she answered, sitting in the chair he held for her.

"Excellent. Your staff has made sure I wanted for nothing."

She smiled as she reached for the cup of hot tea one of the servants poured for her.

"May I fill your plate?" Rafe asked.

Hannah glanced at his heaping plate and laughed. "I wouldn't dare trust you to fill my plate. I'd be so stuffed I wouldn't be able to do any work for the remainder of the day." She nodded to the footman who stood beside the serving table. "Graves will do it. Just some coddled eggs and toast, Graves."

"Yes, miss," Graves answered.

Hannah turned her attention back to Rafe. "I'm glad your appetite has returned. You went without a proper amount of food for too long. You need to eat in order to build your strength."

"Is that why you allowed me to come here with you?"

"Partly."

"There's another reason?"

"Yes, but for now we'll concern ourselves with making sure you eat properly so you build your strength."

"You don't have to fear on that account. My stomach is encouraging me to make up for the meals it lost."

"Good," she answered as she reached for the marmalade to spread on her toast.

Rafe continued eating, then paused to ask another question. "What are your plans today, Hannah? Do you have anything special in mind?"

Hannah looked out the window and saw that the day promised to be beautiful. The sun was already shining brightly, and there were no threatening clouds anywhere that she could see. "Perhaps," she said, looking back at the hopeful expression on his face. "I'd like to show you one of my favorite spots on the estate."

"I'd love that," he answered with a smile. "So far everything I've seen has been impressive."

"It is beautiful, isn't it?"

"Yes, I've never seen an estate like it. The windows in my room overlook the garden, and the view is remarkable."

"Then you have several more to discover. There are five gardens in all. Each of them is unique."

Rafe put another fork filled with sausage and eggs in his mouth and chewed. "However did you discover this estate?" he asked when he finished chewing.

"I didn't find it. It was a gift. It was given to me," she said, then watched to see the surprise on his face. He was obviously trying to decide who would have gifted her such a magnificent estate—and why. She realized the moment he understood.

Hannah nodded in Graves's direction, and the room cleared. She was alone with Rafe.

It wasn't that she didn't want to tell the story of how she'd acquired Coventry Cottage in front of the servants. Several of them had been employed by its former owner and knew exactly how she'd acquired it. Which meant that the newer members of the staff were also aware. But she still preferred telling Rafe the story without an audience to listen to her words.

"A gift," he said. He placed his fork beside his plate. It seemed he'd lost his appetite.

"Yes, Rafe. A gift."

Hannah lifted her cup to her mouth and took a sip of the tepid tea. She struggled to appear as relaxed as possible. "When I first came to Madam Genevieve's, I worked as one of her girls. I had different clients every night. Some of them I enjoyed being with. Some of them I prefer to forget."

Rafe's gaze lowered to a spot on the table to the side of his still-filled plate. He was uncomfortable when she talked about her life as a prostitute, but she refused to pretend it had never happened. She'd accepted the life she'd been forced to live, and Rafe would have to as well. Or…

Perhaps this was the ugly truth he needed in order to realize how different they were from each other, and that there was no hope for a future between them.

"One of my favorite clients was an elderly gentleman who visited me regularly every week. Sometimes more than once a week. He was a very special person, very intelligent as well as extremely wise about all things. I enjoyed talking to him and learning from him. He deserves the credit for encouraging me to purchase Madam Genevieve's."

"You don't have to go into detail about your former life, Hannah. I know who and what you were. You don't have to remind me."

"*Am*, Rafe. Who and what I *am*. I am Madam Genevieve. I am one of London's most well-known courtesans. Being a prostitute isn't an occupation you can pretend you never had. You can lose many things in life and find them again. But your good name isn't one of them. Once you lose your reputation, it's impossible to get it back."

Rafe's features hardened. Hannah knew she could stop. She'd made her point. But she wasn't finished. It was important that Rafe knew all about her. And about Coventry Cottage.

"Coventry Cottage's former owner was the gentlest of men. He was slight in build, and his features were often referred to as being on the effeminate side. I think he'd gone through life having his masculinity questioned. A topic that humiliated him."

Hannah rose from her chair and walked to look out the window. "One evening when I went down to meet him, I overheard the cruel jests made by one of Society's more outspoken gentlemen, suggesting that my friend return home and let the males who were more adequately endowed satisfy the girls at Madam Genevieve's."

Hannah remembered the night as if it had happened yesterday. She remembered how outraged she'd been on her friend's behalf. She turned to face Rafe. "I lost my composure and suggested that if this bully was concerned with satisfying the girls at Madam Genevieve's, then he would do all of us a favor and allow my client to take his place."

Hannah returned to her chair at the table and sat. "My comments were met with uproarious laughter that censured the bully who'd made fun of my friend." Hannah took a deep breath before she continued. "It wasn't long after that I noticed my friend seemed to have less energy. He'd always been a small man, but he seemed to be getting smaller. And he'd often spend a great deal of time sleeping instead of talking.

"I wasn't surprised one day when I received word that he'd passed away. I *was* surprised, though, to get a letter from his solicitor informing me that I'd been mentioned in his will."

Hannah reached for a glass of water and took a sip. "He'd left me Coventry Estate." She smiled as she always did when she thought of her benefactor. "His family, of course, contested the will, but as Coventry Cottage and the land surrounding it weren't entailed, there was nothing they could do about it. Plus, my friend had his solicitor draw up a document and had it signed by everyone, including the queen, stating that he anticipated that his greedy relatives would challenge his will, but he insisted it remain as written."

She looked at Rafe's shocked expression. "That's how I acquired Coventry Cottage."

His mouth dropped. "You got it from Covey. From the Marquess of Coventry."

Hannah smiled. "Yes. From Covey. Over the years, I'd been here often. I loved it here, and Covey knew it. When he died, he left it to me to do with as I saw fit."

"And you saw fit to turn it into a home for the girls you rescued off the streets."

"Yes. Heaven knows there's enough room. One wing houses the girls' rooms. They are required to care for their rooms and keep them spotless. The classrooms are on the west wing. The girls spend four hours each day at their studies. They learn to read and to do basic numbers. Then in the afternoons, they do various household duties. While there, they are evaluated by the staff.

"The girls who show an interest and the aptitude for running a household are given the opportunity to work with Mrs. Grange, the housekeeper. Those who show a talent for cooking are sent to the kitchen to help Cook. Those who show an interest in outdoor work are encouraged to tend the garden and take care of the produce. And those who enjoy tending the babes go to the nursery to take care of the children."

"Babes? There are babes here?"

"Yes, they are kept in the east wing. There are always babes. They are the smallest victims in this tragedy. Would you like to see them?"

"Yes," Rafe answered. "I'd like to see all the girls. I'd like to visit with them."

Hannah rose to her feet. "Follow me, then."

She turned to the door, but stopped short when Rosie rushed into the room.

"I think you'd best come quick, Miss Genevieve. Jenny is having her babe, and things aren't going good."

Hannah rushed to where Rosie held open the door. "Is the doctor here?"

"Yes, but he says he doesn't think he can save her."

"And the babe?"

"Probably not the babe either."

"Damn Skinner," Hannah said as she rushed across the marble-tiled floor and up the stairs that led to the rooms where the girls expecting babes were housed. "How much longer will he be allowed to murder innocent young girls?"

When Hannah reached the top of the stairs, she ran to Jenny's room. She wasn't sure she could go through this again. Wasn't sure she could hold another young girl's hand while life slipped from her body. But she had to.

Someone had held her hand while she'd been delivered of her babe. Someone had held her hand as life slipped from her body. And from her babe's.

And that hand had kept Hannah from giving up.

Especially when her babe had died in her arms.

Chapter 18

Rafe had never prayed as hard in his life.

Several hours passed, and he paced the floor outside the room where the girl, Jenny, struggled to give birth to a new life. He knew it wasn't going well. Everyone who exited the room wore a look of despair.

At first he'd heard muffled sounds coming from the room; now—nothing.

He turned as the door opened again and one of the servants walked out with a bundle of soiled linens in her arms. "Has she had the babe yet?" he asked, praying it was over.

The girl nodded. "She had a wee little lassie, but the doctor says it probably won't live. The birthing was too hard on it."

"And Jenny?"

She shook her head as more tears streamed down her cheeks.

Rafe felt a wave of desperation. He'd been at the bedside of several good Christians leaving this world, and for those who knew what awaited them, it was a joyful occasion. He wanted to make sure Jenny knew that comfort.

And there was the babe to baptize.

Rafe opened the door and took in the sight around him. The doctor was preparing to leave, and Rafe stepped aside as one of Hannah's servants escorted him from the room. Mrs. Rosebury sat in a rocker in the corner of the room and held a small bundle in her arms. Hannah sat on the bed and held Jenny's hand.

Rafe walked forward.

Hannah saw him first and looked up. Tears filled her eyes and streamed down her cheek. She tried to smile, but Rafe saw how difficult it was for her.

"Hello, Jenny," he said, smiling down on the young girl. Death was near. He knew it. And so did Hannah. "My name is Vicar Waterford."

"Did you come because I'm going to die?" she asked in a weak voice.

"Only God knows if and when we're going to die, Jenny. I came to tell you how special you are and tell you how happy you'll be when God takes you to heaven."

"That's what our vicar said when my granny died. He said she was happy now."

"Your vicar was right. Your granny is very happy. And you will be too."

She looked at him as if she wanted to believe him—was *desperate* to believe him—but wasn't sure.

He sat in a chair beside the bed. "Have you seen your babe yet?"

"For a minute. She's awfully tiny. The doctor said she more than likely wouldn't live either."

"Have you given her a name?"

She shook her head.

"Have you thought of a name you'd like to give her?"

Jenny nodded. "Rachael. I heard it once in a story from the Bible and thought it was pretty." She breathed a deep sigh. "I want to call her Rachael."

"That's a beautiful name. Would you like me to write her name in God's book?"

"You mean baptize her?"

Rafe nodded.

"Would you? My granny said that's what happened when I was baptized. My name got wrote down in God's book so He'd know who I was when I got to heaven."

"That's right, Jenny. He's waiting for you and so is your granny."

"I miss her," Jenny whispered. "Everything changed after she died."

"Then you'll be happy because she's waiting for you." Rafe stroked his fingers across Jenny's damp brow. "You'll be happy forever."

Jenny was losing strength. The end was drawing nearer. He nodded to Mrs. Rosebury, and she brought the babe over. "Would you like to hold Rachael while we baptize her?"

Jenny nodded, and Mrs. Rosebury placed the babe in Jenny's arms.

Rafe baptized the babe with clean water from a nearby basin, then let the babe rest in Jenny's arms. He quoted the comforting parts of scripture until God took Jenny home.

No one moved for a long time. Even after Mrs. Rosebury took the babe from Jenny's arms, Rafe and Hannah sat with her. Hannah held her hand, and Rafe stroked her cooling forehead. Tears streamed down Hannah's face, but she wasn't the only one who shed tears for the young life that ended far too soon. Tears streamed down Rafe's face too. Tears he didn't try to stop. Tears he didn't try to hide.

The sun rose high in the sky, and he and Hannah still sat there. A maid brought in a tea tray with small sandwiches on it, but neither of them was hungry. And Rafe knew he couldn't leave until Hannah was ready. They both owed the girl who'd given her life at such a young age to birth a babe who didn't stand any better chance of living than her mother had.

Finally, Hannah lifted her head and looked at him. With a nod she rose and walked to the door.

He followed.

She walked down the hall, then up another flight of stairs and down a long hallway to another wing of the mansion.

What he noticed first were the sounds coming from a room at the end of the hall. Although the sounds were muffled, Rafe knew they were happy sounds—the sounds of laughter. The gleeful sounds of children at play.

He followed Hannah, and when she stopped at one of the doors, he reached around her to open it. The door swung inward, and Hannah stepped inside. Rafe followed her.

He took one step into the room and stopped.

The room was filled with children—not crowded, not throngs, but many children. There were probably upward of twenty children in the room, from infants a few months old, to toddlers, to youngsters of four and five. In addition, Rafe guessed there were six or eight twelve- to eighteen-year-olds playing with the toddlers and those older, and six adults caring for the babes and overseeing the rest.

Rafe looked at Hannah and frowned. "Do you run an orphanage too?"

She shook her head. "Not exactly. These are all babes of the girls who were not fortunate enough to escape Skinner before he tossed them out on the street when they became with child. If the babe Rachael survives, she'll be cared for in this room."

He studied the children. "What will happen to them?"

"Occasionally, someone comes who wants a child so desperately they're willing to overlook the child's parentage. But mostly, all of them will remain and be raised here. They will be fed and clothed and loved unconditionally."

He followed Hannah as she walked through the room. She picked up all the toddlers and babes and gave them each an equal amount of her attention. Then she sat on the floor where she was surrounded by the older of the children and played with them for several minutes. She eventually rose and walked toward him.

"Are there older children?" he asked.

She nodded and walked to the door.

Rafe followed her to another wing of the mansion. When they turned the corner, she opened the first door they came to. It was a classroom and the children were busy doing problems on a slate.

"These are the five- through eight-year-olds. They are learning to read, write, and do basic numbers. Their instructor is Miss Amanda. We rescued her off the streets when she was fifteen. As she learned, she showed exceptional teaching abilities. When it was time for her to leave to find a position, she asked to stay." Hannah pointed to the little boy in the second row. "That is her son, Timothy. She didn't want to be separated from him, so becoming a teacher at Coventry proved the best solution for them both."

Rafe looked around the classroom, and his admiration for Hannah overwhelmed him. Before he could say anything, she turned and they left the room. They walked down the hall to the next room, and she opened the door. It was another classroom.

"These are the nine- through twelve-year-olds." She pointed at the young man standing in the front of the room. "That is Henry. He's been with us since he was nine."

"You rescued him too?"

Hannah nodded. "Skinner's clientele isn't only interested in young female virgins."

Rafe felt sick to his stomach. More and more he realized how important Hannah's work was. More and more he understood her desperation to save as many children as she could before it was too late. More and more he realized how important it was to stop Skinner.

"He instructs the older children and, with the assistance of Rosie and several other adults, makes recommendations as to what position each child should train for when they leave his classroom."

"Positions?"

"Yes, you might think of it as their *callings*."

She turned, and Rafe followed her out of the room.

"If we would walk through the rest of the Cottage," she said as they moved away from the classrooms, "we would find some of the older girls training to be nannies, some training to be maids or housekeepers, some as kitchen helpers and some as cooks. We train our boys for positions that might be useful for them later on. Some of them work with Higgins in the gardens. Some work with Jeremy in the stables. Some with Danvers in the house as footmen and house servants."

"How many children do you have here now?"

"There are seventy-six, including the older ones who chose not to leave. There are twelve babes and infants, seventeen to the age of eight, twenty-four to the age of twelve, and twenty-three children twelve and older."

"How do you manage?"

"Manage?"

"Yes. Feed them all? Clothe them? Find places for them when they're ready to leave?"

Rafe saw a different side to Hannah, a different side than the Madam Genevieve she pretended to be. It was a side that inspired admiration.

"Actually," she said, walking down the hallway, "finding posts for the children when they're ready to leave isn't that difficult. I have help in that area."

Rafe placed his arm around Hannah's waist when he noticed that she stumbled the slightest bit. It had been a long day, a tiring day. He wanted to get her someplace where she could rest for a while—where they could both rest.

He led her to a window seat in an alcove at the end of the hallway and made her sit. He sat beside her. "What help do you have?"

"The Duchess of Raeborn, the Marchioness of Wedgewood, and all their sisters. When any of them hear of a position that needs to be filled, they offer to assist in finding a suitable candidate. There's never a shortage of openings for well-trained staff members who come with excellent papers. And all of our children leave here superbly trained and with the highest of recommendations."

Hannah rubbed her hand over her forehead.

"Are you all right, Hannah?"

She nodded, but Rafe knew she was lying. He placed his arm around her shoulders and sat back against the corner of the window seat. He took her with him and nestled her close to him.

She curled against him and pressed her cheek against his chest.

"Everything will be all right, Hannah love," he whispered.

They sat together for several long moments. Hannah was the first to break their silence. "What time is it?"

Rafe reached into his pocket and pulled out his grand-father's watch. "It's nearly five in the afternoon."

"It's been four hours," she whispered. "I need to return. There are arrangements to make, and there's the babe. I don't know if…"

Rafe fingered the jewels on his grandfather's pocket watch. He'd wondered about the babe too. He stood and held out his hand for her to take. "Come. We'll face what's ahead of us together."

Hannah rose, and Rafe pulled her into his arms. He held her because he thought she needed to be held. He held her because he needed to hold her in his arms for a little while. He needed to feel her against his body, to feel the rise and fall of her shoulders as she took a breath.

To keep her with him for a little while so nothing could hurt her.

He wanted to kiss her, but he didn't. This wasn't the time. Passion wasn't what she needed. She needed his comfort, his strength. Nothing more.

After several moments, he placed her hand in the crook of his arm and led her back to the room where Jenny had given birth to her babe. Rafe opened the door, and Hannah walked in first.

The room was draped in shadows, but two lamps burned from the opposite sides of the room. Jenny was gone. The bedding had been changed and a new quilt put on the bed. There were no signs of what had happened in this room only a few short hours ago.

Rafe searched for any sign of the babe.

At first he didn't see anything, and he thought his worst fears were a reality. Then he saw Mrs. Rosebury holding a bundle in her arms as she rocked back and forth in a chair near the fireplace.

"Is she still alive?" Hannah asked, rushing to Mrs. Rosebury's side.

"Yes. Little Rachael may have had a hard start to life, but she's a strong lass. I think she just might make it."

Mrs. Rosebury stood and handed the bundle to Hannah. She took it with the ease and familiarity of someone who was used to holding babes.

Hannah pulled the light cover from the babe's face and brushed her fingers down little Rachael's cheek. "Has she taken food yet?"

"Not yet, but she will. I've sent for a wet nurse, and she should be here soon."

Hannah sat with the babe in her arms and rocked her as Mrs. Rosebury had done.

"I'll check on Jenny," Mrs. Rosebury said. "She should be ready now."

Hannah's eyes filled with sadness. "We'll hold a service tomorrow morning."

"If you don't mind," Rafe said when they were alone, "I'd like to conduct the service."

A sad smile lifted Hannah's lips. "I'd like that. We don't have a regular vicar here at Coventry, so we call on one nearby when we need him."

"Do you have a church?"

"Yes. It's a beautiful little church, but we don't hold too many services in it because we don't have a vicar here."

"Then that will be my job while we're here. I'll conduct Sunday morning services as long as we're here."

A smile brightened Hannah's face. "That's your calling, Rafe. I can see by the excitement in your eyes."

He laughed. "Yes, Hannah. As your calling is to save as many children as you can from Skinner's clutches, my calling is to save as many souls as I can from the devil's grasp."

Hannah gifted him with another smile, and Rafe thought his heart would burst. He could get used to her smiles. He could survive on them instead of food for the rest of his life.

Chapter 19

❧

*H*annah sat in the front pew of the small church while Rafe greeted the parishioners outside. This was the third Sunday he'd preached at Coventry's church, and today even some of the local residents came to listen. He had a gift. Even the younger children sat still while he spoke. And from the youngest to the oldest, he made everyone feel as if he were speaking to them personally.

No wonder the members of his parishes had loved him. No wonder every mother and father with a marriageable daughter wanted to claim him as a son-in-law. It was a miracle that none of them had snatched him for their daughter.

She lifted her gaze to the cross at the top of the carved oak altar. She loved it here. She always made a point of coming here when she visited Coventry Estate. Sitting here by herself in the peace and quiet was comforting.

She knew that, after what had happened to her, she shouldn't feel that way, and at first she hadn't. Then one of the older women who'd retired from Madam Genevieve's, but still lived there and helped out, reminded her that God wasn't the one who'd raped her. If she wanted to be angry with anyone, be angry with the devil. God wanted everyone to be good and to love each other, but the devil was the one who was evil. He was the one who had controlled the man who raped her. God and his angels were crying tears because of what that sinner had done.

Hannah wanted to believe that. She needed to know that God hadn't abandoned her or the children she loved and cared for.

She said a quick prayer that God would give her an answer where Rafe was concerned, then stood. He should be finished greeting his congregation by now, and they could go back to the Cottage. She'd promised the children she'd take them on a picnic this afternoon.

She turned and stopped. Rafe leaned against the door frame, his arms crossed over his chest and one booted foot over the other.

"Do you know how beautiful you look?"

"I believe you mentioned you found my attire passable when we left this morning, Vicar Waterford."

"*Passable?* Did I say *passable?*"

Hannah felt a bubble of laughter rise to her throat. "Perhaps you used another word. I can't remember."

Rafe pushed himself away from the door frame and walked toward her. "I'm sure I used another word, and if you can't remember, perhaps I should repeat myself. I said you were the most beautiful woman God has ever created."

"Your flattery will not influence me in the least. I still insist that you accompany me on our picnic."

"You think I would try to get out of it?" He reached her and looped her arm through the crook of his elbow. "I've been looking forward to being with the children since I found out you'd arranged a picnic."

She held his arm close to her as they walked out of the church. "I know you have. The children have reminded me numerous times that Vicar Waterford will be there. They're more excited because you're going with us than they are about the promise of a boat ride."

"I'm just as excited."

She smiled. "I know."

His enthusiasm amazed her. His love for children. The way he fit in perfectly with everything here. "You had them eating out of your hand this morning."

He glanced at her with a frown on his face as if he didn't quite understand her meaning.

"The people in church. Even the children. Not one lifted their gaze from you. You had their complete attention."

"Isn't that what speakers are supposed to do? Especially vicars?"

"Yes, but not many realize that." They walked down the path that led away from the church and back to Coventry Cottage. "Every vicar I've ever met thought their purpose in standing up in front of their congregation was to put the fear of God in them."

"Are you talking about your father?"

She lowered her gaze. "Yes. As well as all the speakers he forced me to listen to."

"You must have had a horrible experience growing up. I'm amazed that you can even step foot in a church."

"For a long time, I couldn't. Then I remembered all the passages I'd read that said how good God was, how Jesus fed the multitude because he didn't want them to go hungry. How he healed the lepers and the blind and the lame. I thought of all the good things in the Bible and knew my father was the one who had it all wrong."

Rafe stopped. He grasped Hannah by her shoulders and turned her toward him. For several intense moments, he looked into her eyes, then he slowly lowered his head and kissed her on the forehead. "Have I ever mentioned how special I think you are?"

Hannah shifted her gaze from his. He had mentioned that and much more.

"Have I mentioned that I believe I am in love with you?" he whispered.

Hannah closed her eyes. He'd mentioned that too. But she couldn't believe he could be. He knew of her past. He knew what she'd been, what she'd done—what had been done to her. How could he love her? How could any man love her—especially a man as good and perfect as Rafe?

He lowered his head again and pressed his lips to her forehead. "I know how frightened you are, Hannah. I know you think that if you just give me enough time, I'll wake up one day and realize I can't possibly love you. But that won't happen. I know the real you. Not the person you pretend to be in London, but the person you are here, the one who's devoted her life to saving as many children as she can from monsters like Skinner."

Hannah opened her mouth to argue with him, but the words wouldn't come. How could she try to convince him that a future with her was impossible, when a future with him was everything she'd ever hoped for?

She tightened her hold to his arm, and they took their first step back to the mansion. They were together now. For a little while longer, she could dream.

* * *

Hannah sat back on the blanket and watched the children. The younger ones were playing games in the meadow. Several of the boys were holding fishing poles and anxiously awaiting a big fish to gobble their bait. Others were patiently waiting for Rafe to return so they could take their turn in a boat ride.

Hannah knew without a doubt that everyone—children and adults alike—would sleep well tonight.

"The vicar has a way with the children," Rosie said when she sat down beside her.

"Yes. They all adore him. I think all of the older girls are half in love with him."

"Do you blame them?"

Hannah looked at Rosie and laughed. "No, I guess not."

She heard a commotion from the lake and looked up. Three girls were in the boat Rafe was rowing ashore. But Hannah didn't concentrate on the girls. She kept her eyes focused on Rafe and the gentle roll of his shoulders.

He was tired.

"I think I'd better rescue our vicar before the girls wear him out." Hannah rose from where she sat and walked toward the water's edge. "That's enough, girls. It's time we headed back to the Cottage."

She held up her hand to quiet the moans and groans. "Besides, Cook has promised she'd have a special surprise waiting for us when we returned. And I swear I detected the faint whiff of gingerbread baking when I left."

The promise of gingerbread pacified them a little, but it wasn't a suitable replacement for spending several minutes in such close proximity to Vicar Waterford. Hannah couldn't stifle the laugh that wanted to escape.

The girls made a point of thanking Rafe for the enjoyable afternoon, then reluctantly walked to where the other adults were rounding up the younger children and shepherding them back to the Cottage.

"My shoulders and back thank you," Rafe said, climbing onto dry land and pulling the boat onto the bank. When Rafe had the craft adequately secured, he sat down on the grass and flopped backward with his arms outstretched. "There was a time when I thought I could happily row a boat for days on end. Now I know that was a delusion. I'm not nearly as strong as I used to be."

"You haven't completely recovered."

"I've turned into a weakling."

Hannah laughed at him, then took his hand when he held it out for her. She sat on the ground beside him.

"Have they all gone?" he asked.

"The children?"

"No, everyone."

"No. They're still gathering the last of the picnic lunch and the blankets scattered on the ground."

He moaned. "Tell me when they're gone."

"Why?"

"Because I want to kiss you, and I can't until everyone has gone."

Hannah couldn't think of anything to say other than, "Oh."

"That's all? Just 'Oh'?" He turned to his side and rested his head in his palm. "And don't tell me you don't want me to kiss you, because I know you do."

"You do?"

"Yes, I've known it all day."

"All day?"

He lifted his gaze and looked into her eyes. "Yes. At least since we came here for our picnic."

"You're quite sure of yourself, aren't you?" she teased.

"I have to be," he answered. "I have to make up for all your doubts."

"Those aren't doubts, Rafe. I'm simply realistic where you're anything but."

"Do you know what your problem is, Hannah?"

She waited.

"Trust. You don't trust me."

"Trust has nothing to do with this, Rafe. I'd trust you with my life. I just don't want to be responsible for yours."

"It's not your *life* you're unwilling to trust me with. It's your *future*. You aren't brave enough to trust me with your future."

"That's because I can see what *you* are unwilling to face."

"If you think your reputation will make me hate you, or your past will be a stumbling block for me, you're wrong."

"I'm a prostitute, Rafe. A whore."

He stopped. The expression on his face died, and some of the ruddy color left. "You *are* a prostitute?" he asked. "Or you *were* a prostitute?"

"Does it matter?"

He sat upright. "Of course it matters. It matters a great deal."

Hannah turned to look out onto the gentle waters streaming by. It was so peaceful here. So calm. She tucked her knees to her chest and wrapped her arms around her legs. "*Were*," she answered. "I *was* a prostitute. For several years I sold my body to the man who paid me to offer him my favors."

"Then that's in your past. That has nothing to do with who you are now."

"It has everything to do with who I am. I am Madam Genevieve. I own one of the most well-known, expensive brothels in London. I cater to the most elite group of men Society has to offer. And my girls get paid well for what they do."

"You don't need Madam Genevieve's. You can give it up, walk away from it."

"No, I can't."

"You can. This can be your life, helping these children. Teaching them, training them. Finding positions for them."

"You don't understand."

He ignored her. It was as if he couldn't see what was right in front of him. Or that he didn't want to see the whole picture.

"I can't give up Madam Genevieve's."

"It means that much to you?"

"It means that much to the children."

"How can a brothel mean anything to innocent children? I thought that was the life you were trying to save them from. I assumed that would be the last place you would want them to go."

Hannah bounded to her feet. How could he even think such a thing? "They will never go to the brothel. They will never work at Madam Genevieve's. We don't train them for that. And we never will."

He rose to face her on even ground. "Then why is Madam Genevieve's so important to you?"

"Where do you think we get the money to feed and clothe the children? Where do you think we get the money to pay the bills to keep from losing Coventry Cottage?"

The expression on Rafe's face changed. He stared at her for several long seconds before he spoke. "Why didn't I realize that?" He grasped her by the shoulders and pulled her close to him. "I should have known from the start that Madam Genevieve's provides the income you need for your children."

Every instinct told her to step out of his grasp, but she couldn't. She wanted to be close to him. She wanted him to hold her next to him. She wanted someone to lean against. She wanted Rafe.

Instead of pulling away from him, she wrapped her arms around his waist. She pressed her cheek to his chest. She listened to the steady pounding of his heart as he held her, and she thought how comforting the sound was.

He tilted her chin upward, then lowered his head to kiss her. Bending her to his will wasn't difficult. He was an expert at getting her to comply. He was an expert at encouraging her to return his kisses. She was, after all, hungry for the passion he stirred within her. She was eager to experience the emotions he brought to the forefront.

She was desperate to feel the joining of their bodies every time his lips touched hers.

For several long minutes, they kissed beneath the bright sunlight. Each encounter was more intense than the last.

She had fallen in love with him. She'd come to care for him more than she thought it was possible for her to care for anyone. And he loved her in return.

Intimate Surrender

She knew it with the same certainty that she knew the sun would rise every morning in the east. And that it would set each evening in the west. Even if he'd never declared his feelings, she'd have known what he felt for her by his actions. From the way he guarded and protected her. From his attempt to make himself a part of her life. And the reasons she loved him were too numerous to mention.

She wrapped her arms around his neck and clung to him like a drowning man clutching the rope thrown to save him. Except she was the one who needed saving. She was drowning in the depths of her feelings for him. And no rope anyone could toss her was long enough or strong enough to save her.

"We need to talk," he gasped when he lifted his mouth from hers. "I refuse to give you up, Hannah. Don't ask me to."

Hannah placed the palm of her hand against his cheek. Not only didn't she want to ask him to give her up. She wasn't sure she was strong enough to ask.

Not anymore.

Chapter 20

The weeks since the picnic flew by, and Hannah knew it was time she returned to London. She'd never been away from Madam Genevieve's this long, but the time she spent with the children—and with Rafe—away from the troubles with Skinner had been blissful. But it was time to return.

Dalia had sent two girls during the last two weeks. They'd rescued them from Skinner's grasp, but Dalia wrote that it was getting more difficult all the time. Skinner had hired more men to protect his property, which was what he considered the young girls he stole from the streets. She wrote that not only was it more difficult to rescue the girls, but it was more dangerous. The conflict with Skinner had turned into a war. Even though the girls from Madam Genevieve's were accompanied by several bodyguards, problems arose at a steady pace.

Delores had been injured while saving the last girl, and Marjorie had been attacked on a previous attempt. Marjorie had been severely injured and required a doctor's attention.

Hannah was needed in London. She just wondered how she would manage leaving without Rafe insisting that he accompany her.

"You've been terribly preoccupied as of late," Rafe said as they walked through one of the Cottage's many gardens.

This was Hannah's favorite time of the day. The evening meal was over, and the children had retired for the night. She and Rafe made a habit of walking out-of-doors as the sun set, then they sat in the moonlight and talked.

Hannah had never been so happy in her life.

"Are you going to tell me what's bothering you?" he asked when he led her to one of the gazebos that overlooked a quiet pond.

Hannah leaned her head against his shoulder. "I have a favor to ask of you."

"And you're afraid I'll refuse you?"

"Yes."

He separated himself from her and grasped her by the shoulders. "You should know by now that there's nothing I won't do for you, Hannah. All you need do is ask. If I have it in my power to do it, I will."

"You don't know how glad I am to hear that," she said on a sigh, then placed her head back against his chest.

"Name it. What favor do you need?"

"I need to return to London. It's time I went back to Madam Genevieve's. I've never been absent this long."

Rafe chuckled. Hannah heard the laughter from deep inside his chest.

"And you were afraid I wouldn't want to leave? I admit I love it here and would be happy to spend the rest of my life here. But I knew you'd have to go back eventually. And it isn't as if we'll never return. It won't be long and we'll be able to come back."

"That's not what I'm asking from you."

He paused. "Then what is it?"

"I don't want you to come with me. I want you to stay here and help Rosie."

"No, Hannah. I'm—"

"I need you to stay. I need you to teach the children. They love you. You have a gift that very few possess. You have a calling, and this is where you're most needed."

"I won't let you go alone. I know things are getting more dangerous in London. The last girl who was brought here sobbed with terror when she related what had happened when Marjorie rescued her from the streets. She still has nightmares because of how severely Marjorie was beaten." He turned and held her shoulders firmly. "I won't let you go alone. You won't be safe."

"I'm the only one who will be safe," she said softly. "Skinner won't dare hurt me. He'll have every brothel owner up in arms. Even the ones who have not joined us in our attempt to bring Skinner down will have no choice. So far, he's focusing on the people who work for me. He intends to frighten them until they leave him alone. But that will never happen."

"How can you be so sure?"

"Because everyone knows if we don't stand up to Skinner now, he'll control every brothel on this side of London. And no one wants to work for Skinner. His girls are terrified of him."

"Then why don't they leave him?"

Hannah smiled. This was a question only someone completely unfamiliar with a man like Skinner would ask. "A few have tried," she answered. "Their bodies either washed ashore on the Thames, or were discovered mutilated in an alley near Skinner's brothel."

Rafe's hands fell away from her shoulders. "I can't let you go," he said with more force than earlier. "I can't risk that something will happen to you."

"I told you. Nothing will happen to me. I'm off-limits where Skinner is concerned."

Rafe sat back on the bench and stared out onto the still water in the pond. "So you want me to remain here while you go to London?"

"Yes. I need to know that everything is running smoothly here while I'm gone. And I don't trust anyone to do that more than I trust you."

For several long minutes they sat in silence, neither speaking. Neither moving. Finally, Rafe broke the silence.

"How long will you be gone?"

"Perhaps a month. No longer."

Rafe held her close, then leaned down and kissed the top of her head. "If I can help you more by staying here, then I'll stay."

Hannah tipped her head upward and looked into Rafe's face. Oh, how she loved him. She never thought it was possible to love anyone this much. She skimmed her hands up his chest and wrapped her arms around his neck. Then she brought his head down and kissed him.

She knew she was playing a dangerous game. The differences between them were staggering, and yet Rafe somehow seemed to adapt to them. He had overlooked so much that she wondered when they would find the proverbial straw that broke the camel's back. She wondered when she would ask one thing too much from him and he wouldn't be able to grant it—or overlook it.

She kissed him with all the passion she possessed, because she knew that day would eventually come.

There were only so many demands she could make of him.

* * *

The smells and sounds of the city grew stronger as she neared London. Hannah pulled back the window curtain to judge how close she was to home. Except this time it didn't feel like home. Today she felt as if she'd left the life she was born to live and was entering a place she no longer wanted to be.

She breathed a deep sigh. It was Rafe's fault she felt like this. If he hadn't let her glimpse a life so different from the one she was used to living, she wouldn't realize how much she wanted something more.

Hannah swayed with the carriage as it rumbled over the cobblestone streets and leaned back against her seat. She remembered the look on his face when she left. He didn't want her to go. He was worried about her. But she couldn't stay any longer. She was needed in London. Dalia had sent another message saying things were getting worse.

She leaned to the side and lifted the curtain. They were almost home. It wouldn't be long now. Soon she'd be back to her old life and the time she'd spent at Coventry Cottage and with Rafe would seem like a dream.

The carriage slowed, then stopped, and Humphrey opened the door and lowered the steps.

"Glad I am to see you, Miss Genevieve. Things are getting worse by the day."

"Come in as soon as you can, Humphrey. I'll send for Dalia, and you can fill me in on everything that's been going on since I left."

"Right away, Miss Genevieve."

Hannah handed her cloak, gloves, and bonnet to the waiting footman and sent word for Dalia to join her in the Lilac Room. The tea she asked for arrived at the same time that Dalia came into the room. The frown on her face told Hannah things were indeed bad.

"Oh, Genny. I'm glad you're back."

Dalia rushed to give Hannah a warm hug, then sat in one of the three chairs that formed a small cluster.

Hannah poured them each a cup of tea, then sat in a chair opposite Dalia. "Start at the beginning, Dalia. I want to hear everything that's happened since I left."

Dalia took a sip of her tea, then set the cup down. "Everything was peaceful at first. I don't think Skinner realized you'd gone to the country. Then, about three weeks ago, everything changed."

A knock sounded at the door, and Dalia stopped. Humphrey opened the door and stepped into the room.

"Sit down, Humphrey," Hannah said, pointing to the third chair in their group. "Dalia was just telling me what's been going on."

Humphrey sat. "And a lot there's been. Especially lately."

Hannah looked back at Dalia.

"About three weeks ago, we got word that Skinner's men had kidnapped a new girl and were bringing her in. Chastity volunteered to go after her, and two of Frisk's men and one of Razer's men went with her. We've been sending three men to guard our girls each time."

Hannah nodded. "Did word come through our regular source?"

"Yes. It came the same as always."

"Go on."

"Chastity and the guards waited where they'd heard the girl would be transferred, but when the girl showed up, so did a bunch of Skinner's men."

"It was a trap," Humphrey said.

Hannah sat forward in her chair. "Was anyone hurt?"

Dalia and Humphrey nodded. "They were all hurt to some degree or other," Dalia said. "Chastity took a few blows, but no marks that didn't go away in time. The men, though, took the brunt of it. Skinner's men fought them with knives. All of them were hurt. Some bad. One of Frisk's men was hurt the worst. They didn't think he'd live, but he has so far."

A lump fell to the pit of Hannah's stomach. The skirmishes were coming more frequently, but at least no one had died yet in this territorial conflict with Skinner.

"Since then," Humphrey added, "Rauncher has joined forces with us, and so has Tumbler, from the East End. They're all afraid of what Skinner will do if we don't stop him here. He's boasting that he's going to ruin Madam Genevieve's and take over this whole part of town."

Hannah took several deep breaths. "Is there more?"

Humphrey and Dalia looked at each other.

"Last night the Earl of Hanbrooke's carriage was waylaid near here and the earl was robbed."

"Are you sure it was Skinner? It could have been any—"

Humphrey reached in his pocket and took out an envelope. "This came this morning."

Hannah opened the envelope and three gold crowns fell out, along with a folded piece of paper.

These gold pieces belong to Hanbrooke. You can give them back, if he's ever brave enough to visit Madam Genevieve's again.

S

Hannah bolted to her feet and threw the crumpled paper to the floor. "How many has he robbed on their way here?"

"Hanbrooke was the third," Dalia answered.

"In two weeks?"

"Yes."

"Damn him!"

"What are we going to do, Miss Genevieve?" Humphrey asked.

"Is Madam Genevieve's the only one Skinner's targeting?"

Humphrey nodded. "It wouldn't do no good to stop anyone on their way to the others. Their customers don't carry enough coin to make it worth anyone's while."

Hannah paced back and forth in front of the window. She had to think of something. There had to be a way to fight Skinner. It wouldn't be long at all before Madam Genevieve's business would come to a halt if her clients didn't feel safe traveling here.

"Where are these robberies taking place?"

Humphrey scratched his head. "Two of the carriages were stopped when they slowed to turn from Tottenham to Oxford. The other on Crown Street."

Hannah focused on the expectant expressions on Dalia and Humphrey's faces. "How many men does Skinner send to stop the carriages?"

"There have been two each time," Humphrey answered.

Hannah took a step closer to Humphrey. "I want you to round up a dozen men and place half of them in each location. Make sure they keep out of sight. If—rather, *when*—Skinner's men attempt another robbery, we'll stop them. Give the men instructions not to harm Skinner's men. We don't want to start a war. We just want to show our strength."

"What do you want them to do with Skinner's men?"

"Tie them up and take them back to Skinner."

Humphrey laughed. "That will give Mr. High 'n' Mighty something to think over."

Hannah sighed. "That's the purpose. Skinner doesn't have the manpower we do. He's just trying to put up a good show."

"You think once he realizes he's outmanned, he'll give up?" Humphrey asked.

"That's what I'm hoping," Hannah answered. "Skinner's not stupid. He wants power. He knows possessing Madam Genevieve's will give him that power. As long as we don't provide him with a reason to escalate this, I'm sure we can stop his efforts."

"What kind of reason?" Dalia answered.

"Like injuring one of his men. Or killing someone. He's just being a nuisance. A little like a fly that won't leave a horse alone. The horse will swat his tail at the fly to make him leave. For a while the fly ignores the horse's attempts, but, after a while, the fly gets tired of getting swatted and leaves the horse alone."

Humphrey laughed. "I like thinking of Skinner as a fly."

"Well, I don't," Dalia said, clutching her hands to her upper arms. "He scares me. You never know what he'll do next."

"That's why we have to constantly be on our guard. We'll continue to strike him where it hurts—by rescuing the children he intends to exploit. And we have to make sure we don't give him any ammunition to use against us."

"What kind of ammunition?" Dalia and Humphrey asked in unison.

"Like taking risks that allow him to gain the upper hand. Putting any of Madam Genevieve's girls in danger."

"Then shouldn't we stop going after the new girls Skinner brings in?" Dalia asked.

"No, that defeats our purpose in being here. The girls can go out, but they will remain in the carriage. The men will rescue Skinner's targets. Our girls will not take any chances. We can't risk Skinner holding anyone ransom. That will give him the ammunition he needs to gain the upper hand."

Dalia and Humphrey nodded in agreement.

They discussed several other issues that had come up while Hannah was gone. Then, an hour or so later, Hannah left them and went to her rooms.

She was tired. She was unsure of herself. And she missed Rafe.

She wasn't sure if she was doing the right thing where Skinner was concerned. What frightened her most was the possibility that she might be underestimating how far he would go to gain the power he was desperate to have. Because if she was wrong, it could cost someone his life.

Hannah poured herself a glass of dark wine and sat in her favorite chair and took a sip.

Thank heaven Rafe wasn't here. At least he was at Coventry Cottage—where he would be safe.

Chapter 21

❦

*H*annah read Caroline's letter over again and smiled. She almost had the words memorized, but she never tired of reading about Coventry Cottage's successes.

According to Caroline, she'd heard of several positions that were open and had written to Rosie. Rosie immediately sent letters of reference to the homes that had positions to fill.

They'd placed five girls and two young men, all in excellent homes. Three of the girls and the two young men would have positions in country homes of friends and acquaintances of either Caroline or one of her sisters. The other two girls would go to town houses in London. The carriage bringing them to London should arrive any moment now. It would deliver its passengers where positions awaited them, then stop at Madam Genevieve's. The driver would remain overnight, then leave in the morning with a passenger.

They'd rescued another girl from Skinner's clutches last night, and she would be going to Coventry Cottage.

Hannah couldn't help but smile. That had always been her goal—to rescue as many innocent young girls and boys as she could from Skinner's clutches, then send them to

Coventry Cottage where they would be trained with skills that would support them for the rest of their lives. When they were ready to go out on their own, the people at Coventry Cottage would find them positions where they were assured of having a better life than they would have living on the streets. Like the seven young people they'd rescued who were now embarking on a new life.

She wondered what path her life would have taken if she'd had a Coventry Cottage to help her when she arrived in London all those years ago. Perhaps she wouldn't be the infamous Madam Genevieve now.

Perhaps she'd be Miss Hannah Bartlett, a nanny in someone's home. She loved children and had the aptitude to teach. Or, perhaps she'd be a lady's maid. She had an eye for clothes and what to wear on various occasions, and she had a talent at styling hair. Or perhaps she'd be—

She stopped fantasizing about what might have been when there was a knock on the door. "Come in," she said.

The door opened, and Dalia entered.

"Has the carriage from Coventry Cottage arrived?" Hannah asked.

Dalia nodded. "The driver delivered the last young lady to her new post."

"Good. Make sure he gets something to eat, then find him a room. Tell him he'll have a passenger when he returns in the morning."

"I've already informed him."

Hannah recognized the serious look in Dalia's eyes and her hesitation to leave. "Is something wrong?"

"I'm not sure."

Hannah waited.

"You have a guest."

"A guest? Who?"

"Vicar Waterford."

"Rafe?"

"He accompanied the girls from Coventry Cottage."

Hannah rose. "He can't be here now. It's not safe."

"I hoped you'd realize that. Skinner doesn't know he's here yet, but when he does, it's hard telling what he'll do."

"Where did you put him?"

"In the Gardenia Room."

Hannah headed for the door. "Tell the driver he'll have two passengers in the morning. He's not to leave without both of them."

Dalia may have answered, but Hannah didn't hear her if she did. She was too concerned with reaching Rafe and making sure he knew he had to return to Coventry Cottage in the morning.

She walked down a long, narrow hallway to the Gardenia Room and opened the door.

Rafe stood on the opposite side of the room with his elbow resting on the mantel of the fireplace and one booted foot crossed over the other. When he saw her, he smiled.

Hannah's heart shifted in her breast. She should be used to his smiles. Immune to his charm. But she wasn't. She'd missed him more during the last few weeks than she thought she could bear—even doubted she could live one more day without seeing him and considered sending for him. But she knew how dangerous it would be for him to come to London. She knew the threat Skinner was to anything connected to her.

She closed the door and stepped into the room.

Rafe was already halfway to her.

She could almost feel his arms around her, feel the warmth of his body next to hers. Feel how safe she'd be next to him.

The voice of reason told her to avoid his embrace. The voice of reason told her to keep a distance between them and not encourage his overtures. But she couldn't. She was too desperate to be held by him. She was too eager to be a part of him.

She walked into his arms and let him hold her.

"Oh, I've missed you," he said. His finger lifted her chin, and he kissed her on the forehead. Then he lowered his head farther and kissed her on the lips.

She kissed him in return, but kept her kiss short. She needed to remain in control of her passion. "What are you doing here?" she asked.

She needed Rafe to know that she wouldn't allow him to stay in London. She needed him to know that they had tonight, then he had to return to Coventry Cottage.

"When I found out the carriage was coming to London to deliver two young ladies to their new employment, I made sure I was on board."

"You can't stay. When the carriage returns tomorrow, you will be on it."

Rafe dropped his arms from around her, then separated himself from her. "And if I refuse?"

"I'm not giving you that choice."

His gaze narrowed. This was a Rafe she wasn't used to seeing, a Rafe she'd only glimpsed once or twice. This was a stronger, more inflexible Rafe than people usually saw.

On most occasions he was a lighthearted, captivating charmer, whose charismatic personality drew people to him with relative ease. Because of his easygoing disposition, he rarely had to use force. But Hannah knew beneath that good-natured charm lay a steely determination. She'd hoped she'd never have to battle it.

Such wasn't going to be the case here. He wasn't going to allow her to order him about as if he were one of her girls, or one of the youngsters she'd rescued off the streets.

She stepped away from him and walked to a small side table where three crystal decanters sat on a silver tray. She poured some liquid from the middle decanter into two glasses. She held one out to him. He took it.

"I'm sorry, but I can't allow you to stay here, Rafe."

"Why? Because it would be bad for business if people found out a vicar was in residence?"

His words hurt. She bristled. "Yes. I have a business to run, and I refuse to let you interfere."

He took a sip of the brandy she'd given him and turned toward the flames that licked upward in the fireplace. When he reached it, he anchored one outstretched arm against the mantel and stared into the blazing fire. "I want you to consider something, Hannah."

He didn't look at her. Didn't give her the chance to look into his eyes to read what his words meant.

"What is that?"

"Please, sit down. Hear me out and don't say anything until I'm finished."

"Very well," she answered and moved to a chair and sat.

He turned. "Our feelings for each other are obvious. I'm in love with you, and whether or not you will admit it, you are in love with me. There's no debating that point. It's obvious every time we kiss. It was obvious to me the moment you walked through the door and my heart leaped in my chest. And, from the look in your eyes when you saw me, it was obvious to you. Therefore, let's save a lot of time and unnecessary arguing and face what we both know, but you are reluctant to admit—we love each other. We belong together."

Hannah opened her mouth to say something, a rebuttal perhaps, but Rafe's raised hand stopped her.

"Please, hear me out," he continued. "I am more than thirty years of age. I'll be one and thirty in a few months. And you are nearing thirty—if you haven't already reached that milestone. I want to marry. I've never had this compulsion before. In fact, I'd even halfway convinced myself that finding the woman of my dreams and giving her my heart as well as my name was not in my future. Then I met you."

Rafe turned away from her to look out the window.

Hannah knew there was nothing of significance outside, but rather, he wanted to avoid seeing any reaction she might make—the downward cast of her eyes, the shake of her head, her lips forming the word *no*. Therefore, pretending interest in the out-of-doors was much safer.

"I'm well aware of your fears. I understand them, Hannah. Really I do. I know how terrified you are that if we marry, someone will discover your past and I will suffer from embarrassment. You are afraid that your past will act as a wedge that will be driven between us. That in time it will sever any love we feel for each other. But that will never happen. I am not a young schoolboy suffering from my first love. I am a mature adult who has weighed all the consequences of loving you and has decided you are worth any trials that will come our way. You harbor doubts because you do not know the depth of love I have for you. Let me assure you, it is stronger and more invincible than anything the world can hurl at us."

He turned and walked to a chair beside her, then sat. "I don't intend to lose you, Hannah. It took me thirty long years to find you, and I won't let you slip out of my grasp. The only question that remains is, what are you going to do? How valuable is my love to you?"

Hannah struggled with the weight pressing on her heart, the painful pressure that wouldn't let her lungs take in air like they needed to do.

"Can you answer that question, Hannah? Do you intend to continually banish me to the country while you stay here in London and run your brothel? Do you intend to allow me to see only the good side of what you do and not the part I am asking you to give up?" He turned in his chair until he faced her squarely. "Do you intend to keep me in the country like several of the nobility keep their mistresses hidden away, and come to visit me only when you can escape your obligations at Madam Genevieve's?"

Hannah was shocked by his questions. She turned her head until she was looking directly into his eyes. How could he think she would turn their love into something so sordid? But he should also realize that she could never give up Madam Genevieve's. And he knew why. "May I ask you a question?" she said. "A question to which I would like an honest answer?"

"Of course."

"What do you see for our future? How will you support me? Where will we live? What will we do?"

"You need never fear that I cannot support you. Or that you will live in poverty. My grandfather left me money in a trust. It is not a huge amount, but it is substantial. It arrives quarterly."

"The same grandfather who left you his watch?"

Rafe smiled. "The same."

"He must have loved you a great deal."

"He did."

"What do you think he would say about your marriage to a whore?"

Rafe turned on her. "Don't call yourself that," he said. "Ever."

There was a flash of anger in his eyes that couldn't be missed. Hannah nodded. "Very well. What do you think he would say about your marriage to a woman with a soiled past?"

"He would understand. He knew what love was. He loved my grandmother very much. Nothing would have forced him to give her up."

Hannah looked at the confident expression on Rafe's face and wanted to believe him. She really did. But if Rafe's grandfather would have understood, he would have been one of the few men of noble birth who did.

"You haven't answered all my questions," she continued. "Where will we live? What will you do?"

His look was one of surprise. "We will live at Coventry Cottage. Did you think I would ask you to abandon something that was so important to you? Did you think I would ask you to desert the children you've rescued off the street?"

She lowered her gaze to her hands clenched in her lap. "I don't know what I thought."

"I would never ask you to give up taking care of the children who were rescued off the street. All I ask is that you leave Madam Genevieve's."

She lifted her gaze. "The income from Madam Genevieve's is what supports Coventry Cottage. Without the income from the brothel, the children will have to go without."

Rafe was silent for several long moments. When he spoke, his voice was soft, almost a whisper. "I can't permit you to stay here, Hannah. Allowing you to live in a brothel—allowing you to run a brothel—goes against everything I believe."

The energy Hannah needed to breathe drained from her body. He was asking her to choose. He expected her to walk away from Madam Genevieve's, knowing it meant that the children at Coventry Cottage would have to go without.

She thought of what this would mean. Her connection with Madam Genevieve's enabled her to rescue the children Skinner intended to sell in his brothels. Without her, hundreds of children would be sold into slavery.

Hannah lifted her gaze and looked into Rafe's eyes. He expected her to choose him over everything that was important to her. She couldn't do it.

She shook her head. "I can't."

She heard him breathe a heavy sigh. "I see."

"You're asking too much of me. I could never live with myself if I turned my back on the children."

"I'm not asking you to turn your back on the children. I'm asking you to turn your back on your life as a prostitute."

As if a window suddenly slammed shut, taking the light with it, her hope for a future with Rafe suddenly vanished.

She had been right all along. The differences between them were too great. The problems too insurmountable.

"Don't you understand? Running Madam Genevieve's is how I have the money to provide the children with clothes to put on their backs and pay the people it takes to care for them and train them."

When he spoke, his voice was louder. His words more emphatic. "You're not a prostitute, Hannah."

Hannah bristled. "That's the problem, Vicar. You have Madam Genevieve confused with someone else. Hannah isn't a prostitute, but Madam Genevieve is! When I'm in London, I am Madam Genevieve! Just like when you're in London, you are Lord Rafe Waterford, not Vicar Waterford."

"There isn't a difference, Hannah. You're still the same—"

"There's a world of difference. There's—"

Hannah stopped. She needed this to end. She couldn't survive the constant turmoil that teetering between her vicar's world and her real world caused. Rafe needed to face what she was, not what he pretended she was. He needed to see the real Madam Genevieve and stop pretending he could change her into someone she could never be again.

"I won't give you up, Hannah."

"Hannah isn't here, Vicar. She lives in the country. At Coventry Cottage. Madam Genevieve lives in London. She's a fallen woman. A harlot. A famous courtesan."

Hannah suddenly realized she needed to put Rafe out of her life forever. She needed him to leave and never come back. To do that she needed to show him how different she was from the woman he'd created in his mind. The woman he called Hannah.

She swallowed hard. She needed him to hate her.

"If you need to see what the real Hannah is like—the Hannah that everyone in London knows as Madam Genevieve—you will have to attend an event she is hosting four nights from tonight. It's an auction."

"An auction?"

"Yes. The item of value to be auctioned off is the famous madam herself. Madam Genevieve will sell her favors to the highest bidder." Hannah smiled as coquettishly as she could manage. "If you need proof that the Hannah Bartlett you created to fit your dreams and Madam Genevieve are one and the same, you are invited to see the famous madam in action. Perhaps you'll even be tempted to bid on her. But, be warned, Vicar. You will have to pay dearly for the pleasure of her body for the evening."

"No, Hannah! Don't do this. You can't."

"But I can, Vicar. That is what whores do. They sell themselves. If you don't have the stomach to watch, then go home! Go shepherd your saints and leave us sinners alone!"

Rafe opened his mouth to say something, but Hannah didn't have the stomach to degrade herself further. She pointed to the door. "Go."

He walked toward the door, but stopped when he reached her. "I can't let you do this, Hannah. I can't."

"Then be here in four nights, Vicar. The bidding begins at nine." She lifted her gaze to face him, then smiled. "But be warned. I will not come cheaply. If you want me, your pockets will have to be very deep indeed."

His eyes flamed with fury as he glared at her.

She thought he would say more, but he didn't. He hesitated only a moment, then walked past her.

Hannah shut the door with a thud and leaned her back against the hard wood. She wouldn't cry. She *couldn't* cry. She'd already shed enough tears over him. She refused to shed more.

She slowly moved to her chair by the window and stared out the glass panes until the sky darkened. And she sat even longer.

She loved him, but she couldn't give up the income from Madam Genevieve's. And that was the only option he'd given her.

She lowered her head and prayed that when the carriage left in the morning, he would be on it.

* * *

It had been three days since the carriage had returned to Coventry Cottage—without Rafe aboard it. Hannah didn't know what was worse—realizing that she'd lost Rafe forever, or not knowing where he was and worrying that Skinner had found him.

She tried to do what she'd done before Rafe had entered her life, but found it nearly impossible. Her job at Madam Genevieve's was to oversee the customers and match them up with the girl she thought would please them most. Now she struggled at what used to come naturally to her, and Dalia had to assume more of the responsibility.

She used to be in daily contact with the girls and know what was going on with them, and if and when there were problems to solve. Yesterday she'd walked into the breakfast room and found a new girl sitting at the table. When she asked who she was, the girl introduced herself and said she'd been at Madam Genevieve's more than a week. And that she was glad to see Madam Genevieve—again.

Hannah had no recollection of meeting her before. She didn't even remember Dalia informing her that they'd hired a new girl. And Dalia would have. Hiring anyone new was one of the things of which Hannah had always insisted Dalia keep her informed.

It was Rafe's fault her mind was so preoccupied. It was his fault she couldn't think straight. Everything was his fault. If only she could be assured that he was safe. If only she knew where he was and that Skinner couldn't get a hold of him.

She walked to her mirror and studied her reflection. Hannah Bartlett was nowhere in the looking glass. Only Madam Genevieve stared back at her. She took a second look, then made some minor adjustments to the gown she'd chosen to wear tonight.

It was one of her favorites. A gown of deep scarlet that made her look like the renowned madam she was. A gown that accentuated her narrow waist and the curves at her hips. She ran a finger over the material at the gown's bodice. The low neckline left little to the imagination. She would draw the eye of every man in the house. And that's exactly what she intended to do.

But tonight, looking like she did—playing the role she needed to play—didn't feel right. Tonight she felt cheap. Used. And it was Rafe's fault.

He'd forced her to glimpse a different life. He'd given her the choice of being someone other than a prostitute. Other than a whore. He'd let her believe it was possible to have the kind of life she'd only dreamed of having. Now she was terrified that she'd never be satisfied with her life again.

She returned from the mirror and headed for the door. She couldn't stand to remain in her room another minute. She needed to mingle with the clients who'd come for an evening's entertainment. She needed to forget about Rafe. And that would only happen if she got back to the life she used to lead. The life she was dealt at the age of fifteen.

Hannah reached for the knob and stopped when there was a knock on the door. She opened the door. Dalia stood on the other side.

"Are you all right, Genny?" she asked when she was inside.

Hannah thought to lie and assure her friend that she was fine, but something stopped her. She was tired of pretending that she was all right. Tired of pretending that it didn't hurt to know she'd shut Rafe out of her life.

Hannah sank onto the nearest sofa. "I've lost him, Dalia. He's gone and he'll never come back."

"Maybe that's for the best."

Hannah buried her head in her hands. "I'm not sure I can live without him."

"You have to, Genny. You won't be able to keep him alive if you don't force him to leave."

Hannah was startled by Dalia's bluntness and looked at her friend in confusion. She waited for Dalia to explain what she meant.

"Skinner's placed a marker on your vicar's head. You have to make sure he leaves London as soon as possible. If he doesn't, someone will kill him."

Hannah covered her mouth to stop her scream from escaping, then reached for the nearest container and emptied her stomach.

Chapter 22

Rafe sat in the chair behind the huge oak desk in Thomas's study and listened to the voices in the hallway. Some of the servants must be having a conversation, because Thomas was still in the country with Caroline and the children and no one else was in the house.

Rafe lifted his half-empty glass to his mouth and took another long swallow. He wondered if Thomas would notice the missing bottles of brandy from his cellar, and hoped his butler would replace them before Thomas returned.

Rafe drained his glass and refilled it again. He was sure Hudson would replenish the brandy. He was very reliable. All of Thomas's staff were reliable, which was why Rafe didn't doubt that Thomas would eventually find out that Rafe had spent the last three days here—drunk.

But by then maybe he'd be able to talk about Hannah without feeling as if he were falling apart, or be able to think about her without having to numb his emotions with liquor.

Rafe lifted his arm, but stopped before the glass touched his mouth. The door opened and Thomas filled the doorway.

"Good evening, Rafe." Thomas closed the door behind him and walked across the room.

"Thomas, what a shurprise," Rafe slurred.

"I imagine it is," Thomas said when he reached the desk. "Do you mind if I join you?"

"'Courshe not." Rafe handed his brother the brandy decanter and watched as Thomas poured a small amount into a glass. "Do you mine me sitting in yer chair?"

"Could you walk to another if I did?"

Rafe tried to stand but failed. "Doubtful."

"That's what I thought." Thomas held up his hand. "Stay where you are."

"Thanks. What 'er you doin' in Ludon?"

Thomas took a small sip of his brandy. "I just came for a few days. I have a meeting tomorrow with Lord Carlyle."

"Oh. Thas' nice."

"How long have you been like this?"

"Like what? Drunk?"

"Yes, Rafe. Drunk."

"Lesee. What day is this?"

"It's Friday."

"Friday," Rafe repeated, then tried to count backward. "This is day three, so that would make it Wednesday. Yes, Wednesday. Thas' when I saw her."

"By *her* I suppose you mean Hannah."

Rafe shook his head while he was trying to take a drink and his brandy sloshed over the rim of his glass and down the front of his shirt. He tried to wipe it away but only ended up spilling more. "No, Hannah wasn't there. Only Madam Geveneive."

"I see."

"Do you, Thomas? I wish, then, that you would tell me what you see, 'cause I sure as hell don't understand. I don't understand anything. 'Specially where she's concerned."

"That's because you're in love with her."

"Wha's that got ta do with anything?"

"Everything, I presume. I wish you hadn't fallen in love with her."

"She says the same thing."

"I'm afraid she's right," Thomas said.

Rafe tried to sit forward in his chair but wasn't sure he managed anything other than tipping sideways. "I need a favor, Thomas."

"Anything, Rafe. You know that."

"I need a loan."

Thomas took a sip of his brandy. "How much?"

Rafe tried to think, but his mind refused to work. He couldn't calculate how much it might cost to buy her. And he had to buy her. He couldn't stand to know someone else would be bedding her. "I dunno," he answered. "A great deal."

"How much is *a great deal*?"

Rafe shook his head, then looked into his brother's eyes. "Ten thousand pounds."

Thomas's eyes opened wide. "Ten thousand?"

Rafe took another swallow, then nodded. "Ten thousand—I think."

Rafe struggled to stand but only managed to fall forward. The desk prevented him from landing on the floor. When the room stopped spinning, he pushed himself to his feet and staggered precariously.

Thomas moved to reach him, but Rafe held out his hand and Thomas sat back down.

Eventually, he gained control of his unsteady body and attempted to take a step. When his feet refused to obey his directive, he decided it was best not to move.

"May I ask what you need ten thousand pounds for?" Thomas asked.

"To buy her," he answered.

"To buy *what* for her?"

"Not *what. Her.*"

"You're not making sense, Rafe. What do you want to buy for Hannah?"

"Not *what*! I need to buy *her*! She's auctioning herself off tomorrow night, and I can't let anyone else have her."

Rafe pushed himself away from the desk. "I—"

Before he could finish his sentence, his world went black and the floor rose to meet him.

* * *

When Rafe opened his eyes, the sun was high in the sky and streaming through his window.

This wasn't the first time he'd tried to wake up, but it was the first time he thought he might actually accomplish his goal. The other two times he'd attempted to get up, he hadn't made it much farther than hanging his head over the side of the bed and emptying his stomach into the container someone had placed there.

Probably Thomas. That would be like him. He always took good care of him.

Rafe lay as still as he could to keep the throbbing in his head at a minimum, and only opened his eyes. After the third try, he even managed to keep them open.

"Do you think you might live?" Thomas said from somewhere in the room.

Rafe didn't even consider trying to find him. That would have involved moving his head, and that was completely out of the question. "Maybe. Not sure."

"I see."

Thomas rose and stood close to the bed so Rafe could see him without having to move his head. "When you can manage, come down and have at least a bite of toast and some hot coffee. Hudson says you haven't eaten since you started drinking. A bit of food will help."

Rafe closed his eyes again and listened to his brother's footsteps cross the room, then heard the door open and close. Although he didn't want to, he knew he'd eventually have to rise and face the day. There was no other choice.

Dressing was more difficult than he'd expected. Even with Thomas's valet to help him, it took longer than usual. That was because he had to stop twice when the room refused to stop spinning and sweat covered his face and neck. He wasn't an experienced drinker, and after this experience, he doubted he'd ever touch anything stronger than tea.

He was finally dressed and ready to face the day—at least as ready as he knew he'd be, considering his queasy stomach. He tugged at his too-tight collar as he made his way down the stairs, then took a deep breath when he reached the breakfast room.

Thomas was waiting for him. He looked up when Rafe entered. "At least you look better than you did last night."

"About last night…"

Thomas held up his hand. "I'll make this easy on you and we'll get right to the point. Explain why you'd like me to give you ten thousand pounds. I didn't quite understand you last night."

"You understood me fine. You're just having a hard time believing what I said."

Rafe waited while a footman poured him a cup of steaming tea, then placed a piece of buttered toast before him. When he was finished, Thomas nodded to Hudson and the room emptied. He and Thomas were alone.

"Now, tell me what you meant when you said you had to *buy* Hannah."

Rafe took a sip of the tea. It burned his mouth but tasted better than anything had for three days. "Madam Genevieve is holding an auction tonight. The bidding starts at nine o'clock."

"The bidding for what?"

"For *her*. For Madam Genevieve."

A frown deepened across Thomas's brow, and his eyes narrowed. "Hannah's auctioning off herself. But why? She hasn't taken a client for years. Why would she do something like that?"

Rafe rested his arms on either side of his plate and fisted his hands until his fingers hurt. "Because of me. Because I forced her to."

Thomas didn't ask why he thought Rafe had forced Hannah to auction herself off. He just waited for Rafe to tell him. Because he knew he would.

"I went to see her when I arrived in London, and she ordered me to leave. She didn't want me at her establishment. She said I was too good to mix with people like her."

Rafe raked his hands through his hair. "I wanted to prove her wrong. I wanted to convince her that she was good. I asked her to marry me. I told her we could make a life for ourselves away from London. Away from Madam Genevieve's."

For several long seconds, neither of them spoke. Finally, Thomas broke the silence. "Why is Hannah auctioning herself off?"

Rafe raked his fingers through his hair. "We had a terrible argument. I demanded that she leave London, that she leave Madam Genevieve's and never return. She said she couldn't. Madam Genevieve's is what keeps Coventry Cottage running." Rafe looked at Thomas. "Do you know about Coventry Cottage?"

Thomas nodded.

"The cause is wonderful," Rafe continued. "What they do there is admirable. But I can't let Hannah continue to run Madam Genevieve's. Living the life of a prostitute goes against every belief I have. It's a mortal sin. The Bible warns us about the consequences."

"What does this have to do with an auction?"

"Hannah's selling herself to make me hate her. She thinks if she proves she's a whore, I'll be so repulsed by her I'll leave London. And her."

"Is that what the ten thousand pounds is for?"

Rafe nodded. "I can't let her auction herself. I…" He paused. "I couldn't live with myself if she did that. It would be my fault."

Thomas sat back in his chair. "What kind of trouble are you in?"

"I'm not sure."

"Do you realize two men have been watching the house?"

Rafe nodded. "They've been there since I left Hannah three nights ago. I recognize one of them. His name is Humphrey. He works for Hannah."

"In what capacity?"

"A guard, of sorts."

"Is there a reason Hannah believes you need to be guarded?"

"It's a long story, Thomas. One I don't believe has merit any longer."

"Whether or not you think it has merit, Hannah obviously does, or she wouldn't have taken steps to make sure you're safe."

"That's what makes this ordeal so ridiculous. Hannah sent Humphrey here to guard me when I don't need guarding, which only leaves her vulnerable and shorthanded."

"Hannah must think the risk is worth it. So, why don't you tell me what this is all about?"

Rafe breathed a heavy sigh, then told his brother about Skinner and what had happened to him when he first arrived in London. When he finished, Thomas placed his forearms on the table and stared at Rafe.

"Do you realize how lucky you are to be alive?"

"Yes."

"No wonder Hannah has someone guarding you. No wonder she's doing everything in her power to force you to leave London. She knows if you stay, this Skinner will kill you. She's trying to protect you, and you keep stepping back into danger."

Rafe bolted to his feet and glared at Thomas. "Why is it so bloody difficult for everyone to understand that I don't want or need anyone to *protect* me? I'm not a milksop, nor am I a naive country lad who's too backward to realize the danger someone like Skinner poses. Just because I'm a vicar doesn't mean I'm unable to protect myself."

"Hannah isn't doing this because she thinks you're unable to protect yourself. She's protecting you because she loves you. She's protecting you because in this case, you *are* incapable of protecting yourself. You're not solving a squabble between two quarreling brothers in your parish. You're battling a man capable of committing murder. *Your* murder. And Hannah is taking every step she knows in order to protect you. At least I am grateful to her for what she's doing, even if you're not."

Rafe brought his fingers to his forehead and rubbed his temples. Thomas was right. Hannah was doing everything she could to protect him, and he was doing nothing but hindering her efforts. He'd been so sure his love for Hannah would overcome any barrier that he'd raged like the proverbial bull through the china shop. Suddenly, he wasn't so sure. And the thought that Hannah had been right all along scared him to death.

The chance that he'd have to live without her was more than he could bear to consider. Rafe raked his fingers through his hair again, then looked at his brother. "I was serious about the ten thousand pounds. I promise I'll repay—"

"The money's yours, Rafe. You'll have it this afternoon."

Rafe couldn't stop the wetness from filling his eyes. He couldn't let Hannah sell herself tonight. He'd never be able to live with himself if she did. "Thank you," he said in a choked whisper.

Thomas clasped his hand on Rafe's shoulder and squeezed. Then he made a statement that proved how important Rafe was to him. "I'll be ready to leave tonight when you are."

Chapter 23

"Are you sure you want to go through with this?" Dalia asked.

Hannah was dressed in the most seductive, most revealing gown she owned. Her hair was done up in a most stylish design, and all that was left were the jewels she intended to wear.

She reached for an expensive diamond necklace and handed it to Dalia to clasp at her neck. "I don't have a choice, Dal. If I don't force him to leave London, someone will kill him. The price Skinner put on his head is astronomical."

"After tonight he'll probably hate you, Genny. Can you live with that when it happens?"

Hannah tried to smile. "I'll have to. I've survived worse."

"Are you sure?"

Hannah paused, then shook her head. "No. This will be the worst."

Dalia was prepared to say something more, but a knock on the door stopped her.

"Come in," Hannah ordered.

The door opened, and one of the girls from downstairs entered. "Madam Felicity wanted me to tell you that the first of the bidders has arrived."

"Thank you, Elaine. Show them into the formal parlor and make sure they have something to drink."

"Yes, ma'am." Elaine turned to leave, then stopped. "Oh, and I'm supposed to tell you that Delores hasn't returned yet."

"Where did she go?"

"She got word this afternoon that Skinner was bringing in a new girl. A real young one. Delores went to see what she could find."

"She didn't go alone, did she?" Hannah asked, knowing that if any of the girls would head into trouble without being prepared, Delores was the one.

"Oh, no, ma'am. She took two of Frisk's men with her. It's just that Madam Felicity thinks they should have been back before now. You know how Madam Felicity worries over everything."

Hannah smiled. Felicity did over worry about most things, and with the rest, she usually concentrated on the worst possibilities. But where Skinner was concerned, it was always good to be cautious. "Tell Madam Felicity to inform me the minute Delores returns."

"Yes, ma'am. I'm sure Delores is all right. It probably just took longer for the girl to arrive, that's all."

"I'm sure you're right, Elaine. But let me know the minute you hear anything."

"I will," Elaine said, then left the room.

When Elaine was gone, Hannah turned to Dalia and said, "If Delores hasn't returned by the time the auction is over, send every man you can get to search for her. They know where the drops usually take place. Have them start there."

Dalia nodded, then rose. "I'll go below and see what I can find out."

Hannah watched her friend walk across the room, but Dalia stopped before she reached the door. "How many men did you invite to the auction?"

Hannah felt a knot bunch in her stomach. "Four. The Earl of Masey, Viscount Balderford, the Marquess of Referley, and Vicar Waterford, of course."

Dalia's brows shot up. "You chose well, Genny. The other three have some of the deepest pockets in London. There's no way your vicar will be able to outbid them."

"That's what I'm counting on."

Dalia nodded, then left Hannah alone with her thoughts—and her regrets. No matter how this night turned out, there would only be one winner—the man who won her favors for the night.

But she and Rafe would suffer the greatest loss.

After tonight they would lose each other forever.

* * *

Hannah walked around the crowded room, playing a part she'd played often in her life—that of Madam Genevieve. Except tonight she wasn't *playing* the role; she was *living* the role. A role she didn't think she'd ever have to play again. And at the end of the night, she would have to do something she never thought she'd have to do again—be the whore.

"Do you think your vicar might not show up?" Dalia waited until Hannah was away from the crowd to ask her question.

"He'll be here. He'll do everything he can to save me. I just have to make sure whatever he does won't be enough."

"You're playing a dangerous game, Genny. I hope you know what you're losing."

"I know who I'm saving. Word will travel fast enough about the price Skinner put on Rafe's head. By the end of the week, it won't be safe for him to step out of his house."

Hannah's conversation was cut short when Viscount Balderford approached them. The smile on his face showed that he was more than delighted to be one of the few chosen to bid for her favors.

He stepped close and bowed. "Madam Genevieve. Madam Dalia. It is a pleasure to be here. And it will be a pleasure indeed to spend several enjoyable hours in your company," he said as he focused on Hannah.

Hannah smiled up into his laughing eyes and tapped him on the arm in a teasing gesture. "Only if you are the highest bidder in the auction, my lord."

"Never fear. I don't plan on being outbid."

The determination in his eyes left a lump in the pit of her stomach. The thought of giving herself to anyone except Rafe caused shivers to race down her spine. She reminded herself for the thousandth time that she had to make this sacrifice to save him. Telling herself that this was the only way she could save Rafe was the only reason she would survive this night.

"Then be prepared to leave a great deal of your money on the table, my lord, because Masey has vowed the same."

"Has he?" Balderford said on a laugh. "If the prize were anyone else, I might consider letting him win. I consider

Masey a good friend, as I do the Marquess of Referley. But when the prize is the famous Madam Genevieve, friendship, I'm afraid, falls by the wayside."

"Did I hear my name mentioned?" Referley said, walking up behind them.

Hannah turned to face the second bidder she'd invited to the private auction.

"You did, Referley. I was just explaining to the beautiful Genevieve that even though you and Masey and I are all friends, any regard I feel for either of you no longer counts. Not when the promise of such a special evening stands before me."

"Let me assure you of the same, Genevieve. I will not let my friendship for either Balderford or Masey prevent me from parting with as much of the Referley wealth as it takes to win you for the night."

"What is it you're boasting about, Referley?" the Earl of Masey said as he joined them. "Are you trying to convince the lovely Genevieve that your pockets or those of Balderford are deeper than mine?" He turned to grace her with a heart-stopping smile. "Let me assure you, dear Genevieve. You have nothing to fear. You will not have to suffer the attentions of either of these braggarts. I intend to have you for myself tonight."

Both Balderford and Referley laughed.

"Look who's the braggart," Referley said, standing tall.

"Not bragging, Referley. Simply stating a fact."

That caused another uproarious burst of laughter that Hannah tried to ignore. If they had been talking about anyone or anything else, she could have found humor in their boasting. But they were talking about her. Each was bragging that *he* would be the one who would take her to his bed and use her like the whore she was.

Hannah felt sick to her stomach. And this is how she knew Rafe would feel. Sick to his stomach to know she intended to give herself to a man to whom she wasn't married. And she didn't love.

She forced herself to close her mind to that thought and concentrate on playing her part. She was the most desired—and most elusive—paramour in all of London. It was a role she'd worked hard to establish. And tonight would be her finest performance.

She brightened the smile on her face and turned her attention back to the three handsome men who surrounded her.

"I thought there were to be four of us bidding for you tonight?" Masey asked.

"There are." She looked around the room, thankful Rafe hadn't arrived yet. She needed another minute or two to prepare herself for seeing him. She needed to steel her nerves for what she was about to do to him—how she would hurt him. Make him hate her.

A weight pressed harder inside her breast. "I'm sure he'll be here any moment. It's not yet nine o'clock."

"Do we know him, my dear?" Referley asked.

"I doubt that any of you do. He's not a part of the London scene."

"Maybe he'll decide not to come," Balderford joked. "Maybe he's heard how desperately each of us wants to bed you and it's frightened him off."

She forced a laugh. "Perhaps, but I doubt it. He has been one of my most ardent admirers."

"More than me?" Raferley asked, pretending to be shocked.

"Yes, my lord. Even more than you."

That elicited another round of teasing laughter.

"All I can say," Masey countered, "is that if our mystery bidder doesn't arrive soon, he won't be able to fit in the room. I expected that your auction would draw a crowd, Genevieve, but even I am amazed at the mob of onlookers."

"Only because they're jealous that they weren't one of the four men given the honor to bid for you," Balderford said.

Genevieve glanced at the mantel clock and saw the hour hand neared nine o'clock. Her gaze moved to the door as Rafe entered. The Marquess of Wedgewood followed him into the room.

Hannah's heart died a painful death inside her breast. Her gaze locked with Rafe's, and she recognized a number of emotions. But the reaction that affected her most was the disappointment on his face when he looked at her.

And she knew that tonight would be the last time she would see him.

Chapter 24

❧

*R*afe could feel the excitement the minute he stepped into the room. The anticipation was as palpable as anything he'd ever experienced. The noise level was so intense he knew he could roar his frustration as loudly as he wanted and not be heard.

And that's exactly what he wanted to do—bellow his anger until everyone in the room knew how furious he was at what was about to happen. Then he wanted to grab Hannah by the arm and drag her from the room.

He was desperate to stop her from allowing this to go any further. He knew she was selling herself simply to prove how far beneath him she was, and he wanted to forbid it.

He understood why she'd turned to prostitution after she'd been raped, and he accepted that part of her life. He also knew that she'd repented of what she'd done because of her refusal to sell herself the minute she'd earned enough money to buy Madam Genevieve's. Because she hadn't turned to prostitution since.

And tonight he wanted to forbid her to return to that lifestyle because she felt she needed to convince him how unworthy she was of his love.

She was more than worthy. She'd done more good than he could hope to do in ten lifetimes. She'd affected the lives of more children and young men and women than he would ever be able to claim to influence. She'd rescued more children from a life of prostitution than anyone could count. He couldn't let her do this.

He wouldn't.

He looked around and found her at the front of the room talking to three men. Two of them he knew, but not the third.

"If those are the men Hannah invited to bid for her tonight," Thomas said from behind him, "she chose wisely. They are three of the wealthiest men in London. As well as three of the most sought-after bachelors in Society."

Rafe reached for a glass of champagne an elegantly gowned young beauty offered him and took a sip. "I recognize Lord Balderford and Referley, but not the third. Who is he?"

"The Earl of Masey. He belongs to one of the oldest families in England. Very influential. Very wealthy."

Rafe studied the three men talking to Hannah, and his blood heated. She'd handpicked these men with the intention of giving her body to one of them.

He studied each of them, then shifted his gaze to look at Hannah. Their gazes locked.

Rafe had imagined the emotions that would surface when he saw Hannah tonight, but he was unprepared for the riotous reaction that engulfed him. He wanted to place a wrap around her shoulders to cover the flesh that her gown exposed. He wanted to hide her exquisite beauty so that every man in the room stopped lusting over her. He wanted to whisk her from the room and save her from debasing herself.

He wanted to forbid her from taking part in this fiasco and be assured she would honor his wishes. But he knew she wouldn't. For some reason he didn't completely understand, she was so desperate to separate herself from him that she'd chosen to sell herself.

He kept his gaze riveted to hers as she slowly made her way to where he and Thomas stood.

"Lord Wedgewood," she said, extending her hand to Thomas. "What a pleasant surprise."

"Madam Genevieve. Yes, I happened to be in town and thought I'd accompany Lord Rafe, since he was one of the lucky four chosen to bid for your favors."

Rafe thought he noticed a flash of embarrassment on Hannah's face, but it disappeared as quickly as it emerged.

"I'm certain he'll appreciate your advice. Maybe you'll even suggest that there's no need for him to risk his money. As you can see from the men he'll be bidding against, he will undoubtedly be forced to drop out of the game soon after it starts."

"Is that what *you* are hoping happens, Madam Genevieve?" Rafe asked.

He enjoyed watching her cheeks darken with a blushing rose.

"If you knew me better, Lord Rafe, you'd realize it hardly matters to me which of the four men bidding for my favors wins. The winner of the prize is of little significance. Just as the prize is of little value."

The knot that formed in Rafe's gut nearly made him ill. How dare she play the part of a slut? How dare she attempt to make him believe that letting one of them use her body meant nothing to her? How dare she try to make him believe that she wasn't humiliated by what she was doing?

A long pause made the tension in the room even more unbearable. Thankfully, Thomas eased the situation. He looked around the room, then turned his attention back to Hannah. "Your event has attracted quite a crowd."

She smiled. "Yes, it has. It's been a long time since I've offered my services to anyone. Obviously, London's male population is interested in who the winner will be."

Rafe couldn't listen to Hannah degrade herself any longer. He leaned closer to her. "Stop this madness now, Hannah. You don't need to prove anything to me. If I could take back my words from the other night, I would. I didn't mean to insult you like I did."

For a fleeting moment, Rafe thought he saw a flash of regret in her eyes, followed by dark remorse, but he must have been mistaken. Before he could identify with certainty what he saw, Hannah tipped her head back and released a hearty feminine laugh.

"Oh, Vicar! Do you truly believe that you are the reason I am offering my services? Do you think I am taking a lover tonight because I believe I need to *prove* something to you? Oh, no. Nothing could be further from the truth." She stood on her tiptoes and whispered in his ear. "No, Vicar. I am taking a lover tonight because I am a whore and I enjoy what I do."

* * *

Hannah's stomach clenched the second the words left her mouth. What she'd said had a visible effect on Rafe. He blanched as if she'd physically struck him.

Hannah struggled to keep the proud expression on her face, even though pride was the last emotion she felt. "Now, if you gentlemen will excuse me. It's nearly nine o'clock. The bidding will commence in moments."

She turned, grateful for the chance to escape. Rafe was not the only one who disapproved of what she was doing. Wedgewood did too. The dark frown on his face told her he did.

She had taken two shaky steps away from them when Wedgewood's voice stopped her.

"Madam Genevieve. A moment, please."

She turned.

"May I have a few words with you?"

"I don't think—"

"Please."

Hannah filled her lungs with air. "Of course, Lord Wedgewood. If you'll follow me."

She led Wedgewood to the far side of the room, then opened a door and stepped into an empty room. Wedgewood followed her, and she closed the door behind them. He spoke before she could turn to face him.

"Perhaps you'd care to explain what's going on, Hannah. Because none of this makes sense."

"There's nothing to explain, Lord Wedgewood. I decided to offer my favors—"

"No, you can use that excuse to Rafe and hope he believes it. And maybe he will. He's so desperately in love with you he can't see beyond the hurt you're causing him. But I am not that affected. Why are you doing this?"

Hannah squeezed her eyes shut while she thought of what to tell her friend's husband.

"You might as well tell me the truth, Hannah. I'd like to be able to tell Caroline the real reason you're doing this when she asks."

Hannah's gaze darted to his face. "Caroline doesn't need to know about tonight."

Wedgewood laughed. "Do you think that's remotely possible? With six sisters and their connections to London Society, someone's bound to mention it. I can name a half dozen men out there right now who will relish repeating tonight's events, including Viscount Carmody's father and the Earl of Baldwin's brother. How long do you think it will take Lady Josalyn or Lady Frances to hear the news and tell Caroline? Or Grace?"

Hannah swallowed hard. She had no choice. She would have to tell Wedgewood the reason she was offering herself. Perhaps she could even enlist his help to make sure Rafe left London immediately.

She walked to the sideboard and poured them each a drink. "Please sit down," she said as she handed him his brandy. The trembling in her fingers felt foreign, strange, unlike her. She was nervous. More nervous tonight than she'd been in years. But tonight was different. Yes, tonight was very different.

Wedgewood walked to the chair she pointed to, then waited for her to sit first.

"Sit, please," she repeated. "I prefer to stand."

She walked to the window and left him behind her. She stared out into the darkness, even though she could see very little. "I'm sure Caroline has told you part of what I do here—my attempt to rescue as many young girls from a life on the street as possible."

"Yes," he said from behind her. "She's explained your mission. I find it admirable."

"Well, not everyone does. Particularly a man named Skinner."

"I've heard of him. And what I've heard isn't good."

Hannah turned her head and looked over her shoulder. "Whatever you heard was no doubt a compliment compared to his true nature."

"How is he involved in this?"

"Several..." She paused. "No, *most* of the girls I've rescued are very young. Many of his clients prefer young virgins. That shouldn't shock you."

"No," Wedgewood replied. "Unfortunately, it doesn't."

"Those are the girls I try hardest to rescue, before they are ruined. Skinner, as you can well understand, has taken exception to my interference. In fact, when your brother first arrived in London, he followed me when I went to rescue one of the girls I'd heard was arriving. Skinner took note of Rafe's intrusion and ordered his men to teach your brother a lesson."

Hannah turned to face Wedgewood. She wanted him to realize how dangerous Skinner was and how at-risk Rafe was. "They shot him in the back, then beat him."

The expression in Wedgewood's eyes turned deadly.

"He could have died, my lord. More than once I thought he might lose his battle to survive."

Wedgewood rose. "That's why you're doing this. Because you are worried over his safety. You intend to disgust him so completely that he'll leave you and never return."

Hannah breathed a heavy sigh. "There's more." Hannah walked to a chair near Wedgewood's and sat.

"Unfortunately, Skinner knows that Rafe is very important to me. To retaliate against me and to stop me from interfering in his business, he has put a marker on Rafe's head. A significant marker."

Wedgewood sat forward in his chair. "A price? On Rafe's head? That bastard."

"Yes. Word is just spreading about the marker, but in time, every lowlife in London will be hunting your brother. It's not only important that Rafe leave London, but that he leaves London tonight."

"That's the real reason you're doing this—to distance yourself from my brother. To save him."

"Don't make what I'm doing sound noble. There's nothing honorable about being a whore."

"Sacrificing your future happiness for my brother's safety is one of the most magnanimous acts imaginable. Thank you, Hannah. I am in your debt."

"You owe me nothing. If not for me, Rafe would never have gotten into this situation."

"You didn't get him into this situation. Love did. If he didn't love you so desperately, things may have been different. And if you didn't love him so unconditionally, you wouldn't be doing something so self-sacrificing."

"Don't give me too much credit, Wedgewood. My plan hasn't worked yet. The rest will undoubtedly be up to you."

Wedgewood frowned. "I don't understand."

"There's no way Rafe will win the auction." Hannah stopped short. "Unless, of course, you backed him."

"I loaned him ten thousand pounds."

Hannah breathed a sigh of relief. "That won't be enough. Masey will no doubt go that high, if not higher. Needless to say, your brother cannot win. When he loses, it will be your responsibility to take him from London. Preferably tonight. If not tonight, first thing in the morning."

Wedgewood listened, then nodded. "I'll tell him I've been called home and make him go with me."

"Good," Hannah said. Then she smiled and walked to the door. "It's nine o'clock. It's time to begin."

Wedgewood crossed the room and stopped in front of her. "I owe you, Hannah. More than I'll ever be able to repay. I don't know how I'd manage if I lost Rafe. He means the world to me—along with Caroline and the children."

Hannah tried to smile. "I know. He means the world to me too. Saving him is the only thing that will enable me to survive losing him."

Hannah opened to door and left the room before Wedgewood saw the tears that had formed in her eyes.

Chapter 25

*B*ecause Hannah had anticipated a large crowd, and because she wanted to make certain there was no controversy with the bidding process, she'd hired two of the most well-known, well-respected men in London to conduct the auction. One, Mr. Ezra Crumbly, the proprietor of one of the largest banks in London. The other, Mr. Phineas Rummery, of Rummery, Chisholm, and Rummery, solicitors to some of the wealthiest families in London, including at least two of the bidders.

Hannah wanted this night over. She wanted the auction concluded and wanted the hours she would spend servicing a man over. It wasn't as if she'd never let a man use her before. She had, more times than she could count. But that was before she'd earned enough money to escape the life of prostitution. That was before she'd dreamed of loving someone who was good, and decent, and worthy. Before she'd met Rafe. Before she'd given up being a prostitute and vowed never to return to that lifestyle.

"Are you ready to begin?" Dalia said from beside her.

"Yes. It's time."

"I'll tell Rummery to start, then."

Dalia turned to leave, but Hannah stopped her. "Has Delores returned yet?"

Dalia shook her head. "Not yet. But we've got men out looking. We should know something soon."

Hannah nodded, then watched as Dalia walked to the front of the room to introduce the men who would conduct the auction as well as the four men who were allowed to bid.

With each introduction, the riotous cheers from the crowd grew louder. The shouts and applause when Dalia introduced Crumbly and Rummery were respectful. The cheers and ovations for Balderford, Referley, Masey, and Rafe were quite different. Masey seemed to be the crowd's overwhelming favorite. Balderford and Referley were nearly tied with equal supporters cheering them on. Rafe, of course, received the quietest applause. Few knew who he was. None knew why he'd been included in the select group invited to bid for the famous Madam Genevieve's favors.

Hannah stole a glance in Rafe's direction. Wedgewood was whispering to his brother, and Hannah prayed he was trying to discourage him from bidding at all. If not that, at least discouraging him from raising his bid too high, because the ten thousand pounds Wedgewood had loaned him would take Rafe a lifetime to repay.

Rafe's gaze lifted and caught hers. For several seconds they held each other's gaze as closely and intimately as if the past months of turmoil had never happened. As if Skinner's threats had never been issued. As if she and Rafe were still in the country and none of this had intruded on their lives.

But it had, and no matter how desperately she wanted things to be different, they weren't. And never would be.

Hannah moved her gaze first and caught Dalia looking at her. Hannah nodded her encouragement to let the bidding begin. She needed this night over. She needed the painful separation with Rafe to be behind her.

"Gentlemen," Rummery began as he addressed the four bidders scattered throughout the room. "The bidding will now commence. The item being auctioned tonight is the lovely Madam Genevieve."

Thunderous applause and cheering echoed in the room. He held up his hands for silence. That did not happen for several minutes. When it did, he continued.

"Do I hear an offer of one hundred pounds?"

"Two hundred pounds," Viscount Balderford said.

Another loud cheer echoed.

"Five hundred," the Marquess of Referley answered.

An even louder cheer resounded.

"One thousand pounds," the Earl of Masey said, doubling the bid.

A deafening roar reverberated in the room.

"One thousand five hundred," Referley countered.

"Two thousand," Balderford added.

"Two thousand five hundred," Masey said.

"Three thousand," Balderford shouted.

There was a slight pause, and Hannah thought perhaps the bidding would slow to a normal pace. Instead, Masey raised the bid by two thousand.

"Five thousand pounds," the Earl of Masey said.

Booming roars and thunderous applause followed his offer. The shouts of approval were earsplitting.

Hannah didn't think the bellows would ever die down, but eventually the room quieted to a tolerable roar.

"The Earl of Masey has bid five thousand pounds," Rummery announced to the crowd. "Do I hear more?"

"Six thousand pounds," Rafe said, bidding for the first time.

The silence in the room was noticeable as everyone turned to where Rafe stood beside his brother.

"We have a bid of six thousand pounds. Do I hear more?" Rummery said.

"Six thousand five hundred," Balderford bid.

"Seven thousand," Referley bid after a slight pause.

"Eight thousand," Masey shouted, upping the bid by a thousand.

"The bid is eight thousand pounds," Rummery announced. "Do I hear a bid of eight thousand five hundred?"

"Eight thousand five hundred," Rafe said, causing another uproar.

"Do I hear nine thousand pounds?" Rummery asked.

The bidding was slowing, and for the first time Hannah worried that the amount might not reach ten thousand pounds. Referley shook his head and stepped back into the crowd, indicating he was out of the running. Thankfully, Balderford and Masey hadn't relinquished.

"Nine thousand pounds," Masey indicated.

"Nine thousand five hundred," Balderford countered.

Uproarious shouts and cheers boomed through the room.

When the cheering calmed, Rummery announced, "I have a bid of nine thousand five hundred. Do I hear—"

"Ten thousand," Rafe announced.

The room erupted in thunderous cheers and bellows. It took an eternity for the sound to lessen. When it did,

Rummery shouted as loud as Hannah had ever heard him speak.

"We have a bid of ten thousand pounds. Do I hear more?"

Everyone in the room focused on Viscount Balderford and the Earl of Masey. Balderford slowly lifted the corners of his mouth to form a bitter smile, then shook his head.

"My pardon, Madam Genevieve. I regret that I cannot exceed Lord Rafe's bid, but…" He paused. "I thank you for the opportunity to bid for your favors." Balderford shrugged his shoulders, bowed his regrets, and stepped back into the crowd.

Only Masey and Rafe were left, and if Masey didn't raise Rafe's bid, Rafe would win her for the night.

A heavy weight dropped to the pit of her stomach. This wasn't how she wanted her friendship with Rafe to end. This wasn't how she wanted them to part—with bitterness and disgrace and humiliation.

"Lord Masey, the bid is ten thousand pounds to you. Will you raise it?"

Masey paused. Then… "Ten thousand five hundred pounds."

Hannah breathed a sigh of relief. Rafe had ten thousand pounds. He was finished. She would go to Masey. To have to give herself to a man other than Rafe would dishonor the love she had for Rafe and cause him to hate her; it would also save his life.

Thomas had promised her he would get Rafe out of London as quickly as possible. He'd promised to take him where he'd be safe.

Hannah took a step toward the Earl of Masey. She greeted him with a look of satisfaction, her expression indicating she was certain he'd outbid his fellow bidders. She took another step, then—

"Eleven thousand."

Hannah stopped her forward progress and stared at Rafe. She couldn't believe this. Wedgewood had only loaned him ten thousand pounds. How could he bid more, unless…

Hannah looked at Wedgewood. The expression on his face told her he was as surprised by Rafe's bid as she was. The shrug of his shoulders told her he didn't know where Rafe had acquired additional money to bid for her.

The room echoed in thunderous cheering and applause. No one had expected the unknown bidder to push Masey beyond the ten-thousand-pound mark.

"We have a bid of eleven thousand pounds, Lord Masey. Do I hear twelve?"

Masey chuckled, then nodded. "Yes, Mr. Rummery. You hear twelve."

The cheering and applause were now so loud the walls seemed to tremble. The moment their roaring voices quieted, the focus turned to Rafe.

"Lord Rafe," Rummery hollered in order to be heard over the crowd. "The bid is twelve thousand pounds to you. Do I hear thirteen thousand pounds?"

Rafe turned his head, and his gaze locked with hers.

Hannah tried to read the serious expression on his face. She tried to decipher what the haunted emptiness in his gaze meant. Suddenly, she knew what he intended to do. As if he'd revealed his plan to her, she knew his intent.

Somehow, he'd acquired the backing he needed, and he would do whatever it took to make sure she gave herself to no one but him.

Hannah shook her head, praying he'd give up his foolishness.

Rafe turned his gaze away from her and focused on the man calling for the bids. "Thirteen thousand."

Hannah was oblivious to the deafening shouts and riotous roars of the crowd. She no longer heard the calls of encouragement from the spectators for Masey to raise the bid. The only thing on which she could focus was that Rafe had chosen to bankrupt himself rather than allow her to sell her body.

She wanted to stop the auction. She wanted to rush up to Rummery and order him to call the auction to a halt. Instead, she watched in stunned horror as Masey raised the bid to fourteen thousand. Then Rafe countered with fifteen thousand.

For a moment, Hannah thought the bidding would end there. That Rafe would win her for the astronomical price of fifteen thousand pounds, but after several moments of silence, Masey offered sixteen thousand pounds.

Without hesitating, Rafe offered seventeen.

Everything stood still. Hannah couldn't breathe. This wasn't how this night was supposed to go. She'd picked three of the wealthiest men in London to be assured that Rafe wouldn't win her body—that someone else would.

"The offer is seventeen thousand pounds, Lord Masey. Do you have a counteroffer?"

The room was silent.

Masey looked at Rafe and must have read the same unyielding determination in his gaze that Hannah did. It was a look that told the world that no matter how much anyone bid for Madam Genevieve, it wouldn't be enough.

Masey shook his head. "No, Mr. Rummery. I regret that I am going to have to allow Lord Rafe the pleasure of Madam Genevieve's company."

For one moment, the room remained so quiet that Hannah swore she could hear her own sigh of regret. Then the crowd of men broke out in uproarious shouts and bellows of congratulations. Those nearest Rafe clasped him on the shoulder and clapped him on the back, but there was no look of triumph on his face, no gleam of accomplishment in his eyes. Only a dark, hollow expression that told Hannah that although he'd won the wager, he hadn't won at all.

She tried to play the part of the gallant host. With shoulders high and back straight, she turned to Dalia. "Show our guests to the parlor," she said loud enough to be heard by everyone around her. "I regret I will be unavailable for the remainder of the night."

Loud guffawing followed her statement, and the crowd of men slowly made their way to the door. When the room was cleared, Hannah faced the man she loved—but had lost.

"Congratulations, Lord Rafe," she said with as sincere a smile as she could. "I hope you find I am worth the amount of money you paid for me."

The expression on his face remained rigid. His eyebrows arched, and she saw a look of disappointment in his eyes she'd prayed she'd never see in him.

"I'm afraid there is only one winner here tonight, Hannah," he said softly. "You. *I* have lost everything."

He turned away from her and walked to where Mr. Rummery and Mr. Crumbly stood, waiting to collect the wager. Wedgewood was at his side.

Hannah watched Rafe accept their words of congratulations, but there wasn't a hint of satisfaction on his face, not a glimmer of joy. Only regret.

He reached into his pocket and handed Crumbly a piece of paper. Hannah knew it was the ten-thousand-pound note Wedgewood had given him. Then he reached into another pocket, no doubt for the remainder of the wager.

He hesitated before bringing the object into the open. Then he pulled it from his pocket.

He held the object in his closed fist for a moment, then held his hand out and dropped the object in Mr. Crumbly's hand.

It was his grandfather's watch.

"No! Rafe, no!"

Hannah rushed toward him. "No, you can't." She turned toward Crumbly and Rummery, who were both examining the watch with great interest. "You can't take that watch."

"The workmanship is remarkable," Crumbly said. "Its worth is far more than the seven thousand pounds Lord Rafe wagered. The jewels alone are—"

"No! I won't let you give up your grandfather's watch." She turned to Crumbly. "I won't accept Lord Rafe's watch as payment."

Crumbly and Rummery exchanged a serious look. "I'm afraid the call is not yours to make, Madam Genevieve," Rummery said. "Crumbly and I were hired to conduct the auction and accept the wagers proposed, and Lord Rafe made his wager in good faith. We have no choice but to accept this watch in lieu of payment."

"But—"

"Give up, Madam Genevieve," Rafe said. His voice was stern, his words clipped. His anger evident.

"Rafe—"

"Like I said, I'm afraid there is only one winner here tonight." He gave her a small bow. "I hope you are happy."

He turned and walked away.

Hannah watched him leave the room with Wedgewood at his side. And she knew...

...she knew she would never be happy again.

*　*　*

Hannah stood where she was for several long minutes. Perhaps it was hours. She had no idea how long she'd stood staring at the empty doorway where Rafe had gone. When Dalia rushed into the room, it was empty. Crumbly and Rummery were gone—along with Rafe's grandfather's watch. All Hannah had left from this evening was a hollow space inside her breast where her heart used to live.

"Genny?" Dalia said, her tone urgent enough to pull Hannah from her despair.

"Skinner's got Delores. He just sent a messenger to tell you that if you want her back, you have to come for her."

Hannah struggled to come to grips with what Dalia said. "Where is she?"

"He said if we wanted her back, you were to meet him inside Covent Garden, off the Bedford Street entrance."

"Have my carriage brought round."

"No," Dalia said. "You can't go alone."

"I have no intention of going alone. Send word to Frisk. Have him bring Razer and Tumbler. Tell them to gather as many men as they can and meet me at Hart Street. Tell them to stay in the shadows. I don't want Skinner to know they're there."

Hannah rushed to her rooms. She quickly changed from the dress she'd worn for the auction. When she finished, she unlocked a drawer in her desk and took out a gun. She made sure it was loaded, then put it in the pocket of her skirt.

"Hopefully, you won't have to use that," Dalia said to her.

Hannah nodded. She'd never killed anyone in her life and hoped that wouldn't change tonight. But if it did, Skinner would be the man most deserving to die.

Word came that Frisk and Razer and Tumbler were on their way to Covent Garden, and Hannah rushed down to her waiting carriage. Every man employed at Madam Genevieve's followed her.

Nothing about this night had gone as she'd planned. Now her greatest fear was that what happened next would be something she couldn't live with.

Chapter 26

Clouds covered the moon, and when they reached Covent Garden, the sky was more black than starlit. Hannah wished there would be at least a little moonlight so she could make out more than shadows, but that wasn't to be.

Humphrey was atop, and he drove her carriage down Bedford Street to the north Covent Garden entrance. The other men had gone to where Frisk and the others were waiting.

When the carriage slowed to enter Covent Garden, Hannah clutched the pistol she had in the pocket of her skirt. She wasn't fond of weapons of any kind, but that didn't mean she wouldn't carry one, or that she didn't know how to use it. She did. Any female who lived on the streets of London for any length of time not only knew how to use a gun, but wasn't afraid to fire it.

The carriage drove a distance into the Garden, then stopped. Hannah waited until Humphrey climbed down and opened the door.

"Do you want me to go with you, ma'am?"

"No, Humphrey. I won't go far. You stay with the carriage. I'll call when I have Delores."

"Do you think she's still alive?"

269

Hannah considered what answer to give to the question she'd refused to ask herself since she heard Skinner had Delores. "If Skinner is lucky, she is."

Hannah took a few steps into the darkness and stopped. She wouldn't go any farther into Skinner's area than she had to. Instead, she'd make Skinner come to her.

She waited.

Somewhere in the distance, Frisk and the others should be making their way toward them. Hopefully, they'd be in place before anything happened.

Hannah waited a while longer, knowing patience was her friend. Knowing that Skinner would undoubtedly tire of waiting before she did.

Eventually, her patience paid off.

"Well, Madam Genevieve," Skinner voiced in a raspy tone.

Hannah couldn't see him, but that wasn't necessary in order to recognize the menacing tone in his words.

"Delores, are you there?"

For a second or more, there was no answer. Then the response wasn't a word confirming Delores was alive and well, but a barely audible moan that proved the opposite. The pitiful whimper in the darkness sent shivers of anger and fury raging through Hannah. Delores was barely able to utter a sound.

"Bring a light, Stump," Skinner ordered one of his men. "I'm sure Madam Genevieve would like to see her friend and make sure she's all right."

Within seconds, a man carrying a lantern walked toward Skinner and held it over Delores's head.

"You bastard," Hannah growled.

Delores's face was so bruised and swollen she was hardly recognizable. The dress she'd been wearing was torn and hung in strips on her body. Hannah didn't want to imagine what had been done to her.

"Bring her over," Hannah ordered.

"And if I don't?"

"You're dead."

Skinner laughed. "Such threats, Madam Genevieve. And from a delicate creature such as yourself."

"You won't think I'm such a delicate creature when you have a bullet lodged in your flesh."

Skinner laughed again. "I believe it's time for you and me to come to an understanding, Genevieve." Skinner pushed Delores forward and stepped closer so Hannah could see her more clearly. "I'm giving you back your whore because I want you to make sure the rest of your girls see her. This is what will happen to every one of them if they dare try to steal any of the girls I recruit to work for me."

"Recruit?" Hannah asked. "You don't recruit them, Skinner. You *steal* children from their homes and families. You take advantage of the weak and helpless and destroy any hope they have for a future."

When he spoke, Hannah could tell her words struck a spot with Skinner. The tone of his voice turned harsher, and he spoke through clenched teeth.

"You're terribly brave for a lone woman facing me and my men. Or is your vicar hiding in the shadows waiting to come to your aid?"

"No, Skinner. My *vicar* is not here. I made sure he is no longer where you can harm him. Unlike you, if he had discovered you'd put a marker on his head, he would have faced you man-to-man. Instead, you hire the dregs of humanity to do your work for you because you are too much of a coward to face him yourself."

"You bitch," Skinner bellowed. "If I didn't know it would cause such an uproar, I'd kill you myself."

"Try it and you won't live long enough to take your next breath," Hannah replied.

Hannah looked at Delores, then turned her gaze back to Skinner. Her fingers itched to pull out the gun she had in her pocket and put a bullet through his heart. But she hadn't reached the point where she could kill someone who wasn't armed.

"I think I have let you be the thorn in my side long enough, bitch," Skinner said. He pulled a pistol from his pocket and pointed it at Hannah.

"I wouldn't try it, Skinner," a voice bellowed from behind her. She recognized it as belonging to Frisk.

"What the hell," Skinner said, staring at the movement from behind her. He motioned for his men to come forward. About twenty men came from the shadows, all carrying pistols.

Hannah wasn't sure how many men Frisk and the other bordello owners could gather on such short notice, but from the surprised looks on Skinner's men's faces, they were outnumbered by more than just a few.

"You'll regret this, Frisk," Skinner threatened. "You'll regret siding against me."

"You've bullied and threatened us long enough, Skinner. We're through taking orders from you."

"You think you can stand up to me?" Skinner bellowed. "None of you are big enough."

"Maybe not alone," Tumbler said. "But we're not alone any longer. We've joined forces against you."

Skinner snarled a low growl, then focused his rage on Hannah. "This is your fault," he roared. "You'll pay for this."

Before Hannah could move, Skinner aimed his gun in her direction and fired.

She waited to feel the pain from the bullet she knew had struck her, but she felt only a small sting, as if her arm had been pricked by a needle.

She wasn't sure what happened after that. The firing of gunshots echoed in the air. When she looked up, Skinner was lying on the ground in a pool of blood and his men were nowhere to be seen.

"Are you all right?" Dalia whispered from behind her.

Hannah tried to turn, but her legs suddenly didn't want to support her. She staggered, then dropped to her knees.

"Genny?" Dalia called out again.

Hannah looked up to see Dalia and Humphrey rushing toward her.

"Genny, are you all right?" Dalia asked.

"I think so," Hannah answered. "Where's Delores? Is she all right?"

"I'll get her. Humphrey, help Miss Genevieve to the carriage. We'd better get out of here before the authorities come."

Dalia ran to help Delores, and Humphrey helped Hannah to her feet.

"Can you walk, Miss Genevieve?"

"Yes, Humphrey. Just give me your arm."

Humphrey held out his arm, and Hannah leaned against him as they made their way to the carriage. She climbed inside and sank against the cushions as Dalia helped Delores inside.

"You're safe now, Delores," Hannah said. She tried to sound confident, but she didn't have enough strength to speak louder than a whisper. "We'll be home soon," she said when the carriage lurched forward.

"I'm glad he's dead," Delores muttered bitterly. "I would have killed him myself if I'd have had a chance."

Hannah opened her mouth to tell Delores she understood, but no words would come out. She tried again, but blackness overtook her and she knew no more.

* * *

"It's about time you woke up," Dalia said from a chair beside her bed.

Hannah looked around the room and noticed the sun peeking through the draperies. "What time is it?"

"Nearly four o'clock. You almost slept the day away. How do you feel?"

"Like I've been shot."

Dalia laughed. "Doctor Blevins said that's what you'd feel like." Dalia rose from her chair and poured some water into a glass. "Are you thirsty?"

Hannah nodded.

Dalia helped her take a drink of the water, then Hannah dropped her head back against the pillow. "How's Delores?"

"She's as fine as she can be after going through what she did."

"Tell her I'll come to see her as soon as I'm able."

"She knows you will. She's more worried about you than herself. All the girls are."

"Assure them that I'm fine."

Dalia sat again. "Do you want me to send for him?"

Hannah didn't pretend not to know who Dalia was talking about. She knew her friend meant Rafe.

Even though she knew Dalia's intention was good, the reality of what had happened was still painful. Rafe had walked out of her life. She'd made sure he'd seen her for what she really was—a prostitute who sold her body to the highest bidder.

"No, Dalia."

"He may not be gone yet, Genny. Maybe he hasn't left London. Skinner's dead now, so he's not a threat to your vicar any longer."

Suddenly, Hannah's heart ached more than her arm. "It's too late. He made that clear last night when he won me but didn't want me. And he won't change his mind. I finally convinced him that I'm a prostitute."

"But maybe now that Skinner's dead you can—"

"Go, Dalia. Assure the girls that I'm fine. Then tell Delores I'll come to see her as soon as I can get out of bed."

Dalia didn't insist again. She knew Hannah's mind was firm as far as Rafe was concerned.

Hannah closed her eyes and waited to hear the door close behind Dalia.

When the latch clicked, she allowed the last tears she would shed over losing Rafe to run down her cheeks. She allowed herself to mourn, because the only man she would ever love was dead to her.

Now if only she could survive long enough for her heart to discover a reason to continue beating.

Chapter 27

Rafe leaned his back against a tree near the stream and remembered the first time he saw Hannah sitting on the bank with her feet dangling in the water. He could still see her lithe figure as if she were still there, still see her tipped-back head as she let the sun's rays beam down on her. Still see her long lashes as they rested on her cheeks.

He breathed a painful sigh as he tried to ease the heavy weight that pressed against his chest.

It had been nearly two months since the night of the auction, and he missed her as much today as he had the day he'd left her. He wasn't sure then that he could live the rest of his life without her, and he was less sure today.

He'd expected Hannah to do all the changing, expected her to believe that he could pretend her past had never happened. Pretend that she was a different person than who she truly was. That was why she'd held the auction—to put who and what she was in terms he couldn't misunderstand. To show him that she was a famous prostitute, and if he wanted her, he had to accept that.

He remembered asking her to go away with him and pretend to be someone she wasn't. He knew now that she'd been right all along. There wasn't a chance in the world that she wouldn't be recognized. Or that he wouldn't have to leave one congregation after another in disgrace when the parishioners discovered that the vicar's wife was the famous Madam Genevieve.

But most humiliating of all was that he had truly expected her to sit in the front row at Sunday church services and pretend to be someone she was not. How could he have been so insensitive? How could he have been so cruel?

He'd only been thinking of himself—what he wanted, what he didn't want to give up. Not what *Hannah* would have to give up to leave with him. Not what *she* would have to suffer to make him happy.

And, most important of all, not rescuing the scores of innocent children from the streets of London. That made him the sickest—that he had put his own happiness before the welfare of children.

Hannah's goal to save the children Skinner would sacrifice to the most evil of humanity was a thousand times more Christian than his goal to build a parish overflowing with saints. He counted his accolades by the number of praises he received after ever Sunday service. He measured his worth by the admiration and acclamations he received from the saints he shepherded.

Why hadn't he realized before now that the *saints* didn't need him? The *helpless* needed him. And he'd turned his back on them.

But Hannah hadn't turned her back on them. She had more Christian compassion in her little finger than he had in his entire body.

Rafe pushed himself to his feet and took a step toward Wedgewood Manor. There were times when he couldn't stand to think about what he'd done. This was one of those times. He was glad Caroline had invited him to join them. Her sister and brother-in-law, the Duke and Duchess of Raeborn, were visiting, and for this one night at least, maybe their conversation would distract him from thinking about Hannah.

He cast a final glance back to the place where he'd first seen her, then walked through the grove of trees and across the meadow that took him to Wedgewood Manor. He handed his hat and gloves to the Wedgewood butler, then made his way to the parlor. He could hear voices coming from inside and knew that's where they'd gathered.

"Did you see her when you were in London?" Caroline asked.

"Yes. We met the same as we used to. It was so good to see her, although…" The Duchess of Raeborn paused.

"Is something wrong?" Caroline asked.

Rafe waited. He knew better than to eavesdrop, but he thought the women were talking about Hannah, and he wanted to hear what they said. He knew if he joined them, they wouldn't be as honest with him there.

"She's not happy, Caroline. The laughter that used to be in her eyes was absent. The excitement I always heard in her voice wasn't there. Even the delight at seeing me wasn't as evident."

"Did she say what was bothering her?"

"She denied that anything was bothering her. But it was obvious that something was. And I think I know what it is."

There was a long pause before Caroline spoke. "It's Rafe, isn't it?"

"I'm sure it is."

"Oh, Grace. I wish I never had invited her here last summer. If I hadn't, she and Rafe would never have met."

Rafe couldn't stand to listen to any more. He stepped through the door, then stopped when everyone's gaze focused on him.

"Don't ever be sorry that we met, Caroline." He walked toward them. "My life is so much richer because I met Hannah."

"But you are both so unhappy."

Rafe shook his head. "That's not your fault. Nor is it Hannah's. The fault is mine."

"No, Rafe. You're—"

Rafe held up his hand to stop Caroline's words. He slowly shifted his gaze to where the Duchess of Raeborn sat. "You understand what I'm saying, don't you, Your Grace?"

The Duchess of Raeborn didn't speak, but the look in her eyes said she knew exactly what he meant. "Would you please offer your opinion? I would truly like to hear what mistakes you think I made."

"You won't like what I have to say, Lord Rafe."

"No, I won't. But you will probably not say anything I have not already told myself." Rafe sat in a chair facing the duchess. "I would appreciate your honesty and forwardness."

The duchess smiled. But it was not a happy smile. Rather, a smile filled with regret. She looked him in the eyes and began.

"Unfortunately, you tried to change Hannah, Lord Rafe. You tried to make her into something she's not. You refused to accept the fact that Hannah is Madam Genevieve. And Madam Genevieve is a whore."

"Grace!" Caroline clasped her hand to her breast. "Hannah isn't—"

"Yes, she is, Caroline. She is a prostitute."

"Your Grace," Caroline said, addressing her objection to Grace's husband, the Duke of Raeborn.

"I'm afraid my wife is correct, Lady Wedgewood," Raeborn answered. "Hannah is a fallen woman. She has been for nearly fifteen years. Whether or not she still practices her illicit trade doesn't change what she is."

"And you tried to change her into something she's not," the duchess continued. "It's impossible for her to take her place in the front pew of your church when you preach. And that's what you wanted her to do. Am I correct?"

Rafe nodded. "Completely."

"You were ready to accept her past as long as she *pretended* to be a good, pious Christian to the people in your congregation." Her Grace paused. "Your mistake was that you tried to make her into something she wasn't. You expected her to live in fear every day of her life that someone would discover her past. And what was your answer if her past was discovered?"

"I told her we would move to a place where no one knew her."

The four people in the room sat in silence. There was nothing they could say. Nothing that could shed a more favorable light on what he'd expected from Hannah.

"Oh, Rafe," Caroline said. "Why did you want Hannah to change? Don't you realize how much good Hannah does? She rescues children from a life on the streets. She helps the people who really need her and tries to make a difference in their lives."

"I know," Rafe answered. "But I loved her so much I was desperate for the world to know her and see her as I did. I wanted her to be accepted for the wonderful person she is. I didn't realize that by doing what I wanted her to do, she would have to give up what was the most important to her. I didn't understand what wanting these things for her would seem like to her."

"She's in love with you, Rafe," Caroline said in a choked voice. "You're the first man she's ever loved."

"I know," Rafe whispered. He took several deep breaths, then lifted his gaze to meet the duchess's. "How is she?" he asked.

"She's miserable. She's hurting. She misses you. But she won't admit it."

Rafe nodded.

The five people in the room sat in silence for several moments. Thankfully, the Wedgewood butler interrupted to announce that dinner was served.

Rafe rose with the others, but stopped. "I'm afraid you'll have to excuse me, Caroline. I can't stay."

"What are you going to do?" Thomas asked.

"What I should have done from the beginning. Except I was too blind to know it."

"Are you sure—" Thomas tried to ask, but Rafe held out a hand to stop him.

"Don't worry," he said as he left the room. "I'll write."

Then Rafe left to do what he should have done a long time ago.

Chapter 28

❧

Hannah walked through a side door of the large parlor where several of Madam Genevieve's girls were visiting with men who'd come to pick out a partner for the night. There was a time when she enjoyed joining in on conversations with the guests. But that time was long over.

She hadn't felt like taking part in anything since the night of the auction. Since the night Rafe had won her, and she'd lost him.

She climbed the stairs to her rooms and opened the door. After she closed the door behind her, she walked to her favorite chair that sat in front of the fireplace and watched the flames lick upward.

When would Rafe stop haunting her every waking and every sleeping moment? When would she be able to get on with her life? Living without him was a torture as difficult as anything she'd ever endured. There were days she wasn't sure she could survive.

She leaned her head back against the cushion and closed her eyes. She hadn't been sitting long when there was a knock at the door. "Come in," she said.

Dalia entered, then closed the door behind her. "Are you up to talking for a bit?"

"Of course. There's tea on the cart. Would you like a cup?"

"Would you?"

Hannah shook her head. "I've had enough for the night."

Dalia sat in the chair next to Hannah, as she often did. Hannah enjoyed her company, although evening visits were rare, since that was the busiest time at Madam Genevieve's.

"How are you doing, Genny?"

"You mean my shoulder?"

"Yes, that, and...everything else."

"By everything else, I assume you mean, am I getting over my vicar?"

"Yes, that's what I mean. It's obvious that you haven't been the same since he left."

"I'm sorry, Dal. I'll try harder to be like I used to be."

"I'm not complaining, Genny. I just hate to see you so unhappy."

Hannah knew Dalia was concerned. That was the kind of friend she was. "I've never asked you before, but have you ever been in love?"

Dalia smiled. "Once."

"How did you deal with it?"

"I married him."

That news shocked Hannah. "I didn't know you were married."

"No one does. It's not something I feel people need to know."

"What happened to him?"

"He died. His name was Jamie. He worked in a brewery, and one of the boilers exploded. The building caught on fire, and he didn't make it out."

"I'm sorry," Hannah whispered.

"We'd only been married six months and were still very much in love. I was expecting his babe, but when I got news that Jamie was dead, I lost the child."

"Oh, Dalia. I'm so sorry."

Dalia was silent for a few moments. "There are things we can't control. That was one of them."

"How did you end up here? Doing this?"

"After Jamie died, I didn't have any money, so I came to London. The same as the girls we rescue. I thought it would be easy to find work. Instead, no one wanted a starving female without training and without papers. So I came here."

"I see."

"And this is where I want to stay."

Hannah smiled. "I'm glad to hear that. I wouldn't want you to leave."

Dalia hesitated, then continued. "There's something I want to talk to you about. Something important."

Hannah turned to face her friend. She could tell by the sound of Dalia's voice that what she wanted to talk to her about was serious. "Yes?"

"I've been watching you lately, and I know you're not as happy here as you used to be. That's understandable. If, however, you'd ever like to leave…"

Hannah sat forward in her chair.

"I'm not suggesting you leave," Dalia continued, "or hinting that I think you should. I'm just saying that if you'd ever *like* to leave, I'd be willing to buy Madam Genevieve's from you."

Hannah sat back in her chair and tried to digest Dalia's offer.

"I'm not sure I can, Dal. There are the children to consider."

"Nothing would change. I'd continue to rescue the children from the streets, and I'd send to Coventry Cottage the ones who didn't have homes to return to."

Dalia turned her gaze to the flames in the fireplace. "Every time we rescue one of the young ones from the life of prostitution, I think of my babe. I think of what it would have been like for her if she were forced to live on the streets. If someone wasn't there to save her from having to sell herself to earn enough money to eat."

Hannah's mind was filled with a hundred questions—a hundred possibilities.

It had been years since she'd worked at Madam Genevieve's, and there were times when she dreamed of leaving. But she knew she couldn't. She needed the money Madam Genevieve's brought in to run Coventry Cottage.

Hannah breathed a heavy sigh. A home to send the children she rescued off the streets meant too much to her. "I can't, Dal. Even if I wanted to, I couldn't. The money Madam Genevieve's takes in is what supports Coventry Cottage. It takes a great deal of what we make here to keep it running."

"You'll still get the money we take in. Maybe even more than before."

Hannah frowned.

"You know how profitable the night of the auction was."

Hannah nodded.

"The girls have been talking. They'd like to continue that tradition. Any money they raised would go to Coventry."

Hannah didn't know what to say. Dal stopped her from having to say anything.

"I'm not offering to buy Madam Genevieve's to make any changes in how it's run. Or to get wealthy."

"Then why are you offering to buy Madam Genevieve's?"

Dalia smiled. "I have two reasons. One selfish. One not quite as selfish."

Hannah smiled. "I can't imagine you being selfish, Dal. I'd like to hear the reason you think makes you selfish."

"Very well. My selfish reason is that I've always dreamt of owning my own business. Call it whatever you want, but to me, a business of my own provides me with security and stability. It's something I've never had, and always wanted."

"That's not selfish, Dal. That's normal. When you've had to live on the streets like we did, it's only natural to want to make sure we never end up there again. That's why I bought Madam Genevieve's. Because I wanted the security that owning my own business gave me."

"That's why I want it too. I want to know I'll always have a home."

Hannah leaned back in her chair and considered everything Dal had revealed. "You said there were two reasons you wanted Madam Genevieve's."

"Yes. The other reason is because of this." Dal reached into her pocket and pulled out a letter. "This is yours. I don't know what it says, but I wanted you to be aware of all your options before you read it—just in case."

Hannah stared at the letter. She recognized Rafe's handwriting, and her heart skipped a beat.

Dal handed her the letter, and she took it. With trembling hands, she reverently placed it in her lap.

"I'm going to go now," Dal said, rising to her feet. "Just know you have more than one option for your future."

Hannah thought she answered her, thought she told her they'd talk later, but she wasn't sure. She couldn't think.

Rafe had written her a letter. He'd contacted her, and she wasn't sure why—wasn't sure she wanted to know why. It wasn't to ask her to give him another chance. He would have done that in person. Which meant the letter undoubtedly contained his final words of good-bye.

She sucked in an unsteady breath. Couldn't he just leave her alone? Did he have to add another connection to their tortured past?

She gently ran her fingers over the words on the letter. Over the way he scrolled her name. She wanted to open the letter, but wasn't brave enough just yet.

She sat for several minutes, perhaps hours. The next time she looked up, the sky outside was dark. Someone had come into her room and lit several lamps and the fire in the grate. She was glad. She didn't want to read Rafe's words in a cold, dark, empty room.

She slowly opened Rafe's letter.

Dearest Hannah,

There are several things I'd like to say to you, but I know that it's too late for words. It wasn't until I lost you that I realized how badly I handled the differences between us. As Caroline and Grace so vividly, and sternly, pointed out, I tried to change you to fit into my world, when you had made a place for yourself in your world so perfectly.

For years I thought I could judge my worth by preaching to a congregation overflowing with saints. My dream was for you to be at my side. I expected you to sit in the front pew along with the other good, pious Christians in my congregation, because that's how I saw you, as the best of all the Christians in the world. As you know, I was only thinking of myself. Never of you.

You told me that you could never fit into my world, that we would both live in fear every day of our lives for fear that someone would discover your past. But I refused to believe you. To accept your rationale meant I would have had no choice but to give you up. And living the rest of my life without you was unthinkable. Yet, that's what happened.

You are so much wiser than I am. You were right all along. You don't belong in my world. And I don't belong in yours. I wish there were a world where we both belonged, but I know now that there isn't.

The love and devotion you have for the children who need you to help them taught me a valuable lesson. It opened my eyes for my place in the world. It showed me with stark clarity what my purpose should be.

The saints of this world don't need me. But the children at Coventry Cottage do.

Because of this, I beg that you'll allow me to make Coventry my home. I have been here for more than a month now and find that not only do the children need me, but I sorely need them. I have found great joy in working with them and realize this is my true calling.

I never anticipated this for my life, but I've found a peace and contentment I never knew was possible. I ask that you consider the good I can do here and not reject my offer of help because of any lack of feeling you may have for me. I beg that you will please allow me to stay.

I know you visit Coventry Cottage from time to time and would prefer that I'm not here when you are. I respect that. Please send word of your arrival, and I will make sure I am absent while you are here.

> *Your servant,*
> *R*

Hannah carefully folded the letter and placed it in her lap. She thought it was impossible to ache more from loving Rafe—and losing him. But the tears that streamed down her cheeks told her how wrong she was.

Chapter 29

Rafe walked along the narrow path with the six young lads who had, because of their excellent reading progress, earned an afternoon of fishing at the stream.

"Vicar Waterford," a youngster named Bobby asked him as they walked back to Coventry Cottage, "can a feller earn a living by fishing all day? I think I'd like to find a job where I could do that."

Rafe laughed. "I'm sure you would, Bobby. But if you fished all day, every day, what would you do to reward yourself for working hard and getting all your work done?"

"I'd..."

Bobby stopped on the path to think, and the other five boys paused to listen.

"I don't know," he finally answered. "I can't think of anything I'd like to do better than fishing."

"So what does that tell you?"

Bobby thought for a few seconds before he answered. "I think it means I should work hard to do what I have to get done so I make sure I have time to fish."

"Me too," another boy answered. "I like fishing more than anything, so that's what I have to do too."

"Me too," the other boys answered.

Rafe ruffled the hair on the heads of as many of the boys as he could reach. "That's the right answer, fellas. Doing what you enjoy most is your reward for doing a good job."

"What do you like doing best, Vicar?" Bobby asked.

"Ya, Vicar. What's your favorite thing to do?" little Timothy echoed. "And don't say read from your Bible. You do that all the time."

Rafe laughed. "Well…" he said, trying to think of an answer he could give them. He could hardly tell them that his favorite reward would be to walk through the gardens at Coventry Cottage with Hannah at his side and hold her in his arms and kiss her until neither of them could breathe and…

He pushed his thoughts from the path they were taking. "I think my best reward would be to spend time with the people who are most important to me."

"Who's that?" Bobby asked.

"Why, all of you," he said, ruffling more hair.

"I knew you were going to say that," Bobby said amid the laughter from the other boys. "You always tell us we're special."

Rafe smiled. "That's so you never forget it." Rafe handed Bobby the basket with the fish they'd caught and cleaned. "Now, run ahead and give these to Cook. Tell her I won't be in for supper."

"Where you going, Vicar?"

"Nowhere. I'm just not ready to come in yet. Tell her to save me a piece of that peach cobbler she made. I'll eat that later."

"All right, Vicar. But don't stay out too long. It'll be dark soon."

Rafe couldn't help but laugh. Bobby kept a close watch on all the boys. He was as near to being a mother as any of them had ever known.

Rafe ruffled Bobby's sandy-brown hair, then the ten-year-old took the basket and ran toward the house. When the boys were out of sight, Rafe walked to a nearby log that looked out onto the stream, and sat.

He didn't know why, but he'd felt restless all day. And there was no reason for it. For the first time in his life, he felt as if he'd found his place in the world. He was working with youngsters who really needed him—not serving as the figurehead in a church where the people came each Sunday morning because that was where they were supposed to be.

Even though there were many who would argue with the choice he'd made, he knew deep in his heart that guiding the youngsters who had no one else to lead them was what God wanted him to do. And yet…

For several days something had gnawed deep inside him. He'd been plagued by an unsettling emotion that refused to go away. And today it was even worse.

Rafe rose to his feet. The sun was sinking low in the sky, and it was time he returned. The evening meal would no doubt be over by now and the children in their rooms getting ready for bed. He would go to the kitchen and steal some of Cook's peach cobbler, then retire to his room to read. Or to think. About Hannah.

Rafe walked in through the kitchen door and took in the busy scene. Several of the older girls were helping Cook clean up after the last meal of the day. When he walked into the room, they stopped what they were doing and smiled. Rafe couldn't help but smile in return.

"Those were some mighty fine fish you sent in with the lads, Vicar. And they were cleaned slick as can be. Not a bone in 'em."

"We had a good day," Rafe answered. "I think each of the boys caught at least one fish, so no one went home disappointed."

"The lads are never disappointed when they can spend the day with you, Vicar. You're just what they need in their lives. But you know that," she continued, wiping her damp hands on her apron. "Now, here's that peach cobbler I saved back for you. Bobby said that was going to be your dinner, but a man like you can't get by on just dessert, so I fixed a little something else and put it on your tray."

Rafe looked to where Cook pointed and saw several dishes on a tray. The cloth covering hid their contents, and he didn't doubt there was probably a full-course meal waiting for him.

"There's a pot of hot tea for you to take with you too," Cook said, pointing to the pot warming by the stove.

"Thank you, Cook." Rafe put the pot on his tray and picked it up. "I think your goal is to fatten me up to sell me at market."

The girls in the kitchen clamped their hands over their mouths to hide their laughter, but Cook didn't try to muffle her laugh.

"Oh, Vicar. I can't imagine you ever getting fat. You work too hard. I know it was you who chopped all that wood that's in the corner."

"Only because I knew you'd need it for my cobbler."

"Then I hope you'll enjoy it."

"I will," Rafe said as he headed for the door. He stopped when the housekeeper, Mrs. Grange, came into the kitchen.

"Oh, there you are, Vicar. I've been looking for you."

"Is something wrong, Mrs. Grange?"

"Oh, no. I just wanted to tell you that Miss Hannah arrived a few minutes ago."

Rafe clutched his fingers around the edge of the tray. "Miss Hannah's here?"

"Yes. She's retired for the night, but said to tell you that she needed to see you in the morning before you started your day."

Rafe made several attempts to fill his lungs with air before he finally felt as if he could breathe. "Thank you, Mrs. Grange. Tell Miss Hannah I look forward to visiting with her in the morning."

Rafe walked up the stairs to his room and set the tray of food on the table. Instead of pouring himself a cup of hot tea, he reached for the bottle of brandy he kept in the back of his bottom desk drawer. When he'd poured some into a glass, he sat in front of the fire and took a sip.

There was only one reason Hannah had come unannounced. Only one reason she hadn't met with him tonight. Only one reason she'd left word that she wanted to see him in the morning.

And the only reason he could think of was the last reason he wanted to hear.

Chapter 30

❦

R afe lay in bed with his arm beneath his head and his eyes focused on the ceiling. He had no idea what time it was. All he knew was that the fire in the grate had died a long time ago. He'd given up on sleep long before that—as soon as he heard Hannah was here and wanted to see him.

He took a deep breath when he thought of his conversation. He wondered how she'd tell him she no longer wanted him anywhere near Coventry Cottage or the children. He wondered if he should save her the trouble and offer to leave.

The thought of leaving the children settled inside his chest like a heavy weight. In the time he'd been here, he'd come to love each and every one of them. They were the sheep he wanted to gather around him. They were the flock of little saints he wanted to care for.

He wondered if Hannah would allow him to plead his case, or if she would simply demand that he leave.

Rafe couldn't stand to think about it any longer. He couldn't stand to lie in bed and worry about what was going to happen tomorrow. He reached for the corner of his covers to toss them aside. He stopped when the knob on the door turned and the door opened.

Hannah stood in the doorway, her golden hair flowing loosely down her shoulders and back. She was a vision he'd only dreamed of ever seeing again. His heart began a race in his chest.

She wore a robe that didn't quite reach the floor, and her toes peeked out beneath the hem. It was the most sensual sight he could imagine. She looked as ethereal as an angel, as enticing as a siren.

She didn't step inside the room but stood in the open doorway for several seconds as if waiting for her eyes to adjust to the darkness.

"Are you asleep?" she finally whispered.

"No," he answered.

She slowly entered the room and closed the door behind her. "I was going to wait until morning to talk to you," she said when she reached the bed, "but I couldn't."

Rafe looked up at her, and a hundred conflicting emotions raced through him. "I didn't get a message that you were coming. If I had, I would have made certain I was—"

"I didn't send one. I wanted you to be here. We need to talk."

"I see."

"Do you?"

"Yes, I think I do," Rafe admitted. "And I don't blame you."

The fire had been out for several hours, and there was a chill in the room. Hannah shivered, then rubbed her upper arms as if to warm herself.

"You're cold," he said. "Take that cover on the chair behind you and wrap it around your shoulders."

"I'd rather you kept me warm, Rafe."

Rafe struggled to understand what Hannah meant. But before he could come to any conclusion, she pushed her robe from her shoulders and let it slide to the floor.

Her satiny flesh glimmered in the moonlight with a luminous glow. For several seconds she stood at his bedside—whether waiting for him to pull back the covers and invite her in, or giving him the chance to reject her, he didn't know.

"Are you certain, Hannah?"

"Yes. Are you?"

Rafe pulled back the covers, and she lay down beside him.

"I've dreamed of—"

"Shh." She placed her finger over his lips and stopped him from speaking. "Tomorrow. We'll talk tomorrow."

She brought herself up over him and pressed her lips to his. "Love me, Rafe. I've waited my whole life to be loved."

Rafe kissed her lips, then shared with her the pent-up emotion he'd held at bay since they'd met. He kissed her again, this time with a passion that was as deep and vast as the heavens.

He wasn't as experienced as most single men he knew. Once he'd realized that the church was his calling, he'd turned his back on the ways of the world. But he wasn't totally inexperienced. It had just been a while.

He deepened his kisses and kissed her again and again, then wrapped his arms around her and turned so she was beneath him.

This was what he'd dreamed of for so long. Holding Hannah in his arms, feeling her flesh against his. Touching her.

He came down over her and made her one with him.

* * *

Hannah wrapped her arms around Rafe and held him close to her. She'd known that their lovemaking would be special, known that his touch would ignite a passion she only experienced when she was with him, when he held her. When he kissed her.

He moved inside her. This was the first time she'd made love with a man. She'd had sex often. Men had used and enjoyed her body often. But she'd never enjoyed what they did. She'd only pretended.

There was no pretending with Rafe.

Their lovemaking intensified. His movements became more urgent, more concentrated. He drove into her with a penetrating force that carried her to a level far above anything she'd ever experienced. She'd never felt like this, never knew there was such abandon when loving a man.

She wrapped her arms and legs around his body and held him close.

Someone cried out. It could have been Rafe. It could have been her. She didn't know. She could no more control her voice than she could control the hunger and desire building inside her. Together they soared, past the stars toward the brilliant light ahead of her. And then she exploded. In a shuddering moment, thousands of sparkling fireworks shattered behind her eyes. She couldn't see. She couldn't think. She could do nothing except cry out as her body leaped from the high precipice where Rafe had taken her and dropped her toward earth.

She plummeted in a timeless fall before reaching the earth with staggering unsteadiness. She clung to Rafe for fear she would never stop trembling.

For several minutes neither of them moved. Except for the rapid rise and fall of their chests as they fought to take in the air they needed to breathe, Hannah was too exhausted to move. She thought Rafe was too.

When she could lift her sated body, she placed her head atop Rafe's chest. She listened to the thundering of his heart and knew he was as affected by what they'd just experienced as she had been.

She smiled through her tears and tightened her grasp around Rafe's body.

"Are you all right?" he asked when her tears streamed down her cheeks and landed on his chest. There was concern in his voice, and Hannah's smile broadened.

"I didn't know it could be like that," she whispered.

"Neither did I," he answered.

"That was beautiful. Thank you."

"I love you, Hannah. I have almost since the first day I met you."

"I know. I tried so hard to keep you from getting too close, but I couldn't."

There was a rumble deep inside his chest. He was laughing.

"What?" she asked, running her fingers over his damp flesh.

"Keeping me from falling in love with you was useless. I'd searched for someone like you my whole life. When I found you, I refused to let you go."

"Even when you discovered I was really Madam Genevieve?"

"Even then." He paused. "Especially then."

"Why?"

He pulled her closer to him, and she tucked her head beneath his chin. "Because I loved you. I had to do every-thing in my power to keep from losing you. And…"

"And…?" she asked when he hesitated.

"You're not going to like this."

She hesitated before answering. "Consider me forewarned."

He took a deep breath that raised his chest. "The sec-ond reason was because you were going to be my greatest success. I took great pleasure in believing that I could save you from yourself. From the life you were leading."

"From my life of sin?" she asked.

"Yes."

Hannah struggled to digest Rafe's admission. "When did you change your mind?"

"When I discovered what your mission really was. When I saw Coventry Cottage and saw the children you'd rescued. When I realized that the saints I preached to every Sunday morning could get along without *me*, but the children liv-ing on the streets couldn't survive without *you*. You do a thousand times more good than I ever dreamed of doing, Hannah. And I had some mighty big dreams."

Hannah breathed a deep sigh. "I'm glad you wrote. Your letter explained several things."

"There is more I need to explain. I didn't understand how much I'd asked of you until Caroline and Her Grace pointed it out."

Hannah smiled. "I pity you. Having either Grace or Caroline chastise you would be difficult enough. Having both of them against you is unimaginable."

"It was rather uncomfortable. But their harshness made me realize how unfair I'd been to ask you to change. I hadn't thought of what I was asking you to do."

"Have you changed your mind?"

"Yes. Now I know how wrong I was. Saving children from the street is your passion. And it's become mine too."

Hannah snuggled against Rafe and breathed a deep sigh. For a long time, neither of them spoke. Finally, Hannah said what she knew they were both thinking. "What's going to happen now?"

"We're going to have to get married," he said.

"No, Rafe. We don't have to marry. No one will expect you to marry me."

"Perhaps not." There was a stern tone to his voice. "They may not expect me to marry you, but they will expect you to marry me. I'm a ruined man, you know."

Hannah lifted her head, and her eyes focused on the smile on his face.

"You can't just walk away from a man once you've ruined him for every other woman on the face of the earth."

Hannah reached up to kiss Rafe on the mouth.

"Don't worry, Hannah. I realize the mistakes I made before. I won't make them again."

Rafe's hands gently caressed her. "What future do you see for us, Rafe?"

He didn't speak right away. It was as if he needed to carefully consider the answer he needed to give her.

"We belong together, Hannah. You know that. We love each other." He held her more securely. "I can't live without you. I tried. I was miserable."

"I know," she answered. "So was I."

"I want you with me as much as I can have you, but I know how important Madam Genevieve's is to you—and why I won't ask you to choose between your life in London and me."

"You would let me have both?"

"I will take whatever you can give me. We will make our lives together when you can come here. But I will not go to London. I can't, Hannah. Please understand why I can't."

Hannah swallowed hard. He was accepting her for who she was—for what she was.

"I only have one demand to make," he said with as much resolve as she'd ever heard in his voice. "I intend to make you my wife."

"How can you want me for your wife, knowing who and what I am?"

"I won't live in sin, Hannah. Don't ask me to. I can't."

Hannah pushed herself away from Rafe and slowly rose. She picked up her robe from the floor and covered her body. She tied the sash with great deliberation, then turned. "I can't marry you, Rafe."

Rafe threw the covers back and stood.

Hannah watched as he pulled on his pants. In anger he shoved his arms through the sleeves of his shirt. He didn't bother to fasten every button, but let it gape open to his waist.

"Why?" he asked when he turned to face her. "Is it because of Madam Genevieve's?"

Hannah lowered her gaze and shook her head. She couldn't look at him. She'd known this conversation would come up. She swallowed hard. "Because I have nothing to give you."

"What?"

"I have nothing to give you." She lifted her gaze to face him. "I can give you *nothing*."

"What is it you think I want? Madam Genevieve's?"

Hannah laughed. It wasn't a joyous laugh, it was a laugh filled with irony. "No, Rafe. I can't even give you Madam Genevieve's—because I don't own it any longer."

His eyes opened wide. "You've sold Madam Genevieve's?"

"I sold it to Dalia. She offered to buy it, and I sold it to her."

"What about its income? What about the children?"

"Nothing will change. The children will still be provided for. Dalia will still rescue the children from the streets. She will handle everything in London, and I can…"

"Yes? You can what?"

"I can stay here."

A smile broadened across his face. "Oh, Hannah," he said, reaching for her. He pulled her into his arms and held her. "That is perfect. Perfect! Then there's nothing to stop us from marrying."

Hannah pushed against his chest. When he didn't immediately release her, she pushed harder. He loosened his hold but didn't separate himself from her. She twisted out of his arms and took two steps away from him.

"I will be here for you, Rafe. I want nothing more than to live at Coventry and work at your side to care for the children. But I won't marry you. I can't."

His eyes narrowed. "Help me to understand this, Hannah. You love me. You want to live with me. You want us to work together to raise and care for the children. But you won't marry me?"

She nodded in the affirmative.

"In other words, you're willing to prostitute yourself to me?"

"Don't," Hannah said, struggling to keep the wetness from filling her eyes.

"I don't understand, Hannah." He grasped her by the shoulders and held her. "Make me understand."

The first tear streamed down her cheek, but she let it fall. She couldn't stop it from spilling over her lashes, just as she couldn't stop the tears that followed. "I can't marry you, Rafe. You have to be free to marry if you ever find someone else."

A shocked expression covered his face. Confusion followed. "Why on earth would I want to find someone else? I love you. I want to spend my life with you. You, Hannah. Not someone else."

"But I have nothing to offer you. I can't give you what you will want."

"You can give me love. What more could I ask?"

"There's more. You know there is!"

"What? What more is there?"

Hannah twisted out of his grasp, then turned to face him. "A son! I can't give you a son!"

It took only a second or two for her admission to register. She couldn't give him a son. Today was the first time she'd said the words aloud. The first time she'd admitted her inability to anyone. The first time she shed tears because she couldn't have children.

She watched his face for the disappointment she was certain she'd see. An emotion appeared, but it wasn't disillusionment. It was more understanding. More empathy than regret.

Silence engulfed the room as he looked at her. Then he slowly lifted his outstretched arms. "Come here, my love."

His voice was little more than a whisper, but it beckoned to her to come to him for comfort. She didn't hesitate, but ran to his embrace.

When she reached him, he wrapped his strong, muscular arms around her and pulled her close to him.

This was the comfort she needed but had somehow survived without.

Rafe lifted her in his arms and carried her to a large wing chair that sat before the lifeless fire. He placed her on the cushion, then walked to the grate and added some wood. It wasn't long before a fire came to life. When he was assured it would keep burning, he returned to the chair and lifted her in his arms, then sat with her in his lap.

"Tell me what happened," he said softly.

Hannah shook her head. "It doesn't matter. It was a long time ago."

"It matters to me. And I know it still matters to you."

Hannah nestled against him and tucked her head beneath his chin.

"Tell me, Hannah."

She took a deep breath and forced herself to remember a part of her past she'd tried to forget. "I made my way to Grace and Caroline's after I was raped. They took me to a woman who lived near the village. Everyone called her

Granny. She was a healer. I overheard her tell Grace and Caroline that she didn't think I'd live. But I did."

Rafe's hand rubbed gentle circles on her flesh, and Hannah thought how comforting his touch was. She didn't ever want to give that feeling up.

"I was with Granny almost three months before we knew for sure that I was carrying a child. Knowing that I'd have a child to care for terrified me. I wasn't able to take care of myself, let alone a babe." Hannah wiped a tear from her cheek. "But I didn't have to worry. Not even a week after I realized I was carrying, I lost the babe."

"Oh, Hannah."

"I'm not sure what happened, Granny said she didn't know, but she told me I would never be able to have children. That my body wouldn't carry a babe."

"And you think that because you can't give me a child, I won't want you?"

She buried her face deeper against him. "Every man wants a son to carry on his name. I can't give you that, Rafe."

Before Hannah could continue her explanation, Rafe held her so she had no choice but to look into his eyes. What she saw wrapped around her heart like a warm blanket to protect her.

"I want you, Hannah. I want to spend every day and every night with *you*. Haven't you learned by now that I'm not like every other man you know?" He lowered his head and kissed her on the mouth. "I love you. I want you. If I want children, I only have to go to the nursery and hold any one of the precious babes there."

Hannah tried to stop the tears from streaming down her cheeks, but it was impossible. How had she found a man so perfect? After the life she'd led, why did she deserve to be so blessed?

She wrapped her arms around Rafe's neck and brought his head closer to her. "Kiss me, Rafe. Love me."

"Whatever my lady desires," he whispered, then rose with her in his arms and carried her to the bed.

Epilogue

❖

$\mathcal{R}$afe looked across the room to where his bride stood talking to Grace, the Duchess of Raeborn, Caroline, the Marchioness of Wedgewood, and several more of Caroline's sisters. If any members of Society would walk in on the gathering, they would swoon at the sight. Joining the conversation alongside Lady Wedgewood and the Duchess of Raeborn were several of Madam Genevieve's prostitutes. Rafe recognized Delores and Savannah and Constance and…

"It's quite a gathering, isn't it?" a familiar voice said from beside him.

Rafe looked down to see Dalia, the new Madam Genevieve. He smiled. "Yes, quite a gathering." He nodded to the opposite side of the room where most of the children and young adults from Coventry Cottage stood near the refreshment table. "I'm not sure Society would believe the report of a gathering that included a duke and duchess, a marquess and marchioness, more than one earl and countess, and a viscount and baron thrown in for good measure, along with a half dozen of London's most well-known ladies of the night and Madam Genevieve herself."

Dalia laughed. "What I think Society would find even more unbelievable was the news of the nuptials of Reverend Rafael Waterford and London's former Madam Genevieve."

Rafe laughed. "That would set them on their ears, wouldn't it?"

"Yes, it would."

Rafe turned serious. "I'd like to thank you, Dalia."

"For what?"

"For offering to take over Madam Genevieve's. For giving Hannah back to me."

"You didn't get her *back*, Vicar. You always had her."

He shook his head. "I thought I'd lost her when she held the auction. That was her intent. To drive me away. To prove to me that she wasn't worthy to associate with me."

A frown covered Dalia's face. "You don't know the real reason, do you?"

"The real reason?" This was something new. There was something Hannah hadn't told him, and he knew it was important that he find out what that was.

"Skinner."

"Skinner?"

"You're correct in that she wanted to drive you away. In fact, she was desperate to have you gone. But not because she didn't love you. Because she loved you so much."

Rafe shook his head. "I don't understand."

"Skinner was dogged in his determination to put a halt to Genevieve rescuing the children before his perverted customers could ruin them. She'd taken a huge bite out of his income, and he was desperate to stop her. And he used you to accomplish that."

"Me?"

"Yes, he put a ten-thousand-pound marker on your head."

Rafe found it impossible to speak for several moments. "He offered money to have me killed?"

"A lot of money. Hannah knew if she didn't do something to force you to leave London, you wouldn't live. Men who do that kind of work would kill someone for a tenth that much."

"Where is Skinner now?"

"Dead. After the auction, Hannah received a message saying that Skinner had Delores. Hannah went to get her."

"By herself?"

"You know Hannah. She would have faced the devil himself if he intended to harm someone she cared for. Luckily, the other bordello owners arrived before any real trouble started."

"She didn't tell me that."

Dalia smiled. "That shouldn't surprise you."

"No, I guess not."

"At least Skinner can't destroy any more lives," she said. "And the streets are, if not safe, at least a little less dangerous for innocent young girls who arrive."

Rafe looked over to where Hannah still stood talking to her friends. "She's a remarkable woman," he said, realizing for the hundredth time that he was the most fortunate man on the face of the earth.

"Yes, remarkable."

Hannah chose that moment to look at him. Their gazes locked, and he hoped she read in his eyes the love he felt for her. He thought maybe she did, because she excused herself from the other women and walked toward him.

"I hope you spent a great deal of your conversation with Dalia telling her how fortunate I am that you agreed to marry me," she said with a smile on her beautiful face.

"Absolutely," he said, quickly kissing her on the lips. "Except I may have mentioned once or twice that I consider myself the luckiest man on the face of the earth to have you as my wife." Rafe kissed her again, but broke off their kiss when their friends and family applauded.

"I think," Rafe said, placing his palm beneath Hannah's elbow, "that we had better spend some time with our guests before this perfect day comes to an end."

"It has been perfect, Rafe," Hannah said, tilting her head to look him in the eyes.

"And I promise you, the most perfect part of the day is yet to come."

* * *

Several hours later, Rafe lay with Hannah in his arms. They'd stayed below until all their guests had retired to their rooms, then made their way to the room they would share for the rest of their lives.

But before they retired for the night, they stopped at the nursery, as was their nightly habit, to check on little Rachael and the other babes. Rachael was special to them—especially to Rafe. She was like a daughter to him, and Hannah often found him in the nursery holding her and talking to her. Hannah may not be able to give him a babe, but he would never lack for a family. Their home would overflow with children.

Their lovemaking had been perfect. How could it not be when he had the most perfect woman for his wife?

"I love you, Hannah," he repeated again. "You've made me the happiest man alive."

Hannah rose above him and kissed him on the mouth. "And I love you. You've given me everything I'd always dreamed of. Everything I thought was beyond my reach."

"Nothing is beyond your reach, Hannah. You've proven that over and over."

"Oh, Rafe." She kissed him again, then rolled to the side and opened a drawer in the table nearest the bed. "I have a gift for you."

"A gift?"

"Yes, something I think you'll like very much."

"I have everything I'll ever want or need, Hannah. Right here."

"But this is something special." She pulled a small box from the drawer and handed it to him.

Rafe sat up in bed, then unwrapped the box. He looked at the expectant expression on Hannah's face and knew whatever was in the box was special. He vowed he would love her gift no matter what it was, simply because Hannah had given it to him, and because he could tell it was important to her that he like it.

"The wrapping is very nice, Hannah. Perhaps I should put it on the mantel to look at it for a day or two before I tear the paper."

She punched him on the arm. "Open it. Now. Please."

Rafe laughed, then tore the paper from the box.

He lifted the lid and looked into the box. His heart skipped a beat and his fingers trembled as he reached into the box and lifted out his gift.

It was his grandfather's watch.

"Oh, Hannah," he whispered, fingering the jewels and the raised filigree. "How did you—"

"It doesn't matter," she answered. She placed her hand on the watch and turned it over in Rafe's hand. "In all things, be *noble*," she whispered. "You are the only person I know who fits those words. You are the only one who should carry your grandfather's legacy."

Rafe's heart swelled inside his chest. He felt as if he'd been given the most special gift in the world. And by the most special woman in the world. A woman beyond any price.

Acknowledgments

❦

A special thank-you to my editor, Eleni Caminis, and the Montlake author team for their help and support.

And to Mary Schwaner for her incredible computer ability, and for not hanging up on me when I keep her on the phone after midnight.

You are all the best!

About the Author

*aura Landon taught high school for ten years before leaving the classroom to open her own ice-cream shop. As much as she loved serving up sundaes and malts from behind the counter, she closed up shop after penning her first novel. Now she spends nearly every waking minute writing, guiding her heroes and heroines to happily ever after. She is the author of more than a dozen historical novels, including *Silent Revenge*, *The Most to Lose*, and *Intimate Deception* from Montlake Romance. Her books are enjoyed by readers around the world. She lives with her family in the rural Midwest, where she devotes her free time to volunteering in her community.